Dedication

This book is dedicated to my son. You gave me the vision while I was pregnant, my dreams still inspire me today. I would also like to thank my family for supporting me through this unbelievable journey. And to my coworker, who I now consider a dear friend, thank you for encouraging me to introduce Phantom to the world.

Copyright © 2019 by Katherine Bond

First paperback edition March 2019

Book design by Germancreative
Editing by Tam Jernigan

ISBN 978-1-7337906-1-1 (paperback)
ISBN 978-1-7337906-0-4 (eBook)

Phantom Knights Series Book One:
Electric Pulse

Every urban fable begins with a little bit of accuracy. Unless you're human, then you can't begin to comprehend our truth. To you, we are creatures created to be feared or romanticized–paranormal beings created through your imagination for entertainment. I'm here to tell you my story, our story. We are strong, independent, harpy fairies, tasked with the job of protecting those that don't believe in our existence. Defending humanity against creatures from our world, the Phantom realm that would love nothing more than to turn Earth into their own personal playground. In a world surrounded by darkness, we are the light. We aren't sparkling, damsels in distress, but beautiful, bloodthirsty, ruthless Knights ready to send any man to their knees. I hope you're ready.

-Sky.

Chapter One

"Once upon a time...." Seriously? Who fucking starts a story like that? Katrina Thorne, aka Kat, sat on the edge of the roof on top of the highest sky rise in the city, doubting people were truly that dense. She was reading a sappy Disney princess story called Cinderella as she pondered. How humans could believe in such an obscure fantasy? Why would women romanticize a man swooping in at the last minute to save a poor damsel in distress; then assume they're going to live happily ever after with the man of their dreams? Bullshit stories like that just weren't realistic. And why teach women that one needed a man to empower them. Hell, women were much stronger than men. Even human women. Physicality aside; there was nothing women couldn't conquer.

Kat sat, swinging her booted-black-bitch-kickers in the wind; chewing her favorite strawberry bubble-yum while reading this so-called fairytale. Her electrical current, which usually laid dormant, pulsed from the pit of her stomach to the top of her fingers. She couldn't remember any of the Disney princesses being able to cause destruction and mayhem with just the flick of their wrist. If human women could produce catastrophic events, without technology involved, then maybe they wouldn't think they'd need a man to save their fragile little hearts if they had the power to protect themselves. Come to think of it, maybe there was one ice queen that could let it go. Now she was badass.

Glancing towards the hand that crackled with power, Kat

regarded her curse or that's how she thought of her "gift." Every Phantom Knight inducted into the league possessed a gift. A special ability that gave them the skills they needed to protect humanity from immortal creatures. The power to create lightning and manipulate electricity belonged to her.

She tried as a child to hide her gift, ever since she realized she had her abilities, knowing the leaders of her kind would come for her with demands. However, the electrical current always showed itself when her temper flared, and Kat had a legendary temper. Hell, all harpies had legendary tempers. And that's what Kat was, a harpy, a mythological creature with small delicate transparent wings, retractable thick black claws, and a top velocity speed that rivaled a fighter jet.

Yes, they existed, almost every mystic creature humankind believed was fiction existed. Vampires, werewolves, demons, trolls, witches, shifters, the list continues. Some humans knew the truth, the smart ones anyway, but others were oblivious to the fact that they shared an Earth with creatures that had the power to destroy them all with a single thought, beings like her for example. They'd freak, go utterly bat shit crazy, then the wars would ensue, and the hunting would commence.

That's what humans did to anything they feared or couldn't comprehend. Fight or capture. Therefore, it was their job, as Phantom Knights, to ensure their other "world" remained hidden, stop those who threatened their existence; while protecting the human race from phantom creatures that wanted nothing more than to see the humans fall so they could rule their planet.

The elders of their new planet managed to eliminate those who threatened the Earth, well before it's complete annihilation. They fought honorably for years, eventually, forcing immortals back to their realm where they belonged. The higher powers wanted to make sure Earth remained untouched while the mortals were created.

Yes, the two worlds were created simultaneously, but due to the impatience of the Goddess, only phantoms existed at the time. Kat was still unsure of how some knew of God's prophesied creation, but the elders knew Earth was not meant for them, despite the portals that allowed them access between the two realms. And that is why, thousands of years later, the Knights fought to make sure the separation remained.

Immortals discovered early on that there were hidden tunnels that allowed them to jump from the Earth to Phantom. And it only happened when a wormhole through space was opened by one of their kind. And since the hidden underground tunnels stayed open, after the war of worlds, it was easy for any immortal to roam the streets of Earth unchecked.

Most were simply curious to discover what the almighty fashioned. When the dinosaurs inhabited the planet things were easy, but life didn't become so complicated until the first mortals touched the surface. Things got a whole lot more interesting after the coming of man. But not even the elders could've predicted how perfectly God had created the planet just for them.

Kat wasn't a huge fan of the world she called home for centuries. No, there wasn't anything wrong with her home planet, it was just, what's the word, ordinary. Besides, every creature that lived there had a God, or Goddess complex. They were all "fear me or die, weakling," Kat rolled her eyes. *Give me a break.* So, the human realm was where she called home. With this new generation of Knights and phantom creatures, it was much more common for their kind to try to hide and blend in on Earth. If they didn't cause trouble or reveal they weren't mortal, living on the human planet was accepted amongst their species.

Like herself, others just preferred to live among humankind, even though Kat despised mortals. They just were so blah. Each of them fighting to live a dream of happily ever after, working themselves to death to acquire what they perceive they needed to be complacent. To her, each exhibited the seven deadly sins to the tee.

But oh, sweet Bliss, the Earth was beautiful, with the many oceans, forests, mountains, and wildlife. The pyramids, the Great Wall; each of the seven wonders of the world were all breathtaking. The vibrant life of it all was fascinating, especially in the city she lived. Lake Powelton was right on the outside of New York City. A little island oasis that was far enough away from the noise of the bigger cities, but close enough where all Kat had to do was hop on a ferry if she wanted to be close to the action.

Kat looked down from the top of Fall Heights, a new tech company, envying the busy streets; knowing she would have to get to work soon, but damn was the view spectacular. She decided to take just one more min -

The wind changed then, and the sudden breeze silently licked along her long flowing fire red hair, startling her into dropping her book. Kat looked dejected seeing her novel floating down the forty-floor building, and she inwardly cursed herself. Not because she'd just lost her sappy ass book, but because she had been caught slacking on the job. She dreaded who was behind her, and she didn't dare turn around.

"Hello, oh fearless leader." She said to Sky, leader of the Phantom Knights, not bold enough to even peek over her shoulder.

"I thought I'd find you up here." Sky sneered behind her.

Kat could practically feel the holes Sky was drilling into the back of her skull, giving her even more of a reason not to turn around. She knew she was fucked, no point in rushing to her untimely demise.

The harpy decided, after a few beats of breathless silence,

to cast a look under her long thick black eyelashes. Turning slightly, Kat peeked over her shoulder. Yep, there she was, standing tall, all six-feet-one inch of her. She was wearing a black leather catsuit, with kick-ass leather boots that were the Knights signature attire.

The boss was probably the most beautiful harpy Kat had ever seen, and usually all harpies were uncharacteristically stunning. But Sky took the cake. With her long jet-black hair that fell to her ass, her ruby red lips, porcelain skin, and night shadow eyes that looked as vast as space itself, she was perfection personified. She reminded her of Selene in that Underworld movie played by Kate Beckinsale. Hot, hot, hot. But looks meant nothing to someone like Sky. To her, beauty was irrelevant, it served no purpose in everyday life; she valued loyalty above all else.

"Yeah well, you know how I like to live on the edge. Get it? Cause I'm on the edge." Kat threw over her shoulder with a slight smile in her voice after a few more seconds of silence. Sky just shook her head slightly while she continued to stare.

"So, what can I do for you?" Kat spoke as the silence resumed. "I know you didn't just come to loom, even though you're a damn fine loomer." She uttered in the wind.

Sky still said nothing, as that black bottomless gaze promised pain. She did tilt her head slightly though as if to study her words.

"Look I was just about to hop down and kill something evil I swear." Kat finally jumped and stood on the edge of the building to face her courageous leader's scrutiny, and yet still she got nothing but silence. Of course, she knew why but Kat wasn't willing to give in just yet.

"Damnit, really, like in five minutes I was going to hop my happy ass down there and get this shit rolling." That got her an arch of one dark black eyebrow.

"Okay, so maybe I wasn't. I deserve some time off. I've been working around the clock, and I needed a break." She waited and stared her leader down and Sky never blinked, not even once. *Man, that shit isn't natural,* she thought. Sky had a domineering authority about her, and she knew she wasn't going to be able to play chicken with her eyes for long, so she started spilling her guts.

"Alright, I took a few days off already. No big fucking deal, there was a Walking Dead marathon on, and we all know how I love my Daryl." She stomped her booted foot, and that got her a chuckle from her static leader. Great, so maybe she wasn't going to die today after all.

The next thing she knew the air shifted, and she looked down to see her leader sitting on the ledge beside her. She resumed sitting and braced for the lecture she knew she was about to receive.

"Katrina listen," Sky began. *Yep here it comes,* she thought, barely resisting the urge to roll her green eyes to the back of her head.

"I know you hate this job. Nevertheless being a Knight is a high privilege amongst our kind. To be able to help protect our race and defend the Earth is an honor most harpies would kill to have. Think of how many people get to go home to their families because of what we do."

Yeah, yeah. Kat deserved an award for being able to rein in her facial expressions. Not rolling her eyes required great skill and strength. Not because she didn't agree on some level with Sky, but because she liked her eyes right where they were in her head and not in her leader's hands.

Every harpy wasn't born with a unique gift like hers, and those harpies thought their Goddess felt they were unworthy to protect humanity. Kat believed it was the other way around. She remembered what it felt like to be free of the burden of being a Knight. And some days she just wanted to do her own thing without fear of retribution.

"Yeah, I know. I'm soooo honored and shit," she scoffed, "but it's a real buzz kill on my social life."

"Ha! What social life? We rarely see you except for meetings, and you barely show up for those. You never come to the occasional events held on Phantom because you're always on Earth and even here you have no friends." Sky glanced at her as if daring her to disagree.

She mumbled under her breath, even though she knew her leader's pointy ears picked up on her grumble, "That's because people suck."

"If I'm putting too much pressure on you," Sky continued as if she hadn't spoken, "it's because you're one of the best fighters I have, Katrina. Hell, your name alone strikes fear in phantom creatures across the realms."

Oh yeah, that made her shiver with delight. If it was one thing that got her off - and it's been a long time since anything else got her off - was fear from her enemy. She loved it, the screams, the terror, the surprise that a little five-foot six-inch redhead with light freckles could light them up like a firecracker on the nineteenth of June. But damn, life was getting a little redundant. Kill, maim, eat, sleep and repeat. She was... bored.

"We all know I love a good Fear-induced bloodbath, but where's the challenge? All these assholes want to do is prey on the weak. They never want to challenge their strength and come after us, noooooo," she dragged out throwing her hands in the air, "it's always the humans they're trying to pursue. Then they try to hide from us like cowards, like seriously, we'll find you dumbass." She threw her hands outward again to gesture her frustration.

"Yes, well that's what our job entails, Kat." Her leader paused to pin her with her death stare. "That's what you were groomed to do since childhood. Be a warrior, a hunter; we help those who can't help themselves. We are the balance that is needed in the universe. We are yin and yang. Without us to keep the stability amongst our people, the world as we know it will end in chaos." Her leader replied smoothly with her lyrical voice of common sense.

Goddess damnit, she knew she was right. They could not very well let the phantom creatures prey on humans until extinction, because then where would she live? What would happen to the beautiful planet Earth she knew and loved? Earth with all its vibrant colors and shapes, architectural structures and the food, let's not forget about the food–Goddess above what would she do without funnel cakes and Philly cheese-steaks? But damn, what she wouldn't give to have a life, a different experience, one without a unique purpose from the current one she possessed. Maybe the humans did have something going with their pursuit of happiness, living without a care in the world. Perhaps she was experiencing a little envy herself, or maybe she needed to get laid.

"Yeah, yeah, alright, I hear you. Just give me ten minutes, and I'll bring you all the evil heads you want on a silver Fuckin' platter, oh Great One." She put her hand on her chest and bent a little at the waist in a mock bow.

Her leader cut her eyes and exhaled an exhausted sigh. "You have five, and I want blood, guts, and glory. I want you fighting until daylight rises; you had a whole week off." Sky cut her off before she could voice a protest, okay a lie, definitely a lie. "Yes, I know you were off for a week because your quadrants were extremely quiet, so you are to battle until you can't breathe, move, or shit comfortably, or I'll return with a babysitter, and you know exactly who I will send."

Ahhhhh yes, Sia, her lovable big sister, by three damn minutes considering they were twins, not that that would make a difference to her. Sia would kill to hold this over her head, and Sky knew it. She threw up a middle finger salute and drummed out a "Sir, yes sir," as her boss disappeared into the night, no doubt to create her own destruction.

Damn Kat wished she could teleport, but as her wicked electrical current danced on her fingertips triggered by that conversation with her boss, Kat decided out loud "One gift was enough." It was enough to get her a job she knew would eventually get her killed, especially knowing she couldn't live another day with the same old routine. She craved more, something enjoyable and exhilarating. Kat needed something to look forward to in the morning when she came home to her empty loft.

The harpy knew her isolation was partly her fault since she'd shut everyone out of her life, but she just needed time to figure shit out on her own, and well, people moved on too. Time waits for no one. And she never figured her shit out either. Maybe she just wasn't meant to be happy. It's not like she knew exactly what it was that was missing in her life, yet she knew it was something. Out of all the Knights in existence, she seemed to be the only one that was fucked up about her "calling."

Kat gathered her thoughts and stood, then glanced down at all the golden streetlights. And as she slipped from the side of the roof and let her body free fall against the gush of the wind, she thought of happily ever after with Cinderella and her prince. *Yeah, what a crock of shit.*

Chapter Two

If Lucas Mason thought life couldn't get any better, well he'd be right - as he sat at his plain maple desk on the thirty-ninth floor of Fall Heights. He envisioned himself screaming as yet another one of his coworkers was congratulated on a promotion that Luke deserved. Why couldn't that be him?

Luke had a master's degree in computer engineering from MIT, and he was one of the best hackers in the world, his intellect was uncanny. He graduated at the top of his class and was wanted by countless organizations including military establishments - well before he walked across the stage. His resume was stacked and to top it off he was kind of funny, well maybe not funny, but he had an overall great personality. But he chose Fall Heights because he felt his talents could be put to better use at an up and coming tech company. It seemed everyone was progressing but him. Why couldn't he move up in the corporate ladder, especially since he had been with the company for over eight years? Ever since the damn building had only one floor.

Deep down, Luke already knew the answer to his question as to why he wouldn't get promoted. And it didn't have anything to do with his bubbling personality. It was because his boss was an enormous, narcissistic, dick. A vain, self-absorbed testicular cancer that wanted his minions to kiss his ass daily.

Heights, his glutinous boss, wasn't a man that favored those who could hold a logical conversation. Nope, he loved the ones that could tell him how nice he looked today or how remarkable he was to be able to expand his empire in a failing market. Luke knew it was all lies. His boss never looked good, no matter how much he spent on designer clothes. And the success of his business was because he rode the coattails of people like Luke.

The guy barely knew how to turn on a computer. But he was a trust fund baby, which granted him millions. To his credit, he hired the best people around him to show him how to invest his money in a sure thing. Thus, Fall Heights Tech Company, FHT, was formed. In the end, he was just another rich white man that was dealt a slightly better hand in life. Therefore, Luke refused to kiss ass. He preferred to let his work as the best statistical analyst in data configuration, speak for itself. Luke couldn't bring himself to fall at his leader's feet. He didn't have a problem following a worthy leader, but Heights was not worthy.

Because of his unwillingness to cater to his boss's every whim, he was stuck in the same position he'd started with, which was junior VP of statistical analytics. It wasn't that he wasn't proud of his job, he certainly made good money, it just made him feel unappreciated, undervalued. Fall Heights, the new tech company making waves in Lake Powelton, New York, was continuously expanding, and yet he felt stagnant. He loved technology, it was forever changing and enhancing itself as the years rolled by, but damn how he wished there was more to life than his desk.

Luke didn't have many friends, but that was because he was kind of a nerd. No one hung out with geeks unless they were one, especially not women. Most women thought he was the friend type, not the one you'd like to throw up against the wall and fuck until you couldn't breathe type.

Luke knew he was partially to blame for his persona. He was incredibly shy around the fairer sex; therefore, he didn't try to form intimate relationships with women. Lucas wore the same style since college as well, which made him look young and boyish–wearing a shirt, blazer, tie, and slacks. Mostly sticking to all nude colors since Luke didn't like to stand out.

He was, however, equitably handsome, with his short choppy dark-brown hair. Luke was about average height for a male at six-two, and he was built well in the body department. His love of athletics gave him a swimmer's physique. And running during his free time, while occasionally lifting weights, gave him a more muscular tone. However, no one ever saw under his clothes, just what was on top, which was average. At least, he thought that's what Casey Dash saw.

Casey was the most stunningly beautiful blond he'd ever seen. Lucas had secretly loved his stoic friend and coworker for months. Heights hired Casey as his secretary a few weeks ago, and he'd been mesmerized ever since. She had gorgeous dirty blonde hair, sky blue eyes, and a body to die for. Every male in the building, himself included, wanted her. She, of course, saw him as nothing more than a friendly coworker. Caught enthralled once again, he had to blink his eyes a few times to stop from staring at her deliciously long bare legs as she glided towards his desk.

"Hey Luke, after work everyone's going to Tony's bar across the street for a drink to celebrate Justin's promotion. You coming?"

To Luke, her voice sounded like an exotic instrument; whimsically playing along with the wind towards his ear. Damn, Casey was lovely with her blond hair tied like a crown atop her head. She was wearing a tight ass black pencil skirt suit, with a blouse that showed her a rather generous breast cup size. And those lips, God those beautiful, voluptuous lips, what he wouldn't give to have those lips wrapped around his di -

"Luke, hey Luke!? Did you hear me? Bar... drinks... Are you coming?" Casey waved a polished manicured hand in front of his face. Oh yes, he was supposed to speak, huh?

Clearing his thoughts, he looked up at her and spoke: "Ummm yeah, sure why not? I don't have anything else planned tonight."

"Great, see you there, buddy."

Luke watched as Casey sashayed away, leaving the "friend-zone" endearment spinning in his head. *Buddy*? That's pretty much what all women saw him as. Gracious, what he wouldn't give for a woman that saw him. *Alright, Luke,* he thought to himself, *it's time to stop wallowing in your self-pity and get back to work.*

As he dove back into his work, his boss, Roman Heights, walked out of his office and loomed in his doorway. As Luke looked over at the slightly obese man he zeroed in on his tight jacket button. Luke grinned as he thought if Roman took just one deep breath that fucker would fly.

"I just wanted to congratulate Justin on his promotion," his boss began, "it was well deserved. And there is more where that came from. The company is mounting, and we need more bright minds that will allow us to continue to cultivate, so make sure you show me you want it and we may be celebrating your promotion next."

Yeah right, show him as in, "drop to your knees before me, peasants." Okay, maybe a drink is exactly what he needed. Luke was becoming cynical. It was time to become engrossed in his work once more. Because, let's be honest, that's where he shined. He was doing what he loved and no one, not even Heights, could take that from him.

Hours seemed to roll by and his coworkers started to file out, one after the other. Luke was so preoccupied with his work that he didn't realize he was the only one left on the floor, well almost the only one. He looked to the window and couldn't believe how late it was, but he turned back once he noticed someone coming towards his desk. Casey walked over to him with a smile.

"You know you're always the first one in the office and the last one here," She placed her hands on his desk, leaning forward towards him, "you're so dedicated I bet you're the next one to move up."

He just shook his head and smiled, locking eyes with her over the rim of his glasses, and yeah, not going to happen. Roman liked him right where he was. He knew his boss couldn't stand him and the feeling was mutual. His boss only recruited him because his father told him he was the best. And hiring the best would help Roman's company move in the direction he wanted. But Luke couldn't help but believe that Height thought if he were promoted, he'd come for his position as CEO. Which wasn't the case at all. He wasn't trying to run a company; he just wanted to use his gift to help advance technology. He couldn't do that pushing papers and answering a thousand phone calls.

"So, you still coming out tonight?"

"Um sure, I just got a few more things to finish up here, and I'll be right down," he smiled again. "Don't worry, you'll have your wingman there tonight, I promise."

Any time they went out together he was either her fake boyfriend that warded off the aggressive men or the reserved best friend that helped weed out the losers. If only he could be the one she was looking for. But for some reason, he couldn't muster up the courage to tell her how he felt. Luke always thought he'd be able to say to the woman he was interested in that he wanted to be romantically involved. But with Casey, he couldn't.

"You're the best. See you soon."

As she waved and walked away, he pushed his comfy black leather seat back from his desk and swiveled to face the window again. Damn, he was in shambles. One of his closest friends was a girl he couldn't have, his job was at a standstill, and his love life was none existent.

Luke took off his glasses and rubbed his face. Once he removed the irritation from his thoughts, Luke glanced towards the windows and saw something the color of fire fall out of the sky. *Fuck, was that a body?* He hurried to the window and looked down and saw nothing but the busy streets and luminous colors of the street lights. Weird. He really could use that drink, but getting laid would probably be better. It had been months since he'd been with a woman and he knew it was probably not going to happen again anytime soon.

Chapter Three

Damn, vampires were stupid; Kat chuckled as she followed her prey down the end of an alley. All they had to do was feed from their victims, then seal the wounds with their healing saliva, wipe the humans' mind with mind control, then send them on their obliviously merry way. The vampire species possessed multiple gifts that would allow them to keep their world a secret.

The leeches were a powerful batch of immortals. They didn't burst into flames at daylight like the myths predicted. They could blend in during the morning hours with no problem, but the sun did drain some of their energy. They were practically invincible on Phantom since the burning rays didn't affect immortals has harshly on their planet as they did on Earth. Vampires could have lived out their existence in peace, yet so many fell victim to bloodlust. The uncontrollable thirst that ruled their kind after a certain age.

Creatures like the one Kat hunted who would lure humans to the dark corners of the shadows and ripped their throats out as they fed. The parasites could have tried to control their impulses, but most never fought the urge to feed. They got off on the terror they caused in their victims. Evil beings using their power to lord over their prey. They salivated over their object's terror because vampires didn't have to kill to survive. Hell, they didn't even need to drink blood every day if they didn't want to. Blood to vampires was like water to humans. They needed it for the nourishment of their bodies, and while going long periods without it would eventually lead to death, missing a day or two wouldn't cause any lasting damage. Because of this, they were powerful phantom creatures. And even harder to keep in check when they went astray.

Not all vamps were bad. However, even the phantom realm had its good and evil creatures, just like the human realm had moral and sinful humans, but the level of evil out there with the powers they possessed were dangerous. The Earth would plunge into darkness if they allowed evil to prevail. That's where Kat came in. She'd been after this specific rogue for weeks. Sky pointed him out to her in a meeting months ago, but Kat could never fucking find him. After countless hours of planning, tracing, and strategizing, she was finally able to corner her quarry to this dark alley behind Tony's Bar.

As she squared off with her alluded nemesis, she gave the vamp a good once-over. He was tall dark and oh so handsome, like so many of his kind were. They needed the glamor to lure their victims to them. Sight–which made them drool-worthy–and their smell made them nearly irresistible. And oh boy, did he smell good. His scent, which caught in the breeze, caused a constant throb between her legs, and as the vamp caught her eye, he knew he turned her on. His devious smile said as much.

"Ahh harpy hunter, how fare thee tonight?" Mmmm even his voice was tempting. She involuntarily shivered.

"So, you know who I am," she exhaled.

"But of course, my sweet, everyone who's anyone knows the warrior women dressed in black with wings."

Licking his lips, he cast his eyes down her leather clad body. No catsuit like Sky, but she wore leather pants and a black muscle shirt that hid the numerous blades she carried. Kat also wore black gun-straps, one on each upper thigh, that harbored her magnificent set of twin forties with bullets dipped in chromium. Her famous Kusanagi was sheathed on her back. Only a fool in her line of work would rely solely on their supernatural abilities to protect them, and she was no fool. Sliding her hands down her hips, she slightly crouched an inch, so she could rest her hands on her terrible twos.

"So, if you know who I am, we can just skip the formalities and get right down to business." She cracked her neck and took a step forward as he took a step back.

"Why must we battle, my beautiful temptress? I'd much rather take you up against this building and plunge my cock into you instead of my fangs."

Yeah, she was tempted to take him up on that offer, and had he not been a murderous fiend, she would've been spread-eagle. But she was never one to mix business with pleasure. Not even if it's been forever since she'd experienced such delights.

"You know, I'd have thought that'd be possible if I didn't just see you rip the throat out of that college girl two streets down."

"Ah, come now sweet." He flashed his pearly whites giving her an *"Oh, I'm innocent"* smile. "She was just a mistake; it happens to the best of us." He had taken another step back as she stalked forward.

"Yeah but see, with you it happens a lot. I know who you are and she's not the only one I've heard you've killed. We would be here all night with your list of victims, and I don't have all night." Seriously she didn't, Walking Dead was back, and Negan just showed up. Kat did love a bad boy. Maybe that's why she was so turned on by Count Dracula over here. She had to end this fast; Sky would forgive another unscheduled vacation if she bagged, not banged, this big fish. Okay, probably she would forgive... maybe.... definitely not, but did she care?

"Well, in that case, since you don't want to play...."

Count moved in a blink of an eye. Kat dodged the throwing star that sailed past her head then backflipped and spun away from the five other stars that flew past her as well. Her dodging gave Count enough time to hit the roof at a dead run.

Goddess, she loved it when they ran. Vampires were fast, but harpies, especially Kat, were faster. Unconcealing her wings, she let them flutter freely then jumped, landing smoothly on the roof. Kat cast her eyes around in search of her target. She found him almost immediately; he was just a white blur in the night moving faster than the human eye could detect. Letting out a battle screech, she took off after him. Vampires were one of a few phantom creatures that could rival their speed, but Kat had always had an edge up on her fellow harpy sisters.

She caught him fairly quickly and took him down with a tackle to his back, impelling him in the shoulder blades with two daggers forged from chromium kept at her back. The metal was the only thing that could hold a vamp immobile, it wouldn't kill them, but it hurt like a son of a bitch. He yelped as the daggers struck flesh and Kat smiled diabolically at the sound. She stood up keeping a boot to the vamp's back and looked down at her prey.

"Now why would you go and do that, hmm? I hate runners, it would've been way hotter if you had stood your ground and fought me like a good little lamb."

The vamp struggled under her weight, which wasn't much. She may have weighed all of 145 pounds, okay fine 152, but she did take a week off a few days ago, so she had gained TV marathon weight. However, it wasn't her weight that helped her keep Count down, it was her extraordinary, inhuman strength.

"Now, now, now." She tapped her index finger to her chin. "What's a girl like me to do with a pretty little thing like you?"

He tried, unsuccessfully, once again to wiggle out from under her boot, so she applied more pressure to his back while she thought about her choices. Kat was so caught up in her own personal game, she'd let her guard down. She never felt her unwanted company appear at her back.

"Kill him, sister-mine."

Kat swiveled around and what would you know, her infamous big sister Sia was standing behind her. She narrowed her sharp green eyes at her twin in greeting. Kat needed to be more vigilant.

"Well, hello, sister. And to what do I owe this privilege?"

"Sky put me in this quadrant, and you're hunting on my turf." Her twin spoke, folding her arms across her chest with a look of annoyance. Kat looked around. Yep, she was outside of her sector. *Hmm, guess that's what happens when the fuckers ran.*

"Sorry, sister-mine, I must have chased him further than I thought." She shrugged in indifference.

"Which means you wanted to chase him further. Bloodsuckers can't outrun you, Kat." Sia gave her an exasperated look.

Sia was right though; she loved running. The further away the prey got from her, the better. Enemies always seemed to believe they could get away from her by running, but they were wrong. She just wanted a few minutes to play. Damn, her big sister knew how to take the fun out of everything.

"As much as I love this conversation among you two, I'd much rather you'd use those pretty tongues of yours to suck my....."

Kat didn't give Count Dracula a chance to finish that sentence. She called upon her gift feeling the warming sensation course through her body, traveling through the palm of her hand. Kat created a fist then captured her prey with her electrical pulse - burning him to nothing more than a pile of ash at her feet. Goddess above, at moments like this she loved her gift. There was nothing better than being able to end such a vile creature's life. On Earth, she was judge, jury, and executioner. She was the red queen. Taking a deep breath, Kat turned to face her delightful big sister, Sia.

"Sooooooo, how you've been?" She questioned through clenched teeth.

"You'd know if you'd returned any of my calls." Sia spat, while still having her arms folded across her chest. Someone had a slight 'tude.

"Now why would I do that?" Kat replied cocking her head to the side in indifference.

"Oh, I don't know?" Sia threw her hands in the air, "maybe because I'm your sister? Maybe because I haven't seen or talked to you alone in months? Maybe because mother and father are worried?" Sia said the last part quietly knowing, at that very moment, she'd fucked up.

"See that," Kat jabbed her finger in the face of one that matched her own. "That stuff right there is bullshit. And the main reason I don't pick up the phone when you call," she fumed. "They don't care about me. I haven't heard from either one of them in months. Hell, if it weren't for the meetings, I probably wouldn't hear or see mom at all!"

"They do worry Kat; you know that," Sia added even more gently than before.

"Yeah, they worry, sure," Kat utter sarcastically. "They worry about why I keep disobeying Sky. Why on Phantom do I keep breaking our fearless leaders fucking precious rules?" she spat through her teeth. "They don't care about me, sister-mine. I showed up at their doorstep bloodied, broken, in need of their guidance and love, and you know what they said to me? 'Sky said you broke protocol. You could've gotten everyone killed,'" she replied with her mother's deadpan expression.

What about her? Kat needed her family to be there for her. What she saw that day. What she'd had to do. She'd needed them, and they weren't there. None of them were. But this wasn't the time or place to reminisce. Kat shut the memory down before she could manifest even more hatred for her family, but Sia's next words had her seeing red.

"Yeah well, maybe if you'd stayed in formation, she wouldn't have said that." Her sister mumbled, looking down while kicking imaginary rocks with her silver-buckled boots.

"Yeah and that five-year-old little boy would've been dead alongside his mother, too!" Kat shot back ferociously. Goddess, her sister brought out the best of her temper, but nowadays it didn't take much. All one had to do was bring up her parents and ding ding ding, let's get ready to rumblllllllllle.

"Look, okay, I get why you hate them, but what about me? You could at least speak to me, like seriously, we're sisters. I went through the same grueling training you did, with the same parents." Sia pointed at her angrily.

Of course, she was right, Kat thought to herself. Sia did go through the same cutthroat training to become a Knight once they reached puberty. And she went through it first, alone. Sia's boot camp began a whole year before her own; even though, Kat discovered her powers far sooner than her sister had. She didn't want a life of drills and unending commands. Sia, however, was excited to show their unbeloved parents she was chosen. Ever since her parents had seen Sia pull a flame from a candle and manipulate it, their lives had changed. Her parents went from stoic drones to commanders in chief.

During Kat's whole adolescence, she'd prayed for a hint

of their love and acceptance. All she wanted to do was make them proud, but when they conceived and neither of their twins showed signs of being gifted, they were discarded. Sia and Kat were left to fend for themselves as soon as they were old enough. They were never a happy, delightful bunch, and the only one that ever showed her the slightest affection was her twin. They were all each other had. Their parents, mainly her mother, were dedicated to the Knights and having children always seem to get in their way. That was all until Sia held that flame in her hands. Sia's childhood after that was over. And Kat had officially lost her best friend to the very people she later grew up to hate.

Sia had a schedule for everything. Hell, Kat didn't think she could even wipe her ass if it weren't on the agenda. Sia, to them, was the golden child. Their whole world revolved around her schedule. Kat was often left by herself while they were training outside in the field. And she had grown accustomed to being the lonely rider. Kat had convinced herself she was better off alone. That's when she knew she'd have to hide her power over the lightning strike. Sia's life was one that she didn't want for herself. And Kat gained sick satisfaction from her mother's inability to produce twin Knights. She got off on being a defect, at least that's how her mother saw her.

One night while Kat was supposed to be sleeping soundly, she couldn't have been more than eight years old, she snuck out of bed to get a glass of water. A burning flame coming from the living rooms fireplace drew her to shadows dancing alongside the beach-sand walls. Those shadows produced the quiet voices of her mother and father. Kat crept closer, so she was able to hear their words since she rarely listened to either one of them talk to each other. It was a wonder they were ever married, either for convenience or love she did not know. If Kat had to wager a guess, it'd be for convenience, since she did not believe her mother was capable of love. As she tiptoed barefooted forward in her flowing flowered pajamas, the voices became more distinct.

"This is not what I wanted. Those children are not what I wanted," she heard her mother sneer.

"We talked about this. The girl's powers may be dormant. They could manifest once they've reached adulthood. We should start training them now," Kat's father rebutted.

"Why waste our time on defects? If they were gifted, their powers would've surfaced by now. I've seen traces of gifted harpies at birth. Those two are simply ordinary. What have I done that the Goddess deems punishable? I have given up everything to carry and birth future Knights, and I am rewarded with shame," her mother muttered in disgust as she exited the cover of the flames.

Kat hurried back to the room she shared with her sister before she could be discovered by one of her parents. She jumped back under the wool quilt quietly, as to not wake her still sleeping sister. Kat tried desperately that night to fall back asleep and forget the horrific words her mother had spoken. As a child, she had felt so small then. Yes, Kat was merely a child, but at that moment, she was nothing.

She had tried obsessively back then to make her mother proud, whether it was by mastering new skills or learning combat training on her own. Kat had wanted nothing more in life to have her mother look at her with pride. But everything had changed that night. That night she was no longer a small adolescent child. That night Kat grew up, and thus her defiance was born. She'd prayed to the Goddess every day that she wasn't gifted. Her mother didn't deserve such glorification. Unfortunately for Kat, their Deity's vision aligned with her mother's.

Shortly after finding out her mother viewed her as an object to contort and control, Kat realized her prayers to the Goddess had gone unheard. The moment had startled her a little in the beginning. She'd always wondered why she was captivated by thunderstorms–spending late nights pondering why she was still chasing the lightning strikes in the sky. Why she was enthralled by the patterns, tracing the outline of the blue-white bolts in the air, while she laid in the grass as the rain kissed her rosy, red cheeks.

Kat finally got the answer while playing outside in the field as the rain barreled down against her bare feet. She was twirling around with her face to the sky, letting the rain cascade down her nightgown, when the most beautiful lightning bolt she'd ever seen lit the air. The luminous colors of the streaks as they stripped across the night sky, had her spellbound. Everything froze at that instant. The rain stopped pouring, the winds soft musical breeze stopped flowing, and she stood still staring up into the infinite universe. Kat was enticed by the bolt that retook shape before her eyes. She reached at that moment towards the sky just as the bolt started to subside, whispering towards the light to remain. And it did.

The young harpy didn't understand at the time that the bolt halted because of her plea, but when she asked the beautiful blue streak to move towards her, she quickly began to realize that she was in control. The Goddess had cursed her after all.

Kat supposed it could be worse. At least she was given something she loved. The storms calmed her rambunctious nature, freeing her angelic spirit. And finding out Kat could create her own storm when needed was a treasured gift, whether she thought it was at the time or not.

Drawing up the same feeling she used to steady the wave of the bolt, she summoned the fluorescent blue light to her small delicate hand. The rod came down and paused in the middle of her palm and awaited her next command. She studied the colors more closely, allowing static to course through her body, stopping in the pit of her core. As the energy settled in, she had finally felt at peace.

Kat played outside for what felt like an eternity, throwing the bolt up to the sky and watching it hurtle down so that she could catch it and send it flying once more. Her laughter and joy were infectious. It had been so long since she had just felt like the child she was. She jumped, ran, and twirled for hours until the storm finally started to diminish. Kat walked back home barefoot and soaking wet, wondering how she was going to keep her new powers a secret. As she walked back home, all the happiness she had felt a minute ago started to fade. She knew if they ever found out, her nights of chasing storms were over.

Kat wanted to keep her curse to herself for as long as she could. If her mother found out, she knew her freedom would end. Unfortunately, a year after Sia revealed her flame, Kat's temper exposed her talents to her family. She was punished for talking back to their mother, and as a result, she wasn't allowed outside in the fields for two weeks. Kat was livid, later burning a hole through their house with her lightning bolt. That day was the only day she'd ever seen her mother look towards her with pride. The rest was history.

Kat became another one of her parents' soldiers, trained to become one of Sky's lucrative Knight warriors. One qualified to protect humanity, *blah, blah, blah*.

Shaking herself from her childhood memories, Kat focused again on the only good thing she had going for herself–her sister. Regardless of their current situation, Kat still loved her deeply, but she'd never tell Sia that. Looking at her face now, it seemed as if her sister loved her just the same. Being a twin gave one a better connection with the other sibling, and she could feel her twin's sadness directed towards her. Centering herself back into their conversation she responded.

"Yeah, I know sis, I should've answered. Shit!" She rubbed a gloved hand down her face in frustration.

"Look. I'm sorry, okay, you're right. Yes, our parents are dicks. But they did the best they could according to them. Considering who they were." Her sister cast a dark look in her direction as though Sia were lost in her thoughts on the subject.

Taking a moment to look at her sister, after all this time apart, she noticed how different they've become since childhood. Yeah, they were identical twins as far as harpies features go, however, they still had minor differences. While Kat had wavy fire engine red hair and emerald-green eyes, her sister had midnight black curls and hazel eyes. These small differences camouflaged their lineage. Maybe their looks hinted at how their lives would also differ growing up. They used to be inseparable, two peas in a pod. But Sia wanted to make their parents happy and Kat, well, *fuck them.*

Kat didn't care if Sia thought they did the best they could. She knew they could've done better. Kat had seen better from other parents in the harpy community and their parents, her mother especially, sucked. But she'd let her sister believe in what she wanted. She would never ruin her perception of their parents by telling her that their mother thought of them as defects. No, that moment was meant for her, and her alone. So, she didn't dignify that statement with a response. After a while, realizing that she wouldn't reply, her sister crossed her arms in front of her and eyed her skeptically.

Changing tactics, Sia spoke. "How about we go for a drink?" Sia gave her a look that dared her to refuse.

"Yeah, sure, why not?" she shrugged. "It's not like I have anything else to do. Sky's going to salivate over this beauty." She looked down and kicked the vamp dust at her boot. "Bet she'd be okay with me having an hour to myself after killing this fucker." She hiked her thumb over her shoulder. But she knew Sky wouldn't be okay. Everyone knew Sky wouldn't be okay.

But again, did she care? Well yes, yes, she did. But Sky wasn't going to find out. She hoped.

Chapter Four

Luke stood lounging against the rustic wooden bar, watching all the heated bodies gyrate against each other as the musical lyrics of Rihanna's "Work" blared from the DJ's speakers. Somehow, his coworkers had convinced him to go to the club downtown after drinks at Tony's, when all he wanted to do was go home and sleep. Everyone else wanted to let off some steam and continue celebrating Justin's promotion. So here he was, posted up at the bar, nursing his drink while watching the sweaty bodies twirl on the dance floor. Well, just one figure in particular.

He couldn't take his eyes off Casey, who was moving like a river. Damn, could she dance. She was a natural, the way her body steadily flowed, as she gyrated poetically to the beat. She had him wholly entranced. Hell, he probably would've loved watching her clean a toilet that's how in love he thought he was with her. And wasn't that just sad?

As Luke turned to signal the bartender for another round of gin and tonic, he thought he was a sick son of a bitch. He couldn't keep this up. Casey was never going to see him as anything other than a friend. And Luke wasn't so much in love with Casey as the idea of her. He was over being alone, even though he portrayed himself as a happily single guy. Luke wanted a companion and needed to try and find someone else, hell, anyone else. Whether it was just for a night or eternity, he was tired of sleeping alone.

The bartender, a handsome, muscular, dark-skinned man,

dressed head to toe in black, cut off his personal self-loathing as he delivered his drink. Nodding his head in thanks, Luke rotated back around towards the dance floor just as Justin strolled up, headed in his direction. Settling up next to him, his friend leaned his body over the rim of the bar and signaled to get the bartender's attention. Once the bartender delivered Justin's drink, he turned back around and reclined like Luke; eyes lit up by the strobe lights on the dancefloor.

Luke glanced briefly in his friend's direction before returning his attention to the crowd. He was happy for his colleague. Justin had gotten a promotion a few days ago, and he was one of few who deserved it. He worked just as hard as Luke and was nearly as canny. They had been friends since grade school, bonding over their love of engineering. Even though growing up Justin was the more popular amongst the two, with Luke being the loner, they formed a friendship. With his rugged good looks, keen intellect, and superior athletic skills, Justin was best, all around. And on top of all his accomplishments, he remained humble, which made him a likable guy. Hence why they'd continued their friendship throughout the years. Justin never forgot him. Their friendship had grown stronger in high school, which led them to become college roommates and was eventually what landed them the same job at the same company. The two were brothers in every sense of the word. They were all the family the other had.

Justin's elbow to his ribs drew him from his musing. "Hey man, why don't you just go down there and dance with her?"

Following the direction of Justin's head tilt, he looked over towards Casey. Surprisingly enough, he hadn't been watching her during his musings. He responded as if he was all the same. "Yea, not gonna happen, my man." Luke shifted his eyes to his drink as he brought the glass towards his lips for a taste.

"Why not?" His friend questioned. "What? Like just staring

at her is going to get her to notice you? You gotta take a chance, my guy. Women like that. They want a man that takes control," he said.

Luke just shook his head; he wasn't that guy. He was more of the strong, silent type. Aggressiveness wasn't in his nature.

"Well then, I guess you have your answer." Luke looked over at him questionably. "She's not the one. Because if she were, you'd be down there right now, not standing here holding the bar up." Justin took a huge swallow out of his glass then signaled to the bar attendant for another.

He supposed Justin made a valid point. If there was one thing Lucas Mason didn't shy away from, it was something that he indeed was compelled to achieve. That's how he was throughout his adolescence. In academia, Luke had to be the brightest, the fastest. He valued anything that challenged his mind. That included women. It wasn't like he was a virgin. He'd had his share of women through college, even a few girlfriends. Things just never seemed to work out. Either it was unfortunate timing or lack of interest, he would always favor his work in the end. Which ultimately led to the majority of his breakups.

"Yeah, I guess you're right, huh?" Luke countered, after his internal contemplation.

Turning back towards the bar for a refill, Luke quickly changed the subject from his love life to his buddy's new position. Being a senior analyst would come with numerous perks, one of which was his office. A private office was something Luke desperately wanted since he hated working in a crowded environment. The many employees made it hard to concentrate, but he made do.

As his friend begun speaking enthusiastically about his new advancement, Luke felt a chill gently caress his spine causing a slight shiver. He peeked around to see if anyone else noticed the draft, but it seemed he was alone. Drawing his attention back to Justin, luckily before he saw his distraction, Luke became enthralled in his happiness once more. That was until that eerie feeling reemerged. The tingle wasn't as unpleasant as it was annoyingly unnerving. Perhaps he'd rubbed up against some material of the carpet to create the static shock. Puzzled, he looked down below his feet. Most of the nightclub, known as Phantom, was hardwood flooring. He cast the sensation aside and tried to refocus on his friend's excitement when some unseen force pulled his gaze towards the front entrance.

And there she was, the most amazingly stunning beauty he'd ever seen. Stealing his focus away from Justin completely, his mystery vixen's strong presence froze him to stone, like Michelangelo's David. The woman was wearing faded denim jeans, with mid-thigh leather fuck-me boots with a heel longer than his middle finger. Luke also observed the black long-sleeved crop top shirt that showed toned, tanned, washboard abs. Her hair was the color of the reddest flames he'd ever seen, and her eyes seem to reflect the colors of May. And as her eyes shifted over to lock with his, after surveying her surroundings, it took everything he had in him to remain upright.

****

As Kat walked into Club Phantom, run by creatures from her realm unbeknownst to the humans inside, she had confidence that tonight was going to be terrific. She hadn't gone out in a while, and she needed to relax without the threat of decapitation looming over her shoulders. Being surrounded by allies would help relieve some pent-up aggression. Kat already wasn't a joy to be around, so when she got into one of her moods, it was best to leave her alone. Unfortunately, thanks to a decade of pushing people away, allies were rare for her. So tonight, she would enjoy the few hours she had to lower her stress levels.

Kat and Sia had just entered when the music shifted to a soft tune. The upbeat tempo of the melody had her slowly swaying her hips as she stood looking around. This female was unquestionably in the mood to dance. But with who?

Searching the club for possible prospects, she tactically followed the trail Sia made through the humans who were mingling around the entrance. Glancing around the herd of bodies, Kat glimpsed up towards the bar and locked eyes with a handsome devil leaning up against the bar top. He was standing talking to another young man, slightly angled away, but his focus was solely on her. And Kat loved it.

Sia mumbled something in her ear, probably something about alcohol because Goddess knows her sister loved a good drink, but her eyes stayed glued on the man reclined against the bar. Something about him drew her attention, and it wouldn't let her go. He was simplicity wrapped up as Superman. And she wondered if her Clark Kent had the physique to match.

Continuing to stare, Kat observed the rest of his stature uninhibited. He was wearing glasses and a cream-colored blazer with dark blue jeans. Clark was not the type that usually drew her attention. The harpy usually went for men that were trying to kill her, and this human certainly couldn't cause her any harm. However, there was something about his aura that lured her to him. So just for the night, she would roll with the connection.

Sashaying towards the dance floor, never taking her eyes off her mystery man, Kat started a slow, rhythmic sway to the beat. Once she made it to the platform, she looked over to the bar to see if he was still looking and he most definitely was. She smiled. *You're mine now.*

****

No way. No fucking way was she looking at Luke. There had to be another person behind him because there wasn't a chance in hell a vixen like her was eyeballing him. She was gazing at him like he was the best lollipop she'd ever had. A lollipop she couldn't wait to get another lick of. She was magnificent, he thought to himself. It was like her body was made to move with rhythmic grace, and as she turned her back to him, he noticed the rear view was just as fine as the front. Entranced by her beauty, Luke almost didn't catch his coworker's words in his ear.

"Oh man." Justin hummed, scooting closer as to be heard over the blaring music. "Is she looking at you like that?" He paused. "Yeah, she's looking at you like that. Bruh, you gotta go over there."

Luke stopped staring for a moment to look over at his friend.

"What?" He questioned. "No, she must be looking at someone else. You, perhaps?"

That would make sense too. Justin was the type of guy that piqued women's interest. With his model good looks and his bad boy persona, his friend had no shortage of prospects. Somehow, Luke knew Red wasn't looking at Justin, but indeed looking at him instead.

"No sir, it's you, her eyes aren't trained on me. And believe me, I doubled checked. Correction, triple checked. Go dance with her. What's the worst that could happen?"

Ha! He could faint. That's the worst that could happen. He could drop fucking dead.

Chapter Five

The music selection at the nightclub was perfect. It allowed Kat to continue her seductive dance as she tried to lure her prey to the dance floor. Countless others had tried to approach her as she moved, many men and a few women, but she only wanted him. But he wouldn't bite, even though he seemed attracted. Hmm. It looks like Kat was going to have to get her shy boy, because Clark was not takin' the eye-fucking bait. To make matters worse, he turned back towards the bar to continue his conversation with the gentleman next to him. Unacceptable. Kat was not used to being ignored, especially by someone she'd shown interest in.

Kat stomped her heeled boot. She was giving him her best moves. She knew she was attractive. All harpies were. She had to shoo away nearly every human male on the dance floor. Even the women were hard to push aside. *So, what gives?*

Kat wasn't one to give up though, nope, not her, she was many things, but a quitter wasn't one of them. Besides, this may be the challenge she had been waiting for. Kat had no problem working for his attention. Her electrical current started to hum inside her body in anticipation.

A slow smile crept across her face, swaying her curvaceous hips to the music, as she walked up to the bar right next to her boy. Signaling to the bartender with a manicured hand she yelled over the base of the stereo system to order herself a drink. "Whiskey, neat!" She shouted to the familiar bartender dressed in all black.

Once the bartender got busy making her drink, Kat turned slightly to her side to get a better look at her human. Damn, Mr. Kent was even sexier up close, hell if he took off those Goddess-awful glasses he'd be diabolically delicious. Kat noticed the guy cast her a glance under his glasses but quickly averted his eyes when he saw her gazing in his direction. As he turned his focus away, she spotted a slight half smile that flashed dimples, and the juices between her legs practically began to overflow. He was hers.

"Hi, what's your name?" Kat practically drooled in the most sensual voice she could muster. She got no response. After a beat of silence, she continued her questioning. "You come here often?" Still nothing. "Are you mute?" She probed, starting to get frustrated. However, the dig didn't garner a reply.

That was until the man on the other side of her unidentified man nudged him in his rib, leaning in closely to whisper in his ear. "Man, Luke, she's talking to you."

He finally peered over and damn; she almost swallowed her tongue. He had the lightest ocean blue eyes she'd ever seen, her newfound favorite color, Bahama blue. He was breathtaking up close.

"Ummm hello." He faltered. "Sorry, were you speaking to me?"

It took her a heartbeat to realize he'd spoken since she'd gotten lost in those deep-sea blues.

Recovering elegantly, she propped her elbow up against the bar and replied. "Well, I was." She answered, inching a little closer to catch his scent. He smelled amazing, of course.

"Oh, I'm sorry I thought... yeah, never mind. Hi, I'm Lucas, Lucas Mason, but everyone calls me Luke." He rotated his body around entirely to face her, sticking out his hand in greeting.

Kat shook his hand firmly. "Well, hello Lucas, nice to meet you."

He swallowed hard. Probably liking just as much as she did how his name rolled off her tongue. "Umm yeah, nice to meet you too." He spoke nervously as the bartender placed her drink on the counter.

Kat reached over slightly causing her hand to casually brush up against his, and grabbed her glass. "So, what do you do, Lucas?"

Seeming to notice the mild spark, he glanced down at their hands briefly before looking back up to proceed with his response. "I'm a data consultant for Fall Heights."

Ahhhhh, so she was right. *Nerrrrrd alert!* Kat smiled inwardly. Banking her amusement, she replied with earnest. "Sounds interesting."

"Ha!" He laughed without humor. "It's not, but I love computers, so it fits." He shifted his shoulders in a shrug.

"Hmm." She pondered.

Smart just wasn't usually her type. She'd only had a few one-nighters throughout the centuries, and when she did, she went for those that were young, dumb, and hung, yet something about Luke intrigued her. Kat tilted her head and considered the implications. After all, he was only human, a man at that. He couldn't be that different from other Y chromosomes.

Shifting, uncomfortably, under her unblinking stare, he quizzed. "So, what about you? What do you do?"

Apparently, Kat glared too long, because she allowed the conversation to filter back to her. Too many questioned hailed in her direction would require too much focus. Besides, it wasn't like she could be honest and tell the man she was a

Knight in shiny armor. Because well, she was. And she didn't want to waste the energy on a good candidate for a one-nighter, so she turned the attention back on him.

Remembering to blink, she spoke. "You here with anyone?"

"Um, just some friends." He answered drawing back a little.

She hadn't realized she'd stepped so close into his personal space. Kat must have been making him uneasy. Ask her if she cared. *Nope.*

She stepped closer swiftly. "No girlfriend? Wife?"

"Huh? Girlfriend, wife?" He palmed the back of his neck nervously. "Um, no just some coworkers. No significant other."

Smiling sweetly, Kat noticed he said um a lot, which indicated he was lying about not having a girlfriend or he was, in fact, uncomfortable with their interaction. Going on faith, she decided to believe the latter. Which meant he wasn't used to women being the aggressor. Wasn't that so fuckin' cute. Oh yeah, she was getting laid by Luke Skywalker tonight. He was just too charming to pass up, and as he brought his drink to his luscious lips for a sip, Kat decided to throw it out there. No point in dragging this unnecessary back and forth interaction between them out. She wasn't interested in getting to know him. Kat wasn't interested in getting to know anyone, let alone a mortal man.

Putting her glass down on top of the bar softly, she voiced her next question. "So, you trying to get out of here?"

Seemingly caught off guard by her direct approach, he began coughing in intense spurts, as liquid dripped a little down his chin–*mmmm*, what she wouldn't give to lean over and run her tongue down his five-o'clock shadow.

Deciding it wasn't best to shock him twice, she reached over to pat his back instead. "Are you okay?"

Cutting a look beside him, towards the other guy eaves-dropping, Kat noticed the guy was trying his best to smother his laughter at his friend's expense. Seeing the failed attempt to hide his outburst of amusement, Luke looked over at his associate as well. The death glare he gave his pal seemed to sober him faster than words could've been spoken.

After a few more seconds Luke was finally able to refocus his attention back where she wanted it; which was on her. "Um, yeah, sorry about that."

He grabbed a napkin off the bar, using it to wipe the excess alcohol off his chin. *Pity*. She smiled. However, her disappointment was defused once she glanced down at a noticeably nice sized arousal strangling in his jeans.

Maybe he wasn't used to women being so forward, but damnit Kat took what she wanted, and she wanted him. Even alpha males had nothing on harpies. They were strong, forceful women, and they did not back down from a challenge. Ever.

Stepping in closer once more, using the hand still at his back, she ran her palm delicately over his shoulder to rest on his chest. "So, you didn't answer my question."

He turned to her then with focus. His eyes were beginning to sparkle with interest. "Like where? Um, yes, go where?"

Triumphant, she eased in, her chest brushing his. "How about your place? We could talk or..." *Fuck*. She didn't say that last part out loud, especially since he already looked like he was about to cum in his pants. She had a better place for him to do that.

Kat bent forward and trailed her hand down the front of his jacket. Settling into his space, close enough to be able to plant her feet between his, she moved in for the kill. Coiling her finger through his belt loop, Kat pulled him even closer, so she could hover her lips over his jugular. Inhaling his obvious natural scent, she felt him quiver under her hands.

"Yes." He exhaled breathlessly. "Yes, that would be perfect."

Excitingly, she drew away and went to grab his hand, so she could finally drag him out of there. Unfortunately for her, some blonde Barbie doll came bouncing up, stopping in front of their exit. Annoyed by the delay, she went to step around her until she noticed Lucas had turned to address their unwelcomed guest.

"Luke, oh my God, Luke!" Malibu Barbie bellowed. "You have to come help me on the dance floor. These idiots won't leave me alone. I told them I was going to go get my boyfriend." She stated, resting her hands on her hour-glass figure, while she threw her blonde locks over her shoulder dramatically.

Kats temper flared. Remembering where she was, she tried internally to smother the flame blaring inside. *What the whole fuck?!* Boyfriend, *boyfriend?* This was one of the very reasons she drastically hated humans. They were fuckin' liars. And here she thought choir boy was genuinely innocent. Apparently not, if he pulled blondie as a girl.

Not one for drama, she decided to count her losses and dip. Silently fuming she looked over at Lucas one more time before she retreated. The look on his face, as he gawked at Barbara Millicent, is what froze her in place.

"Hey, sorry Casey." He sputtered. "I can't pretend to be your boyfriend tonight. I was leaving. Ask Justin." Luke hiked a thumb over his shoulder towards the gentleman still standing quietly by his side drinking a beer.

She gave a pout of her flushed cock sucking lips then grabbed his arm. "Ahh c'mon Luke, please." She plumped up her breast as if to sweeten her request. "I want you, Justin's such a grab-ass."

Justin, seemingly unbothered by the blondie's insult, peered over and sneered. "You couldn't pay me enough to grab that ass, Casey."

Kat could practically hear the "as if" tumble off the chick's tongue as she rolled her eyes, focusing back on Luke.

Bored and a little relieved with this whole display, Kat decided it was time for her to step in. Luke looked as if he was about to cave and she was not one to be ignored.

"Look, Carebear." Kat began, stepping forward. Funshine turned her attention towards Kat, as if she just noticed her presence, even though she had caught her peeking in her direction numerous times throughout her and Luke's exchange.

"It's Casey. And you are?" Laa-Laa batted her eyes, with a look of insignificance aimed in Kat's direction.

Ignoring her inquiry, she continued. "Listen, Luke is preoccupied, or he will be very shortly, so why don't you run along, and do as he says? I'm sure you won't have trouble finding another to be your puppet," she ended, shooing her off with a wave of her hand.

The comical expression Casey produced after Kat finished speaking was priceless. She wanted to bend over and help her pick her face off the floor, but she was over the childish bickering of these humans. Grabbing Luke's hand, she pulled him close to her side as she searched the club for her sister.

Zeroing in towards the end of the bar she spotted Sia talking to one of the barkeepers absentmindedly. Several things were going on behind that empty glare, but right now wasn't the time to address it. Drawing on a connection that had laid dormant for years, she waited until Sia noticed she was leaving. Kat knew the moment Sia felt her presence because she looked up directly catching her eyes. Looking back fleetingly at Lucas then the door, she prayed her sister understood her subtle gesture. Raising her drink in the air, Sia nodded once then turned her focus back to the attendant. And that was the only send-off Kat needed.

Chapter Six

Luke had stumbled into heaven. There was no way on God's green earth, was he being led out of the club by one of the most beautiful women he had ever seen. Allowing her to lead the way towards the exit, he brought his other hand up to pinch his forearm. Verifying his reality, he was awakened further once the ice-cold air of winter in New York hit his face. This whole experience was new to him. He rarely went out, and when he did, women never threw themselves at his feet. Luke knew he was attractive, but he'd never put off a one-night stand kind of aura. Sure, he spoke to women, but it never led to anything remotely similar to this.

Turning towards him in the middle of the sidewalk, the object of his affection grabbed him, pulling him close. Effectively pulling him from his musing.

"So, where's your car?" She purred, wrapping her hands around his waist so she could tuck her hands into his back pockets.

Spotting the valet posted up behind a stand, he reached into his jacket and pulled out his orange ticket. Walking up, he handed the young man his slip.

Shifting back, he replied, smoke coming from his hushed breath against the night air. "It should be here shortly."

Wrapping her arms around him, she stared into his eyes, which only made the erection suffocating behind his zipper throb that much harder. Luke never felt such need, such hunger for another. The lust he experienced with Casey was laughable compared to this raw bleeding passion he felt for the goddess in his arms. Something about her drew him closer, and as she continued to gaze at him expectantly, he decided to go with the moment and take a chance.

Oh, so gently, he reached up and cupped her chin with his hand, bringing her lips inches away from his own. The air seemed frozen in place as they both stood there waiting for the other to close the distance. The anticipation was almost worth it, until the parking attendant cleared his throat a few feet away. Still holding his companion, Luke reached and grabbed his keys from the gentlemen. A bit stunned by the near kiss, he didn't realize his lady was speaking.

"..... So, I'll ride with you," his lady exhaled just as breathless as he.

"I'm sorry what?" Luke responded, refocusing.

"I said, I rode with my sister, so I don't have my car here. So, if it's cool, I'll ride with you."

"Um, yes that's perfect."

Luke needed to broaden his vocabulary and stop with the *um*. Damn, he was acting as if he didn't have a master's degree in computer engineering from M.I.T. It was about time Luke started acting like the grown-ass man he was. The time for being star struck was over; if this were going to happen, he'd make it worth her while. Stepping up to his passenger side door, he cupped the handle, prying it open for her to enter.

"Such a gentleman, thanks," she praised, ducking her head so she could settle in comfortably in his plush leather seat.

Admiring her legs as she swung them inside, Luke waited until she was settled before closing her in. Once she was secure, he closed the car door and jogged around his sleek black Audi

A4. Opening his car door, planting himself inside, he cranked up the heat.

After they were settled, Luke drove off into the night, heading towards his condo. Contrary to his pep talk earlier, he was still nervous. Trying to mellow out, Luke flipped the audio over to one of his favorite albums by The Weekend. Releasing some of his tension as "Earned It" boomed through the speaker, he leaned back against the headrest. Luke was at peace, gliding through the empty streets of late New York with only the streetlights to guide him. He finally felt in control – that was until he felt a delicate hand rub up against the inside of his thigh.

****

Kat sneaked a quick look over at Luke, *shit I may have picked up a fucking virgin.* He was entirely too stiff and timid. He'd barely glanced in her direction, and when he did, he'd shift his focus back to the road so fast Kat thought she imagined it. Absentmindedly, she wondered *was this the norm for human men?* Kat rarely interacted with the fairer species, let alone attempted to be intimate with one of their kind. It was just easier for her to stay close to her people. Being a Knight didn't exempt harpies from the death sentence that would be handed down if they let their identity be discovered. Kat always kept to her own world in matters of dating. Besides, she reviled humans, and men were the worst. But tonight, she was willing to change all that.

Hell, her last encounter was months ago with her ex Luther, and yeah, she *so* wasn't going there. Trying to compare the two worlds would be like trying to compare apples to a vulture. They were night and day, which made it more unbelievable that she'd ever let a human draw her attention. But he did, and Kat was willing to give Luke something very valuable - time.

Being a Knight didn't offer much freedom, so when she

finally did find a moment to herself, it was hard to savor the short minutes. Evermore so now, since over the past few years she'd turned into her new favorite character of all time, the Grinch. Wallowing in her own self-loathing was becoming a daily activity; tended to take up most of her time. But after her butt-kissing sister told her that Sky green-lighted their night off, after bagging Count Muppet, she figured this was probably her only chance to do the dance with no pants.

Hopefully, she had chosen well because when she put her hand on his thigh, he tensed up immediately. It didn't bode well for their evening if every time she touched him, he acted as if she shocked him, which would've been possible if she didn't have complete control of her powers. Kat was beginning to question her judgment until he finally settled into her touch. Smiling, she slowly slid her hand further up the inside of his thigh. Kat was pleased to see the imprint of his erection grow more substantial; as she continued her slow torturous seduction with her fingers.

The two drove a few miles, pulling into a garage on the other side of town after a while. As he came on her side of the car to open her door, Kat examined her location, since she was always attuned to her environment. She still needed to be aware of her surroundings, enemies were always around, and she needed to stay alert. If she were going to die it would be on her terms, not by any sneak attacks.

Looking around, as Luke led her towards the garage's double doors, she noted he stayed in a complex building for condominiums, which was somewhat surprising. She would have pegged him for a ranch with horses kind of guy. And didn't that make him a little sexier?

Walking towards the entrance, he pulled out a key card from his jacket pocket to swipe against the keypad. Holding the door for her to walk through first, she stepped into a rather expensive lobby. It looked like something out of a magazine. The lobby contained clean white walls, marble floors, and tropical plants in vases that looked like they were personally picked from the Amazon. It read money, which was another surprise.

The desk attendant, an older white gentleman in uniform, looked up from his computer screen once he noticed their entrance and smiled.

"Hi Mr. Mason, late night. Phantom?" The clerk asked with a rustic baritone voice.

"Hi Dusty," Luke said in greeting, "Yes, you know my co-workers love that place."

Dusty had already tuned out Luke in favor of staring at her instead, gazing at her with a look Kat was all too familiar with. An expression of pure lust Kat put on men's faces plenty of times. She was a strong, confident, courageous woman after all. Kat knew she was appealing, especially to humans. She owned everything there was about herself, and sure she had her flaws, but she loved the hell out of those too. How she felt about herself was never a problem, because as a woman she knew she was powerful, and that made her virtually unstoppable.

Kat gave Dusty a little wave and a wink. She could practically see the drool develop from the side of his mouth and Kat smiled inwardly at that thought. She really shouldn't be playing with an old man's heart like that, but she couldn't resist. The male species was so easy to lure.

Luke took her hand and pulled her towards the elevators, effectively removing her from her flirtatious antics.

"Have a good night Dusty," Lucas told the attendant with slight annoyance in his voice. Aw, was her boy jealous? How adorable.

Following Lucas, they reached the elevator bay doors, hit

the up arrow and waited. Within seconds the stainless-steel doors gracefully glided open, and they stepped inside. Hitting the elevator button for the eighteenth floor, they avoided each other as they ascended.

Lucas seemed nervous, which was probably why he stood so far away. And that was okay, considering Kat was too busy praying he had a window facing condo–nothing like being trapped in a building with no way out. A girl needed to cover her bases, even though he didn't look like the kind of guy to pull one over on her.

The elevator came to an abrupt stop, and Kat let Luke lead the way, while subtly looking around trying to pinpoint her exits. Unfortunately, it seemed as if there was only one exit on the far side of the floor, which more than likely led to the stairwell. She didn't note any other doors which meant he was probably the only one on this floor. That would mean she had one set of stairs and the elevator for exit opportunities. If she had to, she'd make do.

Walking a few feet, they came to a stop at a large crème color entrance. Kat waited patiently as Luke took his keys out and unlocked the door then held it open for her to walk through first again.

Shutting the door behind them, he flipped up a switch on the side wall casting a dim light into a spacious, high ceiling condo. Kat didn't know what to expect about his living arrangements, but what she saw before her wasn't it.

Studying her surroundings, Kat wondered exactly how much he made at Fall Heights. The place was enormous, which was even more of a surprise considering the condo was a fucking studio. There was a giant ass vintage burgundy canopy bed–with a black microsuede comforter. The bed sat upon a black cement platform near the windows.

Walking further inside, the eating area came into view on her left. The kitchen was beautifully simplistic. All stainless-steel appliances, midnight-black cabinets with stunning countertops. In the center of the kitchen was an island harboring the same design, with one side set as the meal prep area and adjacent, a fully stocked bar with two leather stools facing towards the kitchen.

Continuing her self-guided tour, she turned from the kitchen to the living room off to the right. The furniture was all white leather with black upholstered cushions, with a glass coffee table in the center of a villa gray rug. Which was all accented by an electric fireplace and a mounted sixty-five-inch TV.

The place was decked out, and she hadn't even noticed the best part. Refocusing towards the bed, she saw the night sky. The whole back wall was nothing but floor to ceiling glass windows. Windows with two crème color lining glass double doors in the center that led out to a balcony. Exit number three.

Finishing her final survey, with Luke silently shadowing her, Kat threw a look over her shoulder arching one red brow in question.

"I'm very good with computers," he shrugged. "You'd be surprised how much you can make as a tech."

He stepped closer, "But for what it's worth I didn't pick this out." He waved around the room, "My sister did. She thought I deserved to live someplace nice. I was able to get her to settle on this place," he finished, with a little sadness in his voice.

"Settle?" She pushed.

He gave a humorless laugh, "Yeah, she wanted better and grander. Like a mansion or something, but it's just me. I didn't need that much space. So, we ended up here. She liked the building and told me to get the penthouse, but I talked her down a few floors because again, it's just me. She figured since I still had the floor to myself it'd be okay." He stared blankly around his home.

"Hmm," she drawled as she took a step further inside his place for a re-review.

"So, umm would you like a drink? I have whiskey?" He stated anxiously, walking over towards the bar, as he changed the subject. The redirection was cool with her since she could tell it was something he didn't want to touch on. Besides, it seemed private, and she didn't need to get personal. Kat wasn't here for small-talk, and it was about time she let him know that.

"You've never done this before have you, Lucas?" She inquired, pausing his movements.

Luke turned towards her and their eyes locked. Kat had the answer with the uncertainty in his gaze. No, he hadn't, but Goddess knows he wanted to.

"It's okay," she prowled closer, "I'm very, very dominant, and I'll tell you everything you need to do okay?"

He nodded, and some of those chestnut brown curls fell into his face.

"Good, now strip...slowly." She tacked on.

She thought he'd show some reluctance, but trembling hands immediately went to his jacket. *Yeah*, she smiled to herself, *this was going to be a fun night.*

Chapter Seven

*H*mm, *this keeps getting better and better* Kat thought as Luke tossed his jacket to the side. She could see the outlines of his muscular body from where she was standing, and it was entirely unexpected. Her boy was turning out to be full of surprises. Delicious surprises.

As he went to unbutton his collared shirt and reveal even more tantalizing flesh, she knew she'd chosen well. Even more so when he let the shirt slide down tone shoulders and arms. *Yum-fucking-me.* Who knew Kent had a body under all those tailored clothes. Luke seemed to be utterly unaware of how delectable he was. And she planned to take advantage of that. Leisurely.

As his hands went to his belt, all distracting thoughts ceased. She turned her full focus back on Mr. Lucas Mason. He took the belt off, slowly unbuttoned his jeans, then paused at his zipper. He was looking up to her questioningly.

"Did I say stop, Luke?" She questioned, propping her hand under her chin while tapping her index finger to her cheek impatiently.

He shook his head from side to side slightly.

"No, no I didn't. Did I?" She stated sternly.

Luke unzipped his fly, hooking his thumbs on either side of his pants, and slowly, oh so slowly, lowered his dark washed denim jeans. Damn, she underestimated the size of his dick. Kat could see the imprint through his underwear, and it was impressive. She tried to keep a poker face, but the sight of him made her knees weak. Kat bit her lip and moved a little closer to the hallway wall, so she could lean up against it before her legs embarrassed her. Stabilizing, she continued to eye fuck him from head to toe. From her viewpoint, just behind his boxer briefs, he was long, hard, and thick. He certainly fit her quota of young and hung, just not dumb. Two out of three wasn't bad, especially since he had the two that truly mattered.

Not missing a beat, he went to hook his thumbs into his briefs, to pull them down, but stopped once he noticed her shaking her head, mouthing no. She knew once those boxer briefs came down, it was game on, and she had to touch him first. Goddess above, she was dying to touch him.

Mentally putting a lock on her powers, she strolled forward. The last thing she needed to do was lose control and reveal herself during a time of passion.

As Kat inched forward, she sluggishly began to undress. She deliberately went just as slowly as he had, starting with bending down to unzip her thigh-high boots. After gliding her shoes off, she lifted her crop-top over her head, revealing her emerald, sheer-laced bra. Next came her skin-tight jeans, wiggling them down over her plump buttocks, producing matching lace panties. When she stood within a few inches from him, the heated look he was giving her body dampened the inside of her panties. She gave a little twirl, so he could get a better rearview picture, pleased with the slight gasp that left his breath.

Sauntering onward, Kat began unhurriedly moving around his sculpted physique, drawing her fingers lightly across his abs, ribs, up his chest, then his back and shoulders. She circled his entire body all the while loving the hisses and gasps, he made as she caressed his Adonis-like form. By the time Kat made it back around to face him, he was panting heavily, and if she was honest with herself, the tour of his body affected her as well. Kat needed to take this play time up into the next level, and she had just the idea to accomplish that goal. She grabbed his arm and backed him up gradually until his back hit the front door. She smiled a smile she usually only gave her victims, right before she charred off their heads.

"You've been a very, very good boy, Lucas. I didn't even have to tell you not to speak unless spoken to," she purred, running her hand down his stomach with her chest pressed up against his.

Kat boldly cupped his erection, loving how his eyes popped and his mouth opened in surprise, then immediately closed as the pleasure of her caress registered.

"I think that deserves a reward, don't you?" She hummed. Luke nodded his head again but didn't open his eyes. "Mmmm, yes, my Superman deserves a reward, and guess who is willing to play Lois Lane?"

With that, Kat dropped to her knees in front of him.

****

Luke couldn't move, hell he wasn't even sure he was breathing. When this incredible woman dropped to her knees before him, pulling out his erection, Luke knew if he didn't snap out of his immobility he'd fall flat on his face. Who knew his inability to talk would work in his favor? His ability to speak had left him the moment she told him to strip. All he could muster was not cumming in his underwear while doing what she asked. Now, he was getting rewarded for something he couldn't do even if he tried. When he felt her warm, succulent mouth circle the tip of his cock, he stopped thinking and just began to feel.

Luke banged his head on the door at his back, closing his eyes tighter as she dropped back with her wet tongue around his member. Damn, she was talented. His temptress drew his cock to the back of her throat and went back to circle the tip of his erection. She made this motion with her tongue repeatedly driving him crazy. Making matters more intense, she grabbed the base of his dick and sucked with all her might. *Did this woman not have a gag reflex?*

As he felt his climax surge forward, he knew he was powerless to stop it until she grabbed his balls in her other hand and squeezed. Hard. Luke drew out a groan of shock and looked down. God, he shouldn't have looked. The sight of her on her knees before him was such an erotic sight he felt the sensation to explode roaring back. She gave him another squeeze, and it stopped dead at the tip. He winced.

"You cum when I say you cum. If you can hold out just a little while longer, I'll let you taste me." She licked the border of his cock where precum emerged at just the thought of him getting his lips on her.

"Don't you want to taste me, Luke?" his vixen hummed in her siren voice, a smooth melody to his ears.

Damn right, he wanted to taste her. Turnabout was only fair, and as she looked up with that devious crooked smile of hers, he knew he'd do his damnest to do just that.

"Good. Five minutes, that's all you must last. Up for the challenge?" She smirked.

Hell yeah! Shit, what were five minutes? Luke could handle that, no problem. He closed his eyes and took a deep breath. Centering himself, he glanced down then nodded.

Seemingly pleased with his confidence, she took his erection back in her delicate hands. Looking up at him she gave him that small, crooked smirk that rivaled the mischievous grin of The Batman's Joker, and he knew for a fact at that moment he was *fucked.*

Chapter Eight

Lucas, Lucas, Lucas mmmm he was delicious. With his naturally tanned skin and his muscular toned thighs, everything about him drew her in. When Kat set the timer on her wristwatch for five minutes, she placed her jaw and took him into the deepest dark pit of her throat. Gag reflex, nope, not her, she could take all his girth. And Luke had girth in spades.

He would get close to exploding every few seconds, but he would surprise her every time by drawing back at the last minute, encompassing Niagara Falls. He kept his eyes shut, head back, the entire time which was a good strategy, considering he'd almost come in her hands when he'd looked down before.

He tasted exquisite, like the ocean blue of his eyes, salty but sweet. Kat was so focused on his flavor and her rhythm that when the timer on her wrist went off, she practically groaned in disappointment.

Dejectedly, she looked up and saw he'd opened his eyes and was looking down at her sporting a broad smile that showed a full set of pearly whites and dimples. A smile that made her dark heart spark with feeling.

Amused, Kat looked up into a triumphant gaze, "So, I guess you won. How about you relax now and enjoy?"

The smile he had plastered on his face disappeared, and confusion took its place. When she took him back in her slick mouth and sucked with all her might, stroking his balls with one hand while stroking his staff with the other, he quickly got the hint. He came in a rushing wave, shooting an endless array of warm jets down her throat.

Once he was finished, she practically had to hold him up when he began to sag down the door. She knew he wasn't able to comprehend the strength it took to hold up his large frame. He was so drained he didn't notice. She took everything he had to give and boy oh boy did he deliver. When he finally settled, lifting his lids, he smiled down at her with a question.

"Got something to say?" She inquired. He nodded.

"Speak."

"Damn."

An unexpected burst of laughter escaped her lips. An amusement she hadn't felt leave her body in a long time. And it only took one word to draw it out.

"You could have done that this whole time and ended this before it began, huh?"

Yes, she could have, but seeing him struggle was just so freaking cute. Besides she wanted him to win. The whole ordeal left her drenched and needy. She got up from her knees and took a few steps away from him.

Crooking her finger in his direction, she whispered, "Come here."

He moved to walk towards her, but she stepped back. He came closer to her again, this time moving swiftly to try and grab her, but she shifted so fast he missed her again. He blinked a few times in confusion, but recovered, delighting in the chase.

Kat had to watch it; it was becoming increasingly hard to hide her abilities around him; she wasn't used to being caught up in the world of play. This time when he went to take another step towards her, she didn't move.

*****

Luke beamed when his arms finally engulfed his woman. God, she was soft. Her smooth, satin skin was a little darker than his own, which meant she spent a lot of time in the sun or she had an exotic background. He'd hoped soon he'd get the opportunity to find out more, but now wasn't the time. He ran his fingers from her collar bone to her shoulder, flipping her wavy red locks away from her neck, admiring how she began to shiver.

When she tilted her head to the side, exposing the long elegant structure of her neck, in invitation, he didn't think twice. He ran his tongue over the light trail his fingers had previously made. She moaned, and it was the most delightful sound he'd ever heard. It meant he was affecting her as much as she was affecting him. That was encouraging, considering Luke hadn't been with many women throughout his life. He wasn't a virgin by far, but all his past sexual encounters were after months of getting to know each other, never like this.

However inexperienced he was, his touch seemed to please her, therefore, he continued. Running his hand up her smooth back, his fingers landed on the clasp of her bra. Luke grinned, *why the hell not?* He unclasped her bra, guiding the straps gently over her shoulders. Luke stepped back to watch her lacy green bra fall to the ground and the most beautiful breasts he'd ever seen emerge. *Holy mother of God, I am not going to drool, I am not going to drool. Thirty-two-year-old men did not drool.* But damnit, it was hard not to drop to his knees before her in awe of the flawless beauty standing before him. When Luke reached to touch her, he knew her breast were made entirely for his hands.

She arched into him, moaning slightly in acceptance, so he continued to caress her body. As Luke intensified his touch, he wondered if it was possible for a woman to cum from fondling their nipples. Curious, he flicked her erect pink tip, watching it pucker. The sounds of pure bliss escaping her lips, propelled him into leaning forward so he could draw such perfection into his awaited mouth. As her fingers started slowly roaming through his hair, pulling him closer to paradise, he knew without a shadow of a doubt that this was going to be the best night of his life.

Chapter Nine

Sky entered the Phantom nightclub, trying her best to remember to keep control over her temper. But as she immediately located the Knight she was looking for, she knew that would genuinely require restraint. Sia, who was sitting front and center at the bar talking to one of the bartenders, seemed oblivious to the others around. Recently she'd been seen drinking excessively on her off time. Thus, Sky wasn't surprised to see her drowning her sorrows in alcohol.

Because of the recent increase of rogue creatures in the east, Sky decided to check in nightly with all of them located in the city. As a leader, she wasn't able to be everywhere the Knights needed her to be, but she made a conscious effort to be there whenever any one of them was in dire situations. And Sia's message was so illegible Sky figured it was best she tracked her down to make sure she was safe.

What Sky found when she entered the club was Sia utterly drunk off her ass. This was extremely difficult for one of their kind to accomplish. It took a tremendous amount of alcohol to incapacitate an immortal. Their body temperature ran hotter than humans, giving them the ability to burn off manmade alcohol much quicker. Yet here Sia was, fuckin' wasted. Which only intensified Sky's anger.

She glanced down at her phone again and saw the text from her Knight that read "Alllllllllz gooodd at Phan wit Kit."

Sky had rewarded the twins with a night off, forgetting that those two may not have been the best duo to leave unattended.

And after Sia's response and Katrina's no-answer, her best course of action was to find them both. If Sia truly was in the same place her sister was, then why didn't Kat reply?

She weaved her way through the herd of humans grinding against each other, getting a few looks of admiration as she passed. Most of humanity, the smart ones anyway, hurried out her way, seeming to sense the danger she exuded. The other half were seemingly glued to the floor as they gawked in her direction. Looks she ignored.

Sky was aware of what her appearance indicated; she wasn't naïve. She was alluring, yes. To humans, as well as her kind; however, attractiveness meant nothing to her. Physical appearance was fleeting. Unfortunately for Sky, most did not feel that way. Humans still drew near until they reached close enough to look at her eyes. Only then did they navigate elsewhere. Eyes like the bottomless pit of the universe screamed unnatural. If the eyes didn't warrant caution, then the power that always seemed to sizzle around her kept the others at bay. But there were a few brave ones that would still draw near. Curiosity or the lack of respect for their environment would eventually be the end of their race.

Ignoring the humans, for now, Sky gave a few nods to the creatures of her realms she recognized, as she walked towards her destination. She came up behind Sia, giving Dexter the bartender–a bear shifter–a look that exuded pain. He responded to her death stare with one small shrug of his broad shoulders.

There weren't many paranormal creatures alive that didn't know of the Knights' existence. Her harpies were well known amongst all their kind in both worlds, and they all knew she was their leader, the bear shifter behind the bar included. It wasn't the bear's job to keep her Knights sober. Nevertheless, he had a personal relationship with Sky. The bear always looked out for her Knights when they visited, which led her to believe that Sia must have bribed him. The shifter loved his antiques–she'd had to hand over a few herself over the centuries.

If Sky wasn't fuming before, she was now. Sia was one of her best Knights. Unlike her twin, she was disciplined enough to keep her shit in line. Sia should have known better, but then again, so should've Sky. Sia had become increasingly distracted the further her twin pulled away. She'd walked in on her countless times drowning her sorrows with the booze. Sky thought a night out with her other half would be beneficial towards their rocky relationship. She was wrong.

Not only was Sia drunk off her rocker, in public, she was unaware of her surroundings. Sky was standing right behind her and Sia never moved. Taking a few calculated deep breaths, to calm her rage, she approached her pupil.

"Hello, Sia," Sky spoke, more harshly than intended.

Sky's Knight jumped, sending the drink she held crashing down on top of the bar. Sia disregarded the mess she made, electing to scoot off the barstool she was sitting on to turn around and face Sky.

"Mistress, my lady, Sky, hi," Sia responded with slurred words. To her credit, she tried to appear to have her shit together.

"Shall we?" Sky motioned with her hand towards the back of the club.

She could practically see the sweat began to perspire atop her forehead, as Sia swallowed and nodded.

Beyond annoyed, Sky reached out and grabbed her Knight in a punishing hold. She navigated them through the humans still mingling around as she located a quiet place in the back further away from the restroom. Sky knew she was holding Sia a bit too tightly because now and then she would hear her hiss, as her nails dug into her skin. However, she was too pissed to care. Pulling Sia further away from prying eyes, Sky located the club's employees-only locker room, Sky opened the door and dragged Sia behind her. Once they were both in the room, Sky grabbed her forcibly and threw Sia up against the wall. Hard. The jolt effectively sobered her up.

Fully unleashing the anger she'd tried and failed to contain, Sky growled, "What the fuck is wrong with you?! You didn't even sense my approach. I could've been anyone, you imbecile!"

Sia looked up at her guilty, trembling, more than likely frightened by the transformation of her eyes. They constantly altered when she lost control of her temper. Absently, she wondered what color they were now.

"Yeah, I, I know. I'm sorry, I fucked up," Sia stammered out.

"Clearly," Sky spat.

Inhaling deeply, Sky calmed her rage. Her Knights were her responsibility, and she took her job seriously. If anything happened to either one of them, she'd take it as a personal failure. She tried not to get attached because even in her world, death for immortals was possible. It was on her to make it that much harder for those that wanted them dead, which reminded her.

"Where's Kat, Sia?" She pressed.

Sia looked down, not wanting to meet her eyes, which meant Sky wasn't about to like what she was about to hear.

"Umm, she left about an hour ago." Sky's subordinate finally admitted.

"Fuck!" she exclaimed, releasing Sia from the wall. "She didn't check-in," Sky began to pace, dragging her phone from the holster at her hip, to begin putting together a search crew, "She may be injured, we need to find her." The next words spoken stopped her pacing.

"I think she's okay," Sia cut her eyes in every direction but Sky's face.

Focusing her attention back on her Knight, arching one eyebrow, she growled, "And how do you know that?"

"Ummm...." Sia looked away, crossing her hands behind her back while kicking imaginary gravel.

The temper Sky had just regained control over flared. "Sia! I don't have fucking time for this."

Taking a step forward, Sky reached out, grabbing her pupil by the throat, lifting her to eye level and squeezed. Sky pushed Sia against the wall, hard enough to crack the cement.

"Where. The fuck. Is Kat?" Sky demanded through clenched teeth.

"She left with a guy," Sia spat out, with a little dollop of blood trickling down her mouth.

Sky recoiled, tilting her head as if that would better help her understand the response.

"What?"

"She left earlier with some guy, a human male. And I'm pretty sure it wasn't to talk about the weather, if you know what I mean."

Yeah, she got it. And they both were lucky she had started meditation, or her fury would've skyrocketed at that proclamation. At the end of the day, she wanted what was best for her Knights. They were entitled to have lives; however, duties came first, and Kat should have checked in. She didn't care what the Knights did on their off time if they were smart about their decisions–taking no unnecessary risks. Risks like being alone in a club drunk off her ass, or going home with a human stranger from a nightclub, for example. Sia and Kat both fucked up tonight and she was going to make them pay for it. Sky wasn't here to paint each other's nails while they sipped wine in front of a cozy fire. She was their leader. And she was going to enjoy reminding them why.

Releasing the death grip she had on Sia's throat, Sky gave one final squeeze then stepped away. For now, she'd let them have their night. Knowing they weren't in immediate danger comforted her ire.

Once again composed, she shook her head slightly as she replied, "You twins are a thorn in my hide, you know that?"

Sia, shaking the cement particles off her shoulders, snorted. "Thorne? Boss, was that a joke? I can't believe it; you made a joke."

Now was a good time to leave, before she killed one of her favorite Knights. She started to walk towards the exit when Sia grabbed her by the arm to stop her.

"Please don't tell her I told you," Sia fully sober now, fumbled, "she'd never trust me again. I think we have a chance of getting back on good terms. I don't want to lose my sister. I have only her. You see the road she's walking down. Please, Sky," Sia implored.

Sky knew it was only a matter of time before she got the call that Kat had died in battle. No matter how much effort she put into keeping track of her whereabouts, Kat always seemed to end up in precarious situations. Kat had been becoming erratic and careless with her behavior, toying with her victims, leaving herself open, almost as if daring others to attack when she was defenseless. It was a sure-fire way to get a Knight killed, and Sky needed all her warriors to remain alert. Hell, the world needed all of them watchful. She'd seen this behavior many times before, and all of them ended poorly. Far too many of their kind grew tired of immortality, electing to meet the divinity instead. Kat, as she'd come to realize over the passing years, had a death wish. But Sky wasn't ready to let her go.

As Sky looked in the eyes of Sia's sad plea, she knew she was going to be lenient.

"She has until dawn to reply, or I'm bringing every Knight warrior from the North in to find her." Sky voiced, tugging her arm out of Sia's grip

Sia sagged with relief, "Thanks, boss."

Deadpan, she watched her eyes flare in the reflection of her Knights' eyes, "Don't thank me just yet. Because if I ever see you drunk off your ass again in public, you won't have to worry about an enemy catching you unaware. I'll kill you myself." She spared her Knight one last look before pushing her way through the exit door, not waiting for a reply.

Sky trudged through the club, pushing aside two human males that dared to get in her way as she went. She wasn't in the mood to entertain last-ditch efforts to score by night's end. Fortunately for them, they moved out of her way quickly, allowing her to reach the front entrance in a few strides. She could have left through the back doorway leading into the alley, but she needed to take a full breath of the freshest air she could get in New York.

Bursting through the double doors, she was greeted by the night's chill air. Sky barely felt the bite of the wind, as she looked up into the night's cloudless sky. Letting go of a small slice of weakness, she growled her frustration into the night. How could they have been so stupid? Losing one Knight was hard enough, losing two, the repercussions would've been catastrophic.

She couldn't think along those lines for long, because her skin was beginning to crawl with a familiar sensation that she was becoming quite accustomed to. Fear. Closing off her emotions, Sky decided it would be best to regroup. Sky knew better now than to try to reel in her anger alone.

Tucking her hands into her floor-length black leather coat, Sky strolled down the sidewalk until she reached the opening leading to the back alley. She usually was in a rush, but tonight she took her time, leisurely gliding down the passageway. Centering herself, she honed into all the particles that made up her body, shifting the dimensions through space and time, creating her portal through the universe.

Snapping all her molecules to pieces, she teleported outside to a small cottage in Toronto. She could've teleported inside, but she had learned over the years that it was better to not pop in on others without invitation. Taking a moment to admire the seclusion of the cottage, she listened to the quiet sounds of the nearby forest. The surprising large one-story stone bungalow, before her, sat in the middle of nowhere. Privacy was becoming increasingly difficult to achieve on Earth, with the humans continued growth in technology. Everyone over the age of five had a smartphone, which made it that much harder for them to retain their secrecy, which made places like this vital on this planet.

Walking up the stone steps, the soothing aromas from inside seeped through the cracks of the heavy wooden door, instantly calming the tension in her body. Smiling, Sky brought her fist up to knock. Pausing before her hand connected, remembering belatedly she was supposed to use her key. Stepping back, she bent down to retrieve the small key inside of her boot.

Entering the foyer, Sky shut the door behind her, shrugging off her coat so she could hang it up in the closet next to her. As she stepped further inside, she allowed the scents to draw her further down the hall, reaching the archway that led into the seating area. Propping herself up against the wall she gazed around the warm, open space. The cherry hardwood floors complemented the light caramel interior perfectly. Tropical houseplants were littered around the room, giving off smells of sandalwood and lilac. The crackle of flames coming from the rustic built in stone fireplace drew her gaze.

Briefly closing her eyes, she smiled. This was home. Sky loved it here; it was her oasis in the Sahara. And the woman that sat to the right of the fireplace, reclining atop a plush spacious sectional, reading a book while sipping tea was her haven.

That woman was Zafrina, her second in command. Sky tended to always come to the hut after her shifts to decompress. No other Knights knew the location, and Sky preferred it that way. She had a giant mansion in their realm that she welcomed all their Knights to, but this, this was their sanctuary.

Zafrina was Sky's balance in every way. Where she was short-tempered, Z was mellow. When Sky wanted to shout her fury, Z would remain mute. And when Sky wanted to create chaos, well, Z was always willing to join in on the mayhem, if it was warranted. The two fit. And she wouldn't have made it this far in her immortality without the woman before her.

Sky took a moment to gaze at her friend, basking in the warmth that spread through her body. She envied the power Z had to create a tranquil atmosphere. If she had the ability to develop her serenity instantly, maybe she wouldn't have come so close to ripping Sia's head off.

Sky took a few calculated breaths as she watched Z sip her tea, allowing her to gather her thoughts. Zafrina was stunning as always. Her long ebony hair usually kept braided into a low bun was down, flowing loosely over her shoulders. She'd traded in her fighting gear in favor of a soft crème nightgown that complimented her silky mocha skin. Her eyes were a deep hazel that crackled in the burning fire. High cheekbones that framed her oval face perfectly gave off an aura that read of the Egyptian queen she used to be. She was built to be loved, worshipped, and their Knights never failed in their praise.

Every Knight got along with Z famously, even the hard-headed disobedient ones such as Kat. She was the only one that Kat allowed to command her, with little to no complaint. Z was probably the only reason Kat had made it this far.

Recharged, Sky took a few steps into the seating area, plopping down on an accent chair opposite of her friend. The whole time, Z never looked up from her book, yet she felt the moment Sky regained clarity because she spoke.

"Feeling better?" Zafrina inquired with her head down, her eyes speed-reading the pages in front of her.

"Yes," was Sky's one-word response.

"Good," Z followed, flipping the page.

After a few beats of silence, she finally gave in. "You're not going to ask?"

"Do I need to?" She instantly replied.

Sky brought her hands over her face, bracing her elbows on her knees, "No."

"Would you like to talk about how they pissed you off this time then?"

"No," she growled through her hands.

Z flipped another page, casually taking another sip of her tea without a care in the world. Waiting. And Sky did not disappoint. She stood up from the seat and begun to pace. Z softly closed her book, sitting it gently beside her. Clasping her elegant fingers before her, she looked up, giving Sky her undivided attention.

"Why do they like to defy me so? It's like they want me to punish them," Sky thundered out as she continued to pace in front of the fireplace. "You know she didn't check in again? And this time it was because of a male. A human male. Does she want to get herself killed?! I know things haven't been ideal for Kat since that mission, but damn! When will she let that shit go? And don't get me started on her twin. That harpy's been drinking herself into an early grave for decades, and the only person capable of saving her is trying to get her own self *killed!*" Sky screamed in frustration.

Sky stopped her pacing, sitting back down to regain her peace. Grateful for the healing sensation she felt wash over her body, instantly relaxing her once more.

"Thank you."

Zafrina nodded, before speaking. "Kat will find her way. You must be patient and give her time and space to choose the right path. Everything will work out in due time; you will see."

Narrowing her eyes, she studied her friend, "And you know this how, Z?"

She shrugged, picking back up her book to resume reading.

Z occasionally received premonitions that allowed her to see the future, yet sometimes they weren't clear. Most of the snapshots that she translated precisely to paper were somewhat confusing, so they were filed away in her library labeled, allowing them to keep track, just in case they needed to revisit the image later. Sky trusted Z's judgment nonetheless, so if she said to give the twins time, she would try.

"I love them." She admitted reluctantly, through hushed words, sinking back in her chair.

She didn't want to feel anything for her Knights, because having emotions for another was a weakness she couldn't afford to pay. Somewhere over the years she became attached. They wiggled their way into her dark black heart, and the thought of losing any of them was unbearable.

"I know you do, as do I," Zafrina responded, flipping a page in her book yet again.

Sky paused and looked towards her partner in war, "I love you too." Might as well throw that out there.

"Even though you don't want to?" Z looked up, pausing with her hand in her book, holding her place.

Replying Sky hung her head in shame. "Yes."

To her to love was foolish. It served no purpose to their cause to love another. Up till now, she always felt free to make sound judgment calls concerning her harpies, but now everything was encompassed in doubt.

"It's okay to love, my dear friend. You don't have to make it sound as if you killed my dog."

"You don't have a dog." She cocked her head in confusion.

"And you are missing the point. Love doesn't have to be a weakness; on the contrary, it could turn out to be your greatest strength. You will fight harder to defend those you love. You protect them," she paused to look Sky in the eyes, "as I protect you."

Z resumed reading once again, as Sky sat back in the chair to think. Her phone was buzzing at her hip, but she just needed a few more minutes to collect herself. Having Z help her work through her emotions allowed her to see Sia and Kat's situation more clearly. They were adults, and she knew she needed to stop riding them so hard. She was essentially allowing them the time to work through their crap together, without the threat of her wrath.

Regardless, of her personal feelings towards them, they were two of the best fighters she had, if she lost either one of them, the Earth would feel their absence. Sky refused to lose them, but she would give them time to figure shit out on their own. And if anyone interfered with their journey, well then, at least she'd be able to kill someone.

Chapter ten

The night was shaping out to be pretty damn spectacular. Kat hadn't been this entertained in years, which turned her on even more. Lucas was beginning to come out of his shell, and she was pleased with his playful demeanor.

Backing up, Kat stepped onto the platform that held the bed. Grabbing Luke's hand, she dragged him on top of her as she fell backward onto the luxurious pillow top mattress. Enjoying the cradle she made for him between her legs. Goddess above, it'd been so long since a man touched her with care. Hell, Luther, her ex-lover, was all about the turn around and grab the ankles. No touching, no caressing; just wham, bam, thank you, ma'am. That was one of the many reasons they didn't work.

Kat lived for the anticipation, the allure, the hunger, the passion. Werewolves, the King of wolves, in particular, was all about doggy style, which was pretty cliché. But that was only one of the reasons they ended.

Luther was not only a predictable lover, but he was an incredibly dominant male with an ego that far exceeded her own. Hell, she was modest, he was an egotistical, self-centered, bastard, which ultimately led to their downfall. Kat was better off for it; when a girl wanted to self-destruct, she was better off alone.

Luke ran both hands up her thighs, imploring her to wrap her legs around his waist. She obliged, effectively pulling her from her destructive past. Kat ran her nails up his back reveling in the hushed hisses he made as he ran his tongue down her neck.

Mmmm, that glorious body of his was epic. He was all muscle, no body fat. Luke was just a bowl of magnificence. She was utterly transfixed, marveling in the feel of him between her legs, but when he started to trail his wet kisses down her body, she was forced back into focusing on her pleasure.

My oh my, did he have a talented tongue. That was another thing that surprised her. He continued to work his way down her body circling his tongue over her breast, paying equal attention to both, as he nipped and sucked at her nipples. Right before the playful seduction became painful, he moved his attention down her stomach. He was circling his diabolical tongue around her navel, causing her to grip the sheets tightly in her hands. He didn't spend long at her belly-button, which she was grateful for. He traveled further down to the juncture of her thighs placing feather-like kisses along each side.

She usually had more self-control over her body's movements but, *fuck*. The anticipation was killing her. And something told her lover boy knew it too. He knew just where to kiss her to make her writhe under his passionate caress. Her back arched off the mattress as he continued licking at the insides of her legs.

Kat was trying hard not to focus on the magnitude of his touch, realizing belatedly that the sensationally impossible tremors weren't just him. Somehow, she'd released a small amount of her electrical current to mix in with his talented tongue, causing mild vibrations throughout her body and intensifying the sensation. She'd always kept a tight leash on her powers, yet they'd just turned her on in the best possible way. The gradual escape of her gifts had never happened before without her notice. Usually, her skills were only used for more deadly purposes. But this was better. Especially since the escape of her powers seemed internal. Which was perfect, because all thoughts of how's and why's died a glorious death as Luke finally found her pulsating core. She merely threw her head back against the pillow, ran her figures through Luke's silky mane, and let go.

****

Her skin was remarkable. She smelled marvelous, like a lavender field at sunrise, and tasted even better. Luke couldn't comprehend how she smelt this extraordinary after spending all night in a sweaty dance club, but she did. And he was in heaven for it. A body like hers, so toned and smooth, deserved to be admired, treasured. He could've stroked her all night long, but during his exploration of her body he had felt her mind wander. He decided to bring her back in the best conceivable way, by going straight to the core of her essence. When she moaned, hiking her back off the sheets, he knew he had her back.

His lady was still wearing her lace panties, and he loved how wet they were becoming under his mouth. Kissing her through her underwear wasn't good enough for him, even though he knew it was driving her crazy by the way she was pulling his hair. He had to taste her center without any barriers between them. Leaning back on his knees, he slightly lifted her body, yanking her panties down in one fell swoop.

Lying flat, Luke cupped his arms under his vixen's thighs, pulling her back towards his awaited lips. With zero hesitation, he darted in and out of her with his tongue, circling her walls with skilled perfection. Hearing her moan in ecstasy had him throwing up thanks to his ex-college roommate, a sex therapist, that taught him a few things about how to pleasure a woman. Because let's be honest, who better to show a man how to pleasure a woman than another woman, an act he thoroughly enjoyed. Luke felt like he could taste her flavorful juices for hours and never get enough. He continued to draw out the pleasure before he thought it was time to put her out of her blissful misery. With just a few more penetrating thrusts of his tongue, he sucked her clit between his teeth, rapidly licking as he hummed.

****

Kat saw stars, like real life twinkle, twinkle as she came so hard her back bowed off the bed. She felt her electrical pulse course through her body, and she had to close her eyes to keep the spark from shining through her eyes like a flashlight.

She could do nothing but lay there, panting, as she took a moment for her soul to reenter her body. *Damn, Lukie was good.* Once her breathing became even again, she finally had the strength to pry her eyes open to look down. And what do you know, Lukie boy was sitting back on his hind legs, watching her with a deviously handsome grin on his face.

"Well, aren't you full of surprises," his smile grew and so did hers, "Well I think it's time to wipe that smug grin right off your face, hmm?"

Sitting up swiftly, she grabbed both his arms, flipping him over on his back, then straddled his hips. She spun him over with a strength and agility that probably would've been better kept leashed, but when she lifted lightly to pull his boxer briefs off, he didn't seem to notice. Settling firmly back around his waist, she grabbed his member with all intentions of impelling herself on his cock, but his next words stayed her motions.

"Wait. Wait, we need a condom. Top drawer of the night-stand."

Impatient, Kat came close to telling him that her kind didn't carry human diseases but stopped herself before the words slipped out. Nodding, she scooted off him, reached the dresser by his bed, grabbing the little gold wrapper to peel it open with her teeth. Hopping back atop Luke, Kat smoothed the condom on, then smirked down at her lover. Lifting herself, she gradually guided herself down the tip of his manhood, until fully connecting at the base. She had effectively wiped that grin off his face.

Chapter Eleven

Kat jerked out of her sleep, then sat up and frantically looked around. Where the fuck was she? Kat tried to readjust her eyes to the bright sunlight coming in through the windows, so she could fully collect her thoughts. As she looked towards the handsome man sleeping soundlessly beside her, all memories of last night's erotic escapades came crashing back. She'd messed up, big time. She looked out the giant windows towards the sky, groaning as she saw the sun just coming over the horizon. *Fuck, fuckity, fuck, fuck, fuck.*

She looked around desperately, trying to find her phone. After a minute, she finally realized her cell was in her jeans pocket, all the way across the room, by the door. As quietly as possible, she slipped out of bed trying her best not to jostle the mattress and wake Luke. Tip-toeing across the hard-wood floors, she grabbed her phone out her back pocket with care. The last thing she needed after getting this far, was to wake Luke up with a bunch of weapons hitting the floor. His face was angelic while he slept, especially without his glasses.

Thinking back on the night, she wondered when he found time to take his glasses off without her knowing. She got lost in thought, trying to remember. *Oh right, my phone.* Using her fingerprint, she unlocked her cell, going straight to her messages. *Shit!!!*

Twenty missed calls, two voicemails, ten text messages, all but one from Sky. Opening up the column from Sky, she held her breath while she read.

"Nightly report?"

"Why haven't you responded?"

"Where are you?"

"You're starting to piss me off, Thorne."

"You better call me back now, or I will come and find you. And you don't want me to find you."

Kat shivered, and not in a good way.

"I'm calling in the Knights."

"This better not be another one of your unauthorized weeks off, or I'm calling your mother."

Ouch, Kat winced, *low blow.*

"Please, Kat. Enough, I'm worried."

Kat blew out the breath she was holding. Kat believed her. Sky, Z, and Sia seemed to be the only ones that hadn't given up on her. And that pissed her off, even more. She didn't need anyone to care. She was perfectly fine on her own. Well maybe not perfect, but damnit she was close. Okay, she wasn't remotely close, but they didn't need to know that little detail.

It looked as if she waited a few hours before she sent her final reply. "You have until dawn to report in, or the Knights and I are coming for you."

Kat looked to the sky outside and sent off a quick reply, hoping she still had time before her boss found her and killed her, for good this time. She may have a death wish, but she rather not die by Sky's hands. The harpy still had her pride. When she died, it would be in battle.

"Yo boss lady relax, allz good," she typed trying to lighten the mood, "just had a long night, K. Full report in an hour."

Exiting out of that stressful thread, she pulled up the one that had a new message from Sia.

"Hey sis, just wanted to make sure you're okay. You're not answering the phone, so I guess that means you're having a great time. Laters, text me when you can."

After sending another *allz good* reply to her sister, she started to get dressed quickly.

How, in the name of everything that's holy, did she fall asleep next to a stranger? And for hours nonetheless, with weapons on the other side of the damn room? Rookie mistake and being over two centuries' in age she was no rookie. She must have lost her mind. And as a result, Sky was going to cause her pain. Kat had to hurry up and get out of here, so she could figure it out. Hell, if all else failed, she'd plead insanity. It worked for some humans, why not her? A light shift in the mattress drew her attention back in the direction of the bed. Luke had rolled over onto his stomach, his hair falling a little over his eyes as he continued to sleep. Smiling to herself, she figured if the insanity plea thing didn't work, last night would've been worth whatever Sky had in store.

The sex between them last night was mind-blowing. Kat wished she could stay for a few more hours and enjoy some good old fashion morning sex, but staying with the human during the day was dangerous. Not for her of course, but for him. Kat had too many enemies, and she didn't need to be caught with a human even if they were inside all day. He didn't deserve that kind of heat just because she had an itch that only he could scratch. And scratch he could.

Shaking herself from her impure thoughts, Kat finished getting dressed, then walked over to the dresser beside the bed. She grabbed the pen and notepad laying atop and left her lover a note.

Stepping back, she looked down at her sleeping angel and ran a hand over his cheek. It was crazy, but she felt as though she was going to miss him once she left. Kat barely knew this sensational man, yet she felt an emptiness began to fester in the pit of her stomach.

Kat brushed off the warm and fuzzies and walked over to the window. She silently pried open the glass doors leading out onto the balcony and stepped out into the day. Gently closing the door behind her, she used her energy to release her translucent wings. Throwing one final look over her shoulder, Kat hopped the rail and took off down the side of the building.

****

A frigid breeze across his cheek awoke Luke. Rolling onto his back, he laid an arm across his eyes, trying to focus. *Did I leave a window open?* Fluttering his eyes, he groaned, sitting up slightly on his forearms. Gazing out the window, he was greeted by the bright yellows of the morning sun. Which was puzzling, considering he always remembered to draw the drapes at night. With windows like his, it was a necessity, especially on the weekends. So why the fu...? *Oh, right.*

Luke sat up so fast his head spun. He patted the space where his mystery woman had laid beside him. He threw the covers from over his body, got up, then started to look around his condo for his redhead.

Placing his hands on his hips, he looked around his studio. He didn't see her, so he decided to walk over to his master bathroom, past the kitchen. Opening the door, hopeful, he took a look inside–nothing, which was somewhat disheartening.

Realizing she must have left, he walked back over to the door and noticed it was locked. Which was strange, considering without a key it wouldn't close from the outside. Bringing his hand up, he pulled at his chin, as a light breeze tickled his feet. Distractedly, he moved his gaze over to the slight crack in the balcony's glass door. With renewed hope, he strutted over to the patio to take a look outside. Unfortunately, she wasn't lounged out there either. He abandoned his search, shutting the door tightly and drawing the blinds with the remote he kept holstered up on the wall.

Jaded, he walked back over to his bed and plopped down. Luke rested his elbows on his knees, while he ran his hands through his tousled hair. Seriously, what had he expected from a woman like her? That she'd stay and wait for him to make her breakfast as they got to know each other? Deep down he knew it was supposed to be one night, but he had hoped that she'd at least stay until morning. Then maybe he could have.... could have what? Persuade her to stay so they could explore the connection they seemed to have? Stumble over his words, as he tried to convince her that it could be more than sex? Shaking his head Luke groaned, he was a hopeless romantic.

Straightening his back, he shifted his neck from side to side. Luke tried to draw out the kinks in his shoulders when he noticed a letter written on the notepad he left on his nightstand. Moving the pen aside he read aloud.
That was fun. I hope I get to play with you again sometime.
xoxo

Optimism returned until he saw she hadn't left a number. No address, no *meet here*, no nothing. The note was just a subtle way for her to say goodbye. She had no intentions of seeing him again. A fact solidified, once he realized she'd never even given her name.

Chapter Twelve

Sia reached out a hand and pulled a pillow over her head, trying and failing to block the bright light shining through her window. Damn, her head was throbbing, but that's what you get when you go on an all-night binge. Drinking as she did was not a good idea, especially in her line of work. She was a Phantom Knight, for crying out loud. Add to that her strength, speed, and ability to conjure up fire, getting smashed could have serious consequences–for her and everyone around.

She let out a groan as she rolled over on her bed, feeling for her phone. Seriously where was that light coming from? She pulled the pillow from her face, squinting at the window. Was it the sun? *Really?* How many hours did she sleep?

Shit. Sia bolted up, regretting it immediately as her head swam and her stomach lurched. Undeterred, she stumbled out of bed in search of her phone. Sia found it on the floor by her discarded clothes. Putting in her unlock code, she pulled up her messages and groaned again when she saw her boss, Sky, in the lineup.

"Lucky, lucky. Kat reported in right on time... Let's not make this a habit, Sia. I count on you to keep her in line."

She scrolled down some more to read the next message from Sky: "Meeting tonight with all my Knights in the North. Make sure you're there–your twin too."

Double shit. How was she going to pull that off? They didn't have the best relationship, even though Kat lived only two floors up from her apartment. Sia wondered if Kat knew she lived so close. Probably not. Lately, Kat was so wrapped up in self-destructive behavior that she didn't recognize other things going on around her. But it didn't matter, not really. Sia had to stay close to her sister. She couldn't lose Kat.

Her sister was the only one who mattered. They laughed together, cried together, fought in the same war together. They shared a bond that went beyond blood. Sia wished she could go back to the day of that mission—the day she had betrayed Kat's trust. But that was not one of the powers Sia had, and there was no point in dwelling on the past.

What she needed was a shower, some clean clothes, and a plan to get her sister to this meeting tonight. At least two out of three she could handle.

Sia walked into the bathroom to turn on the shower. Before the steam overtook the mirror, she took a good look at herself. She looked horrible, with bags under her eyes and her hair a mess. Without even thinking, she brought her fist back and smashed it into the mirror. Glass shattered everywhere, and blood from her knuckles dripped on the floor.

Your mother would be so disappointed, her shattered reflection in the foggy glass seemed to whisper.

Sia pulled herself away from her distorted reflection and stepped into the shower to wash her misery away, her knuckles stinging from the hot water. The pain combined with the soothing sight of the red water going down the drain calmed her. When she emerged from the shower, she taped up her hand and got dressed, sweeping up the broken glass once she had shoes on. She would buy another mirror when she had the time or when she felt like she could look at herself again.

Sia went to the kitchen and started a pot of coffee. Feeling a little better about her near meltdown, she decided it was time to pull herself together and get her day started before tonight's meeting. Sia needed every minute of the day to formulate a good, get Kat to Phantom, plan.

Chapter Thirteen

Kat laid in bed staring at the ceiling, thinking about Luke. She knew it was time to start getting ready for the night, but she couldn't get him off her mind. It had been a long time since someone had gotten under her skin. Even longer since someone's touched her as if she was wanted above all others, treasured. Kat wanted to see him again. She should've left her number on that damn paper. Maybe Kat could have tried to get to know him outside of the bedroom. He was so timid until she touched him just right, kissed him in the right places. There was just something about him. If only she had more time. However, more time with him couldn't happen.

It was dangerous for him, not just for her. It wasn't unheard of for phantom creatures to get involved romantically with humans, it just caused complications. Complications she didn't need. If one were a warrior like herself, an enemy would do everything in their power to exploit that weakness. Kat had made too many enemies over the centuries and they'd give their left nut to capture and torture someone she cared about.

Wait, what? I cared about? That couldn't be right. She couldn't possibly feel for a mortal stranger. Kat didn't even know him. So why did she care about what one of her enemies would do to him? The harpy knew his touch, the interesting faces he made when he came, the two laugh lines in his eyes that crinkle when he smiled. She knew he was intelligent and took direction like a champ, but care? Ha, Kat didn't care about anyone or anything.

She most definitely didn't care about the meeting tonight on Phantom. There wasn't a need for her to respond to such utter blaspheme. She wasn't going. Not even if they paid her, though technically, she would get paid. There was just no plausible reason for her to be there. It would be the same old tune. *How's hunting? Great. Kill anything? Yep. Are you still my bitch? Damn straight.* The whole thing would be pointless. She'd much rather spend the beginning of her night watching her geek pleasure her with that talented tongue of his. She shivered just thinking about it. Unfortunately, he wasn't hers, and he never would be.

Kat continued to lounge while staring at the ceiling of her loft as her mind wandered. She distantly heard a vibration in the air. She shook herself out of her daydream and went in search of the sound. The wave turned out to be her cell, which was still in the back pocket of her jeans. What commands did her majesty have now? *Hmmm*, interesting, turns out it wasn't Maleficent.

"Helloooooo." She bellowed into the receiver.

"Hey, Kat, it's Sia," her dear sister answered in greeting.

"So, it would seem." Why her sister felt the need to announce herself when Kat had caller ID, she had no idea.

"Hey, listen, you get the text from Sky?"

"Of course, she sent it to all her minions." Kat retorted sarcastically.

"So...."

"So, what?"

"You're going to go, right?"

"Ahhhhhh." The *hell no* was as silent as the G in lasagna.

"Look, Kat, please, you gotta start coming to these meetings, they help."

"Ahhhhhh." She didn't think so.

"Seriously there are some sick fucks out here crossing territories. If we don't share our intel, we might miss something. We can't afford to miss anything, Kat. One mistake could cost a life."

Goddess above, she hated when people spoke logically, mainly when she wanted to be an evil, petty bitch. It wouldn't be her if she played by the rules. Who would Sky yell at if she didn't have Kat to fuck shit up on occasion?

"Look, I get it, okay?" she gritted through her teeth, "I'm just not much of a team player, you know that."

"Yeah, I do; most of us aren't. We work alone, and it's better that way, for everyone, harpies aren't known to play well with others. If you could pull your shit together for one hour tonight, I'd owe you."

Ah ha, it all made sense now. So, it was Sia's job to get her to the meeting tonight. Sky knew her and knew her well. She should have known Sky would pull out the big guns to get her to this meeting. With all her faults, Kat still couldn't turn down her sister when she begged. Even though they still had their issues, she would always love that bitch.

"Fine I'll be there at 10 o'clock, sharp," she yawned.

"9."

"Huh?"

"The meeting's at 9."

"Oh, shit, well I'll be there at 9."

"I'll come to get you at 8." Her sister hung up.

Kat held the phone away from her ear and stared. *Damn, where was the faith?*

****

Kat had just finished waking up from a nap and taking a shower when she heard a knock on the door. She used her essence to put out a feeler and unsurprisingly, it was her sister, punctual as always, arriving at her doorstep at 7:59. She walked to the entrance, towel drying her hair as she turned the security system off, flipping the locks open. Paranormals could blow through the security system with ease, but the extra security was required if they stayed on Earth. Sky thought the extra precaution couldn't hurt. Kat thought it was dumb, but what did she know? She was just a mindless servant.

Kat pushed the door open wide and walked away to finish getting ready.

"I thought you'd be taking your time." Her sister said at her back, coming in and closing the door.

"Yeah, well, we all know how I like to make an entrance."

She could practically feel her sister roll her eyes behind her. Strolling over to her walk-in closet, Kat started to strap on her weapons. She couldn't wait until this meeting was over. Kat was in a piss-poor mood and she needed to kill something. It was hard enough to contain her power when she wasn't a bundle of emotions. Having her mind all over the place was a sure-fire way to get herself killed. Hunting would hopefully clear it.

Kat finished securing her daggers onto her body, then started to get dressed. Donning her traditional battle attire, she strapped on her blades, sword, and favorite silver forties, Hansel and Gretel. Taking a quick look at herself in her floor-length mirror, she assessed her image. Her green long-sleeved skin-tight top concealed most of her blades famously. Her gray cargo pants allowed even more hidden compartments for her weapons. And her thigh holsters were in the perfect position for easy retrieval. Her outfit was complete; she was ready to go.

Walking out her closet, she looked and saw her sister sitting on the edge of her queen-sized bed looking down at her hands nervously. Sia was uncharacteristically quiet, and she wasn't making eye contact, even though she knew her sister sensed her presence in front of her. They remained silent for minutes, but eventually, Kat had to break the tension.

"What's up?" Crossing her arms, Kat waited.

"Mom called."

Kat tried to contain her aggravation before she responded. "Oh," was all she was able to muster once she collected her shock.

"Yeah," Sia replied, to her credit seemingly equally perplexed, "she wanted to know if you were coming to the meeting tonight."

"Huh."

"Yeah."

"Andddd you said...?" Kat waved her sister on with her hands.

"That I didn't know. That she should call you if she wanted to know."

Ding, ding, ding. Her sister was earning her loyalty points back.

"Okay." Kat shrugged, all nonchalantly.

"She's going to be there, you know."

"I would assume so."

Sia recoiled back and finally looked up at her. "You know. And you're still going?"

Kat was starting to get pissed. "I told you I'd go, didn't I? No worries sis," she shrugged her shoulders "I trust she'll pretend I'm not there. She always does."

With a relieved sigh Sia whispered under her breath, "Thank you, Goddess."

"Let's go; we don't want to keep the Queen of Darkness waiting." Kat grabbed her leather jacket from the back of her barstool and walked out the door. This should be a fucking blast in a glass.

Chapter Fourteen

After Luke went for a run to clear his mind from the previous night, he showered and put on a tank with matching track pants, then set out to make himself breakfast. He didn't have any plans for the weekend. Therefore, Luke had already set himself up nicely to stay in. He had gone shopping the day before, so his fridge was stocked and so was his bar. It wasn't often he'd have plans with anyone other than his empty condo, so staying home wasn't anything new to him.

Luke's parents along with his sister had died a few years ago, leaving him with no family ties. They had moved around throughout his entire childhood, so any distant relatives were long forgotten. Despite the familiarity of being in the company of himself, he felt even more isolated today. Last night showed him just how lonely he'd become.

In the past, Luke never had to worry because at least he had his family. He could get lost in his studies, throw himself into extra-curricular activities such as debate class. No one could truly comprehend what it felt like to lose everything in just one day. If he had known, Luke would have treasured those special moments with his family a little more. Perhaps the sting from last night wouldn't have hurt as bad.

He went to the kitchen to pull out the ingredients for waffles and set his coffee pot. Milling around the room, Luke became lost in his thoughts. He had been alone for many years–day after day of the same routine. Being by himself was what Luke was used to. All he had was his work, and until recently, he was okay with that. Last night showed him how much he missed the company of a woman.

Luke had given up on the notion that he would ever find someone that he could fall for. Sure, he had a crush on Casey in his office, yet she in no way made him feel the way his redhead made him feel last night. If only there were a way to find her again. Maybe he should go back to the club to see if she would return. It was worth a shot. Hell, what did he have to lose?

A loud popping noise, signaling that his waffles were done, drew Luke from his thoughts. He pulled out his waffles, gathering the necessary utensils, poured himself a cup of coffee and went over to his glass dining room table.

Luke grabbed the morning paper from the center of his table and began to read as he sipped his coffee. Flipping it open he read the headline, *Serial Killer: Captured or Killed?* on the front page. It seemed the murderer that was preying on young college girls had been MIA these past few days, considering the rapid decrease in killings on campus. Hopefully, he or she was dead. He couldn't believe the monsters that were out in the world. So many young college kids that would never get the chance to fulfill their dreams. What a shame.

Finishing the headlines of the papers, Luke completed his breakfast and began to clear the table and clean the dishes. He looked towards the messy bed that still hadn't been made, which he knew was foolish. Not like keeping it unkempt would change anything. Putting an end to last night's festivities, he went over to tidy up. After making sure everything was as it were, he went over to his seating area to watch TV and try to get his redhead off his mind.

He was settling in on his couch when his phone went off. Pulling out his cell, Luke answered it without looking at the caller ID.

"Hello?"

"It's 1 o'clock in the damn afternoon. I've been calling you all morning!"

Luke had to pull the phone away from his ear because his friend was yelling so loud.

"Justin? Hey, sorry I just felt it vibrate. What's up?"

"What's up?! Are you fucking serious? You go home with that sexy angel last night then go dark for hours and you have the nerve to ask me what's up?"

All he could do was laugh, nothing like this had ever happened to him before, so calling Justin to talk about it never crossed his mind.

"What are we, two gossiping school girls?" He chuckled.

"Damn right! I just bought some gingersnaps a few days ago. Stop stalling and spill."

After a few more bouts of laughter, he gave Justin a general synopsis of his night.

"And then I woke up and she was gone. All she left was a note, but no number."

"Damn, that sucks. But hey, you can't expect much from a one-night stand Luke."

"Yeah, yeah," he ran a hand down his face with a sigh, "I know it's just...."

"You like her?" Justin finished for him.

"Is that crazy? We hardly talked. I'm just going off how she made me feel, and I don't know which head is leading those feelings, if you know what I mean."

"Yeah, I get it. Good sexual chemistry can be intense. But

if she didn't leave a way to notify her, there's a good chance she just wanted the night. Most women aren't the ones to pull the disappearing act, though." Justin responded, puzzled.

As Justin spoke, Luke knew it was the truth. The feelings he experienced last night were one-sided. Luke may have thought they had a fantastic night that warranted another night or two, or forever, but that didn't mean she felt the same. Which clearly, she didn't, since he was alone without even a name. Hell, maybe the sex was just that mind-blowing that it sparked imaginary emotions.

"Yeah, I know, you're right."

"At least you got to blow off some steam. You've been tensed lately, you needed to loosen up and have fun. I worry about you man."

"I'm good. Just been in a rut, don't let my mood worry you. I'm fine." Luke assured even though he wasn't.

"Whatever, you're my friend. So, I can worry if I want, shut the hell up."

Luke laughed again.

"So, you wanna link up later for dinner tonight, watch a game?" Justin asked after Luke forgot to respond after a few beats of silence.

"Yeah, sounds good." It wasn't like he was doing anything else.

"Great! One more question though?"

"Yeah?" Luke asked as he rested the phone between his cheek and his shoulder, as he tried to find the remote.

"Does the carpet match the drapes?"

Luke spat out his laughter, doubling over so suddenly that

he dropped his phone. His friend had no filter. Collecting himself, he sobered up enough to pick the phone up from the floor and respond.

Clearing his throat, he answered. "I wouldn't know," he paused for dramatic effect, "it was all hardwood floors."

"*What!!! Seriously!!*"

Luke hung up.

Still laughing, he tossed his phone to the side and turned on the television, but didn't look at the screen. His mind once again went to last night. Luke's thoughts went to the touch of her skin, the feel of her body. How her mouth felt on him while he stood immobile. She was not of this world. Women like her didn't exist.

Maybe he wasn't putting himself out there as he should. Luke had always been the reserved type; perhaps it was time to change that. Lucas Mason was tired of being alone. He craved more nights like last night. A big family was what he desired, as well as making love to the woman of his dreams for the rest of his life. However, that was not going to happen if he didn't get back on the horse. Maybe the previous night was his new beginning.

Chapter Fifteen

Kat utterly despised the Phantom Realm. Most paranormal creatures of her world thought they didn't need the luxuries humans experienced on Earth. And as she looked around, their lack of architecture was reflected in their world. Most phantoms were simple creatures, with limited needs. One wouldn't see a Starbucks on every corner, no Wal-Mart run at 3:00 am, no nothing. Just a whole bunch of fields and trees. Sounds delightful, doesn't it?

Regardless of the deficiency in style, the two worlds did carry certain similarities. For instance, the Phantom world contained their continents; however, instead of Africa, North America, etcetera, they had species domains. Harpies stayed on harpy land, demons stayed in demon territory, witches with witches, and so on. Less conflict happened in their realm if one remained with their kind. Every now and then creatures of varied species' paths would cross. But rarely ever would an immortal stumble onto someone else's region by accident. They weren't naive. If one was caught wandering around in another's territory without permission, then be prepared to sign the death warrant. So, they generally kept to their quarters unless they were on neutral territory.

There were places where they could all gathered peacefully, like the humans United Nations. Most of that open land consisted of bars or clubs, where they all could congregate or pass information amongst each other if needed. Many of those locations belonged to the witches. They used their magic to make a substantial fortune in their world. So, if one needed something, the Outlands was where anyone would want to be.

Kat stood in the open field and glanced around. She couldn't remember the last time she'd come back to "harpy town," but this was home. For some inexplicable reason, this would always be home. The minute she stepped foot on the land, the tension she hadn't realized she was holding eased off her shoulders. The Phantom Realm was a place they could be themselves. Somewhere she didn't have to hide the best parts of who she was.

Letting her wings break free of her leather jacket, she breathed a sigh of relief. Containing her wings in mystical mist required focus and an unbelievable amount of power, which is why her colleagues didn't understand why she lived in the human world. Hiding their wings was unnatural, and for younger, inexperienced harpies it hurt like a son of a bitch. But for her, the sacrifice was minimal. It's not like she went out much in the day anyway, and she had been on Earth for so long that containing her wings was becoming second nature. Something she didn't want to look too closely at.

Taking a deep-seated breath, she knelt as the warm breeze kissed her cheeks. Running her hands over the moist grass, she looked before her to the forest ahead. The open space and trees called to her spirit. Taking a moment, Kat closed her eyes and smiled as the pure air stilled. The wind calmed, and the forest creatures quieted as the sky ignited with lightning. No thunder, no sound, only the booming white light greeted her. She was at home.

Dusting off her hands, she righted herself and began walking across the field, surveying the area. Here, one never knew who was going to jump out and try to kill you. This, however, was their turf. And no one smart willingly pissed off Sky. She was the phantom's equivalent of the boogeyman. One didn't want to make an enemy out of Sky, which generally kept all the

Knights safe in harpy territory. But outside their land, all bets were off. Keeping her eyes peeled, Kat moved forward towards the trees.

The air behind her became stagnant as another portal solidified. Not looking back, she spoke.

"Nothing's changed." She remarked while still observing her environment.

"What did you expect," Sia walked over, stopping an inch away, so they were nearly shoulder to shoulder, "for Aladdin to come out and show you a whole new world?"

"Funny."

Silence descended upon them once again as they started walking towards the direction of the compound, where the meeting was held. Portals could only be opened to them in specific locations of Phantom. Therefore their landing point left them with a little bit of distance. It was strategic for them to build their compound away from the gateways. It gave them enough of a warning for unwelcomed guests.

As they continued to walk, the sky settled down, and the subtle noise from the forest resumed. The silence between them, although uncommon, was comfortable. She'd forgotten how nice it was to be in the company of her sister. Her twin. They shared a unique bond. A connection that was almost impenetrable. Almost.

"So?"

"So?" She paused in tune with Sia's halt and looked over to her sister.

"Wanna race?"

Kat's twin threw her a cocky crooked smile and changed her stance to a runner's position. Her fingers were twinkling in anticipation of a race.

Kat moved ahead of Sia shaking her head from side to side while placing her hands on her hips.

Looking bored she tilted her head to the side and replied, "Tsk, tsk, tsk now why would I want to do–" She didn't finish her sentence. Kat just took off running at full speed, darting out in the direction of the compound.

"You little bitch!!!" Sia squealed behind her, with a tint of humor.

Kat chuckled, as she sprinted forward at a pace that equaled the speed of a commercial jet at maximum velocity.

Damn, she missed this. The joy of being able to run freely in an open forest, ducking and dodging tree branches and boulders without the fear of being discovered by a human hunter or hiker. She'd spent so much time suppressing her abilities that she'd forgotten how freeing running was for her. The feeling of the soil beneath her feet, the rustle of the leaves as she blew by, the musical sound of the wind as she cut through its inviable silk. She missed it all.

Basking in the moment, she heard the soft crackle of branches behind her as she continued her frantic pace towards the compound. Smiling, she let up on her speed slightly. Her twin was getting faster. Aww, someone was practicing! It would seem living in the phantom world presented an unfair advantage. There was more space to run. And fewer humans to get in their way.

It brought Kat back to their childhood, racing to see who was the fastest. Harpies' favorite hobby was running. For them, it was therapeutic. She couldn't count how many times the two of them snuck out in the middle of the night to race. Kat always won. And today would be no different.

Sia was physically stronger, which propelled her forward until she was once again at her side. Even with the head start, her sister managed to keep pace, which was impressive. But Kat was just getting started. Looking over for a split second, she gave her twin a sinister smile - showing her little pointy side teeth while channeling all her energy to her legs. Arms back, head forward, Kat put on a burst of speed using her electrical pulse to push her forward, she shot off like a rocket, vaguely hearing her sister's squawk of astonishment behind her. *Eat my dust, bitch.*

After a few long strides, Kat burst through the end of the forest and finally pulled to an abrupt stop at the Knights' compound. Breathing evenly as if she hadn't just run fifty miles in under ten minutes, Kat studied the structure ahead. Just as her sister came hurtling through the trees a few seconds later.

"Show off," Sia retorted, shaking a few fallen twigs out of her hair.

Kat laughed.

"You let me catch up to you so that you could do that?"

"Didn't want you to think I cheated," Kat mocked.

"Humph." Sia stomped off, pushing past her to punch in the security code at the front gate.

Taking a hesitant step back, Kat took a moment to take in the massive fortress. The titanium steel border that ran circles around the compound was reinforced with a force field created by witches, which took a code to deactivate. A spell that cost them a pretty penny to cast and required the Knights to get the witches to renew their spell quarterly.

Witches were extremely shrewd. They could've created a permanent protection spell, but where's the money in that?– reason number a thousand to never trust a witch.

Walking behind Sia, she waited until she put her face into the security feed and the gate opened. And there she was—headquarters, where all the Knights came to report in to their master. The compound had stone steal plated walls for reinforcement. It would take a bulldozer the size of Mount Everest to take the sucker down if, by some chance, they got through the defense shield.

Coming up to yet another checkpoint, she waited for Sia to enter a different code that gave them access to the building. Sia put her ugly mug into the camera's feed, and the large brass double doors clicked, then crept open slowly.

Stepping over the threshold, Kat braced herself. Walking into the compound was always a taxing experience. The creepy castle reminded her of something out of the Amityville Horror. That was one of the reasons she never showed. Not that she needed a motive. As she fully entered the entranceway, she recoiled, nearly bumping back into the double doors as they closed behind them. *Wow, guess some things do change.*

Looking frantically from side to side, Kat couldn't believe what she saw. The inside looked more like a comfortable, welcoming home than Dracula's tomb. A marble winding staircase greeted them, with a giant crystal chandelier as the centerpiece above the mahogany floors. A giant bookshelf was plastered on the wall leading to what must be the old prison sitting room, and the walls were littered with portraits, as well as delightful home décor. Although the outside remained naturally untouched, the new renovations to the inside were a pleasant surprise.

When the hell did Sky find the time to pull this off? As Kat walked further in, she took the changes in stride, not letting her astonishment show on her face. It read family to her, something she wasn't familiar with, but desperately wanted to experience. It was kind of sweet, and she did not need Sky to know she thought the improvements were pretty amazing.

Kat kept walking until she realized she didn't have a clue as to where she was going. Looking over she noticed Sia had stopped walking and had arched her eyebrow in amusement. Trying to seem nonchalant, she propped her hand on her hip and looked over.

"What's up?"

"Ummm, the meeting hall is upstairs, on the fifth floor."

Her jaw dropped, *so much for acting unimpressed,* "There are five floors? When the hell did that happen?"

Her sister smiled, "There have always been five floors, well six, we just never used any of them. Z and Sky thought it'd be nice to turn a few floors into rooms where Knights could crash when they were off assignments. There's an elevator right over here; we should get going." Sia pointed in the opposite direction down the hall.

"A fuckin' elevator." No point in hiding her wonder now.

Falling in step with Sia, Kat walked down the hall to their left and halted in front of the elevators. She continued to look around as Sia pushed the arrow up, leaning against the wall, arms and ankles crossed. After a few heartbeats, the doors slid open, and the two of them stepped inside. Kat moved to the back and looked up into the cameras plastered above, as Eminem's "Monster" blared through the overhead speakers. Even the elevator music was a nice touch.

Sia pressed the button for the fifth floor and leaned back against the steel rail as she spoke. "Sky thought it'd be nice to have a touch of homeliness. That way more Knights would be inclined to stay at the compound than in the cities they defend."

That drew her notice. "More Knights are staying in the cities?"

"Yep."

"And Sky's okay with that?"

"Guess so, but she won't admit it."

"Huh." Interesting. It seems Kat had missed more than she thought.

The elevator glided to a stop, and they stepped out into a hallway with crème colored walls that seemed to go on for miles. Maybe she'd take a tour after the meeting... *nope, no way.* She instantly shook herself from the thought. She was here for the conference, and that was all, nothing more, nothing less.

Following in Sia's footsteps as they continued down the hall, Kat noticed prestigious paintings of the Knights' leaders throughout the centuries, both alive and fallen, at their prime. The best of the best, the crème d la crème. All beautiful, respected females, especially the one towards the end. The second before the last portrait. The one that held her mother's face. Kat bit back a growl.

It felt like she was looking in the mirror—same hair, eyes, lips, nose, mouth. Kat was her mother's daughter, if only by looks alone. There was no denying that they were almost identical, but that was where the similarities died. She was nothing like that woman, never would be.

The young warrior knew her mother would be here. She was the last Knight leader before Sky took over. One of the few that lived to retire and have children. And she never let them forget it was an honor that she took the time to have progenies. Like she did them a service for bringing them into a world they didn't ask to be in. Kat could hear her voice so vividly. *You should be honored to be the daughters of a deity, a legend.* Because that's what Kamila Thorne was: a legend. At least that's how the other Knight treated her—everyone except Sky. Sky didn't give a fuck about who her mother used to be. The Knights were hers now.

And the last portrait that remained was that of their infamous leader. Sky let it be known every time her mother tried to voice an opinion that didn't match her own; the Knights were her bitches. And that's why Kat followed her. Sky was the only one that could put her mother in her place, and she loved watching that conflict. Especially since Sky always won.

"C'mon, we're already late. I can hear them talking." Sia pressed, grabbing her hand and pulling her forward.

Kat looked down at her watch which read 9:23. Yep, they were late, and Kat didn't give a flying fuck. She looked at the entrance before her and smiled. Sia opened the doors, and they walked into the conference room.

****

All conversation ceased when the doors swung open and the two of them walked through. Every eye in the room went directly to Kat as if they'd seen a ghost. She knew she was electric, but damn. Did she accidentally use her powers? Because the looks on their faces were shocking. Kat wanted to laugh so badly, but she didn't want to give them the satisfaction of knowing their reactions to seeing her had any effect.

So, she ignored the traveling eyes and spared her boss a glance at the head of the conference table. She went to walk around the other side of its long wood frame, far away from her mother, who was already seated next to Sky and staring as well. Kat found an open seat on the other side of the table, thankfully right next to Sia.

The table she was seated at was enormous, could fit fifty people comfortably, and most of the chairs were already filled. And the one seat she tried desperately, yet failed, to avoid was the one that housed her cocoon. Kamila leveled that dark green stare in her direction never taking her eyes off Kat until she took a seat. She pulled out her headphones connected them to her phone, via Bluetooth, and clasped her hands behind her head. Kat threw her black dirt ridden boots up on the table, while Drake's "Energy" started to blast out from her headphones. Giving her mother a wink, she smiled as she turned her attention back toward Sky. Seeing her mother's hands clench in a fist on top of the table only made her smile that more genuine. Sia shook her head beside her and hid a smile behind her hand. Sky cleared her throat, and all heads turned back to look towards their leader.

"Katrina, it's nice of you to join us. Even though you're late." Sky sneered.

"It's my fault," her sister cut in before she could answer, "we were, ummm, catching up and we lost track of time."

She supposed it was right and she wondered now, was that the reason she wanted to race. So, they wouldn't be later than they already were. Sia was always the model soldier.

Sky lifted a dark eyebrow in her direction in question. Kat shrugged.

"Okay, let's get back on track shall we?" her leader's voice broke through the tension, and that's when her mother got up and started handing out manila envelopes. "As I was saying, we need to be more vigilant. The war between the vampires and werewolves is starting to get out of control, and it's bleeding into the human world. I've already talked to Luther, the leader of the weres..."

Sia cut her eyes at Kat, but she never took her gaze off the boss, not even when mother dearest dropped a file in front of her. With a little more force than she did the others, she might add.

"Luther claims he can contain his pack to the phantom

realm, but if the vamps approach them in the human world then all bets are off. We need to make sure the new leader understands the werewolves' position. The vampire must agree to keep the war in the shadows or they face us."

Kat cut her eyes across the table at the unique harpy that raised her voice to speak. Asia, yeah, she believed her name was Asia. She didn't remember much about this particular Knight, but she did remember she had a wicked gift. No one could forget a gift like hers.

"New leader?" She inquired.

"Yes," Sky replied, "Victor is no more."

Mumbles of astonishment arose as quiet conversations developed. Kat's smile grew. They all had been after Victor for some time now. The old vampire king was a menace to them all. He killed inconspicuously, not bothering to cover his tracks. Most of the vamps could control their blood lust, but Victor had been alive for far too long, and he let his mind lose control. He needed to be put down.

"And who, might I ask, took out our infamous vampire king? I was tracking him for years, and the little fucker slipped through my fingers every time," Asia erupted over the side conversations.

Sky cast Kat a glance... *Oh was it my turn to talk, goodie.* She waited until her mother finally finished dishing out the folders then resumed sitting.

"That would be me," Kat answered smugly turning down the volume on her headphones, and again the room fell silent. All eyes were on her once again.

"C'mon guys. You've got to chill out with all the stop and stare stuff. Is it so hard to believe I'm here and talking? Shit, it's only been, what..."

Sia cut in, "Two years."

"Exactly," she continued, "two years. A blink of an eye in our time, so relax."

Zelda on the other side of Asia cracked a smile and tried to smother her laughter quickly, but she was unsuccessful. Ahh-hhh Zel, she missed her. That harpy always got her wicked sense of humor, even though she rarely spoke, smiled, or, hell, blinked for that matter. She was stationed in Canada the last time she checked, and it'd been a while since she'd seen her expressive face. What a face it was, too. She looked like a porcelain doll and with her long silver-white hair and long thick eyelashes, she very well could be. She sent her old friend a look that was all *really, what the fuck,* and Zel laughed a rare and precious laugh. Everyone looked at the deadly snow angel as the sound escaped with disbelief. Everyone but Kat knew Zel had a sense of humor, she just rarely showed it, opting for quiet and reserved rather than loud and joyful. *My kind of girl.*

"Yes, it was Kat," her boss went on, not missing a beat, "but she had to cross quadrants to do it, which shouldn't have happened. If all Knights were in better communication with each other, we could have ended Victor sooner."

"Yes, Katrina, you know the rules. It was reckless of you not to announce yourself to your fellow warrior. You could have endangered your sisters," her mother mocked.

"Yeah well, that didn't happen, and Victor was put down. So, announcing that little tad bit was unnecessary now wasn't it?" She spat back, never relaxing her *I don't give a fuck about the world* position.

"Everything we discuss here is necessary. We wouldn't want another unfortunate incident to occur; now would we?" her mother replied sarcastically.

Goddess, that female got under her skin. "Whatever," was her reply

"Listen, this argument is moot, in the past. In the end, Kat's right. Killing Victor was a conquest for our side, and it needed to be done no matter the cost." Her boss turned that black soul-less-expression stare on her, "Well done."

Annnnnnnd that's why she bowed down to her master and was a good little girl, most of the time. Looking at her mother again Kat pouted her lips and blew her a kiss. Her mother bared her teeth... Which only made Kat smile brighter.

"Keep your ears and eyes peeled, warriors. We need to know who this new king is, and we need to find him before Luther does. If the war gets worse, I will put you in pairs," groans went across the room, and her leader held up a hand to silence their protest, "so I would advise you all to find the king and fast. All the notes and reports from your fellow fighters are in the folders before you. Any questions?" She paused, the room remained quiet, "Okay, you're free to go."

Finally, she took her feet off the table, pocketed her head-phones then went to get up and leave.

"Kat, Sia a moment please" the dark response that warranted no rebuttal came from her boss. *What the fuck...*

The others started to file out, a few threw her a quick wave, and Zel threw up her pinky and thumb enclosing her other fingers in the symbol of *call me*, Kat nodded then watched Zel walk out with the others. Kat, Sky, Sia, and Kamila were the last four in the room.

"That is all Kamila; thank you." Her mother looked over at the new leader with confusion in her narrowed eyes. "I wish to speak to MY warriors alone."

Her mother neutralized her expression, bowed a little then

left without so much as a backward glance towards her two daughters. Whatever, it wasn't like she wasn't used to the cold shoulder from Queen Kamila.

"So," her leader began. Kat propped herself up to sit on the edge of the table and waited for her boss to continue. "I want you two to start working together, effective immediately." Kat scowled, but kept quiet. Sky had earned her silence after that little display of power, by putting her mother in her place. Her leader raised a brow. "No fight?"

"No," Kat and her twin replied at the same time.

"Good. You are two of my best warriors, and the dark lords are starting to take notice. There have been rumors about taking the two of you out, and I can't have that. I need you both alive."

Kats blood started to run hot at the prospect of the phantom creatures coming after them. A menacing smile lit her face, *bring it on, bitches.*

"Since you both live close it just makes more sense to have you working side by side, yes?"

Kat cut her eyes at her twin, but Sia didn't look her way. So, she was staying in New York with her. She wondered why she hadn't said anything.

"So, can you two handle working together without killing one another?"

"Huh?" Kat turned back to her boss, "Of course we can."

"Great. I'll let you two work out your system. Just don't get yourselves killed in the process. If you do, it'll be oh so fun getting the witches to find a way to bring you back to life so that I can kill you myself." With those parting words of promised death, if Sia and Kat fucked up, her boss left the conference room.

"Wwwoeee," she mock shivered, "was I the only one that got a hard-on?" Her sister again just shook her head and headed for the door.

So, the underworld was plotting to take their heads, were they? Mmmm she couldn't wait for the first one to come and try. Kat palmed Hansel and Gretel at her thighs as she strolled out the door. Yep, her twins were looking for candy, and wasn't this the perfect distraction she needed to keep her mind off Luke.

Chapter Sixteen

Asia left the meeting with a sense of urgency. How the fuck had Kat killed Victor? He was supposed to be hers. It may have been a team victory, but she thought she was the one that got first dibs on the vampire king, at least that's the impression she received from Sky.

It was personal between them. The bloodsucker had killed one of her best friends. Someone she loved dearly, and for Knights that feeling was rare. They didn't have much time for anything outside of their calling, so to find someone that she could just be herself around was ecstatic. With Blazer, a lion shifter, she didn't have to be a Knight, she could just be Asia.

Her and Blaze were best friends, inseparable almost. Most thought they had a romantic relationship, but that just wasn't the case. They loved being around each other. Neither wanted a relationship, seeing how they were both busy in their business lives, but they did on occasion fool around. It never got serious between them though. She couldn't have a relationship that lasted too long, especially with her abilities. They always seemed to scare off her partners when she let them slip while in bed. And even now with more experience under her belt, it was hard to reel her gift in. Every Knight lost control of their powers during sex at some point in their lives, typically during the first two centuries of experience, and at just one-hundred and forty-seven years old, she was still learning her powers.

Blaze, however, never seemed to mind when she let go. She never caused him any physical harm; she just knew at times it was awkward. But he never made her feel weird or shamed her for something that came naturally. They accepted each other's flaws and loved one another, despite their shortcomings. They had known each other since they were kids. Their mothers happened to be best friends, and, naturally, that made them close. They studied together, trained together. He was a true friend.

When word finally reached Asia of Blaze's pack having been attacked by Victor and his minions, she left her post in Rome and headed to the Phantom Realm as fast as she could. Once she got to his village, she realized she had been too late. She knew she should've called Sky for a teleport, but she figured the lions would be able to hold their own. Come to find out a few of their soldiers had been lured out of the village by Victor's bloodsuckers so their master could come and drain those left behind.

Women and children were all slaughter by that fucking monster. He left no one alive in his wrath, not even the infants sleeping in their cribs. It was a total massacre.

Asia went nuclear, marching over to every vampire lair she knew in search of Victor. She'd killed countless of them in her quest for their king before Sky pulled her out. She wanted all of them dead, and she didn't care how long it took to make that happen. No one deserved that ending. Blaze was a fighter, warrior's code was anything goes, but they all had their honor. The righteous ones anyway. No one should die trying to defend children. If one were to perish, it should be in battle, but the stupid king took his right. And now she couldn't even avenge his honor.

Asia hurtled out of the portal in the underground tunnels in Rome and made her way to her little cabin outside of town. She had parked her Beetle close by since she didn't know what time of day she would be returning. Feeling defeated, Asia hopped in and began driving down the quiet road. Asia wanted to scream, fight, kill, but she knew she needed to calm down first.

When she'd first heard Kat admitting to taking her kill, she had the urge to jump across the table and strangle her. In correlation, she wanted to do the same towards Sky. She alone knew what killing Victor would mean to her, so she didn't understand why she would put an open kill order on the detested king.

A small part of Asia knew the leader was doing her job. And Goddess knew she hadn't been around when shit went down with Blaze, so of course, she didn't know what had happened. So, she couldn't take it personally. She never liked Kat, she was just too reckless, but the woman had morals, she would have granted Asia the kill if she'd known.

Pulling up to her cabin, Asia slammed her car door and walked up onto her porch. The harpy stomped inside her home, taking off her leather jacket and throwing it over her accent chair. Her cabin was small and rustic, but she loved it. Walking into her sitting room, she grabbed the darts off her dartboard on the wall, going to line up and throw to release her built up aggression. Just when she cocked back her elbow to throw, the air behind her shifted. Her anger began to sizzle. Not bothering turning around, she threw her first dart which landed in the center of the bulls-eye.

"What?" She grunted.

"I just wanted to make sure you were okay," Sky said behind her.

"Just peachy." Asia threw another dart which also landed in the center.

"You know why I pulled the order to capture, right?"

Yeah, she knew, but it still hurt.

"You went against my orders once again and took the search into your own hands, Asia. That was reckless and dangerous, and you could have gotten yourself killed. This needed to end, so I put the kill order out there for anyone to grab and Kat beat you to it. I know the other Knights may have still captured him for you, but Kat didn't know about Blaze. Hell, no one knew about your relationship to the shifter until you went rogue."

And that's the way she preferred it. No one needed to know about their relationship. It was just them, and that was enough.

"I don't need another lecture boss; I got it. Victor's dead and that's good enough for me." She threw her last dart at the center of the board with frustration.

"Is it Asia? Is it really enough?"

She didn't respond because her boss was speaking rhetorically. Asia already knew the answer to that question. No. It wasn't nearly enough.

"I didn't think it was," her boss replied reading her mind.

Cracking her neck, Asia walked over to the dartboard, pulling the darts out of the circular pocket. Holding them, she clenched her fist as a single tear escaped, rolling down the side of her cheek. Victor took the only thing she had to live for. Her parents were killed way before she reached maturity and she didn't have any other siblings. Blaze was the only family Asia had. Without him, she had nothing. She brought her hand up to her drenched face.

"I have something for you."

She didn't care, but she answered anyway. "Oh yeah, what's that?" Asia choked out.

She remained with her back towards her leader as she tried to collect her emotions. No sense in having her leader see the weakness she still carried. She was a Knight. She should be used to death, even if it was personal.

"He was there that night," Sky spoke, blissfully ignoring her meltdown. "Zafrina and I hunted down every single one for those bloodsuckers that destroyed the shifter's village. But we left one...for you."

Asia spun around rapidly, causing her head to spin. Standing by her boss was an impossibly attractive male with dark hair and pale skin. His pupils were wide with fear, and his mouth and hands were bound. He was bloodied, shaking, and wiggling uncontrollably in Sky's hold. He stopped moving once his eyes fixed on her and he recoiled, probably because she was giving him the nastiest smile she could muster.

"So, I ask you again, little one. Is it enough?" Sky questioned, squeezing the vampire's neck. "Or do you want him?"

Oh yeah, she wanted him. Asia took a step closer to the enemy, loving the way he stumbled back on his ass, trying to get away from her. She could almost hear his whimpers through the gag in his mouth. Stopping before him Asia looked at her leader with love and devotion. Sky didn't have to give her this gift. She was the boss, what she said goes, and there wasn't a damn thing they could do about it. But she did things like this that made them not only have to follow her, but want to.

Casting a look down she smiled at the vamp, then looked back up at Sky, nodding her head.

"Have fun." Sky teleported out in the next heartbeat, leaving her alone with her new friend.

Slowly, Asia knelt in front of her captive, reaching out to pull the binds from her foes mouth.

He wasted no time once his lips were free. "Please, please I didn't want to do it I swear. It was all Victor's idea; I was following orders." The vamp babbled out.

Asia didn't speak. She just continued to look at him, tilting her head to the side to inspect her pray.

"Don't hurt me. I didn't want to kill those kids, it just happened." He was still trying to scoot away, but she noticed his feet were bound as well, making it difficult to move. "If those damn lions would've just listened to us, none of this would have happened; they had it coming. If they'd just complied–AHHHH-HHHHH!!!!!!!"

His bellow as she drove the dagger she kept in her boot into his side was poetic. She hadn't removed the mouthpiece to hear his lies. No, she wanted to listen to his pain. She took out yet another dagger, and this one went into his shoulder blade. The scream was just as agonizing as the first, which was the sweetest melody she'd ever heard. He was bleeding all over her carpet, and his screams were bouncing off her empty living room, save a couch and TV. Her place was in the middle of nowhere, so there was no one around for miles to hear his shouts of agony.

"Please end this quickly, no more pain. I killed them all swiftly, at least give me that."

She sneered, pushing the asshole to his back and putting a boot over his trachea. "I owe you nothing," Asia spoke through her teeth, barring her small fangs.

Closing her eyes, she conjured up her gift from the murky depth of her soul, feeling the darkness surround her. Once she opened her eyes again, she didn't need to see her reflection to know her eyes were solid black. She knew because the vamp just stared, frozen in horror. Releasing her powers on the vampire at her feet, she waited patiently for her gift to begin.

Asia knew the very moment the darkness reached her enemy. His magical blue eyes turned the color of the gloomiest night as his silent screams of terror fought desperately to escape. Kneeling before her prey once more, Asia used her nails to unbind him as he laid paralyzed by the darkness that slowly began to eat his soul. She ran her hands down the side of his face as tears of anguish ran unchecked down the vampire's silky skin. Crouched, with her elbows on her knees she pulled back on her gift just enough to hear the torture come through, and he did not disappoint. His pain would echo around her home for days. And yet, the fun was just beginning.

Chapter Seventeen

Luke entered his spacious condo after yet another uneventful night at Phantom. He'd been to the lucrative club almost every night for the past couple of nights, wishing, hoping that he'd see her. She hadn't shown, and Luke waited patiently while he stood at the bar, glancing towards the entrance every five minutes. He just wanted to see her in those long black leather boots with those heels made from sin one more time.

Luke should've given up, he had told himself to look for another, but he had to find her. She had made him feel alive, more alive than he'd ever felt in the past few years of his life. With just one night she made him forget about his awkwardness and his recent tragedies. He needed to feel her touch, if only to hold her just one more time. Luke wanted to do what it took to get her out of his mind. But it didn't look like that was going to happen.

Pulling his brown suede jacket off and tossing it over his barstool, he went to pour himself a drink as his phone vibrated. Looking at the screen, he saw it was just Justin, so he answered.

"Hey man, what's up?" His friend spoke. "You made it in?"

"Yeah, I'm home."

"Oh good, you got kinda buzzed tonight."

"I only had three or four drinks, Justin." Rolling his eyes, Luke took a drink from his glass.

"Yeah, I know, two or three are past your normal. I was worried you might have had too many," his friend paused, "is it the girl?"

Using his index finger and thumb, Luke rubbed the bridge of his nose. He wished his friend didn't know him so well. He knew the reason he kept wanting to go back to the club. Luke never really wanted to go to Phantom until her, but he never said as much. He only went because Justin and Casey loved hanging out there and they were two of his closest friends. Luke liked staying in, but now and then Luke wanted to hang out. So, he went with little complaint.

"No, Justin, it's not the girl, I just wanted to get out. Roman has been riding my ass lately, so I just needed to get out before I exploded."

"Yeah, I get that," another pause, "it's just Casey thinks you've...changed."

Hmph, translation: he doesn't follow behind her like a lost little puppy anymore. And how could he? After he'd had a taste of his red temptress, blondes didn't do it for him anymore. Once the attraction died, he realized he had nothing in common with Casey, so the silly feelings Luke thought he had, vanished.

"Does she now?" Pulling out his barstool he took a seat and leaned back, swirling his liquor, "I really could care less how she feels, my friend."

"To be frank, me either. I never liked hanging with her. I only did it for you. I knew you liked her, so I never really said anything, but full disclosure, Casey's a bitch. And I don't like calling women out their names, but she is. So glad you finally see that shit too."

"Yeah, I know, somethings you have to learn on your own though. But, hey, J man, listen, I'm about to turn in. I'll see you at work on Monday, okay?"

"Yeah my man, goodnight."

"Goodnight."

Luke tossed his phone on the bar and continued to drink away his hopes of ever seeing his redhead again. New York was a big state. People were coming and going, traveling, tourist, she could be anywhere. It was apparent he would never see her again, yet all week he had hoped that that wouldn't be the case. Maybe she just forgot to leave her number and was hoping that he would come back to the club too. Luke knew he was a sap, but he didn't care.

Knowing that being able to see her again was damn near impossible, it was time to get over that one night and get his life back on track. Luke hadn't been as focused on his work as he should, and numbers were starting to fail because of incorrect data. Obvious mistakes even his boss was picking up on. His work was significant to him; he loved computers and technology. He couldn't keep letting his work suffer because of a nameless face. It was time to get his priorities back in line. And the first step was staying far away from Phantom.

Chapter Eighteen

BOOM!!!! *What the fuck was that?*

Kat crouched on the side of a disfigured wall in an abandoned building on the outside of town. BOOM!!! *Were these bastards throwing fuckin' grenades?* Boom!!! Boom!!! Boom!!!! *Seriously, they're throwing fuckin' grenades.*

Shuffling to the side, she hid next to a whittled down file cabinet as a clicking sounded beside her. Peeking around the filing cabinet, she saw a little silver ball emerged right next to her hiding spot; *yep, definitely grenades.*

Kat darted off the wall as fast as she could, firing off rounds of bullets as the explosion ignited at her back. She found an empty room with a busted-out window and somersaulted through it. Kat landed smoothly on the balls of her feet, backing against the wall, guns raised.

Where the hell was Sia? She better not had gotten herself killed or Sky was going to be pissed. Kat darted behind a fallen metal table, then set off the alert device on her watch and waited. As time rolled by, explosions continued to go off around her. It took forever for that little red light to flash in response letting her know Sia was still alive somewhere in the building.

It'd been three weeks since their boss had let Kat and her sister know the big boys in the phantom world were coming for them. And it took no time for them to realize that they were being hunted. Kill one vampire king, and the underworld went bananas. She was beginning to think that her boss was exaggerating, but as she ducked out of the way of yet another grenade she thought, maybe the boss lady was on to something.

Boom!!!!!!! *Urrrghh* okay, the explosions were getting old. Did they not have any other tricks? They were taking "by any means necessary" too far. Usually, phantoms weren't interested in drawing attention to themselves in the human world. But these fuckers didn't care how much noise they made, as long as they came back to their master with bodies, noise be damned.

Hell, she guessed going after the Knights was a smart move. If they got rid of them, problem solved. The world would be theirs to control, and humans couldn't do a damn thing to stop them. Besides maybe firing off nukes. But where would that get them? The creatures would just run back to the phantom realm, and since the Phantom world was another dimension between planets, they'd be safe. They'd return when the world was in turmoil and rule. And the Knights couldn't let that happen. Kat wouldn't let that happened. But she had to find a way around the bombs and out of this building first.

They wouldn't survive long if this pile of bricks came crashing down on top of them. She was strong, but there were some things even a harpy couldn't escape. And getting crushed by a ton of bricks and cement was one of them. She felt her phone buzz in her back pocket as she was looking through the chaos for an escape route. Who the fuck would be calling at such an ungodly hour? She answered, screaming over the noise the grenades and gunshots were making. Firing off random rounds out of the open window, she fumbled trying to answer the phone with one hand as her gun was in the other.

"WHAT?!!!"

"We've got to get out of here. The building is about to go!" her sister yelled over the bombs.

"Sia?! Oh, hey, girl! What's up? Just kidding. You think?!" She yelled sarcastically, reloading her clips as she balanced the phone between her cheek and shoulder.

"Look, we need to draw them out to the lake around back."

They needed to get a better communication system if they were to work together. She slammed the clip into Gretel, cocked it back and holstered it again at her thigh.

"I'm all ears."

"I'm going to light this bitch on fire. We have maybe thirty seconds tops to get the hell out of dodge before the building comes crashing down."

Man, she loved her sister's mind. Go up in a blaze of glory, huh? And the lake, why didn't she think of that?

"I'm ready whenever you are, sister-mine."

With those parting words, she hung up and waited to see red. Breathing deep, Kat looked for the best exit, which unfortunately was back through the window she came. There wasn't much she could do about finding another alternative door because a few seconds later she saw the flames were beginning to spread. Not taking another moment to think, she took off across the room, jumping through the shattered glass window.

Taking a costly pause, Kat shifted around, searching for another clean exit out of the building. A piercing pain hit her shoulder, and she turned around in enough time to dodge the bullet coming for her head. She found cover and checked her wound. It was a clean shot through and through. Kat would have to patch it up later, but for now, she'll live. Feeling her enemies close in, she darted out of the only viable exit, a glass window to her left. Tucking her arm over her face, Kat burst open the window as her body barreled through the glass, turning in midair, letting off on her twins as a few of her assailant followed her lead.

The ground swiftly hit her back, and she tucked, backflip-ping over a boulder as the building collapsed in a heap a few sec-onds after she escaped. Ducking with her back towards the rock, she cast her eyes around, making sure no human police were sig-naled by the dismantling of the building. Looking into the open night, she was pleased to see they were still alone. Aside from the demon hunters behind the rock, waiting for her to step out so they could pull her apart.

Where was–Sia dropped down in a crouch beside her, pla-cing her back to the boulder as well. Briefly glancing in each other's direction, they nodded then stepped out from behind the rock to face their opponents quickly. She took a mental note of the five demon fighters before her, considering there were a total of eight in the building. Three must have fallen in the structure, but she would keep her guard up just in case they survived.

"Looks like things are just heating up, huh boys?!" she shouted to the five guard dogs dressed in all black ninja suits, horns out, faces covered. It looks like the demon prince wanted blood, theirs specifically. Unfortunately for him, the blood he would receive wouldn't be their own.

"Let's play, bitches."

Kat took off towards the river with Sia by her side. She looked back briefly to make sure the goon squad was gullible enough to follow them. They were. She smiled.

"I'm on the roof!"

Sia jumped high on the buildings beside them, jumping from rooftop to rooftop, disappearing into the night. She used her strength to propel her forward with a swiftness the guards couldn't track. Knowing they were better off on the ground, they decided to follow Kat instead of pursuing Sia. Thinking as the mind of her enemy it was five against one. They figured they'd kill her first then go after her sister later. And that's what they were betting their lives on.

Gradually slowing down as she came close to the lake, she made a one-eighty, walking backward to face the hunters with her hands raised. Looking around with mock confusion on her face, she steadily backed up in the direction of the lake as her assailants started to close in. She could practically hear them salivating behind their masks at the prospects of running back to their master with a Knight's head. But that wasn't going to happen. Not tonight anyway. Continuing the charade, so the bullies would let their guard down, even more, she thrust her arms out in defeat.

"What, you just left me?" she screamed "How could you?! I can't beat them all by myself, damn you." She threw a mock fist in the air for dramatic effect.

Oh yeah, they were smiling now. They started inching closer and closer to her drawing out the swords at their backs. Kat threw her hands up, palms out as she stepped back into the lake.

"Please, don't hurt me," she begged, throwing in a few fake tears, yet they kept slowly approaching her with their blades drawn in her direction.

"Look, I didn't mean to kill your buddies. I mean, they were trying to kill me first. Fair's fair." More backing up into the river. They were almost knee deep - now.

"What does your prince pay you? I'll double it. C'mon, I'm loaded. You could all work for me."

They didn't falter a step, as they all emerged in the water, red eyes twinkling with promised death. *Damn loyal bastards,* that honor would be their demise. What a pity. Following that miserable, self-centered asshole signed their death warrant.

Sia took that moment to drop down off the roof behind them, drawing a flaming line in the grass blocking their exit out the lake. Her opponents took a quick look at the flames and turned back around, so their bodies were facing her once again with confusion.

"C'mon, guys, you didn't think it would be that easy, hmm?" She gave them her favorite murderous smile that flashed her small fangs.

"You may work for the Prince of Darkness, but we work for the Boogeyman. And that crazy Knight will have a heart attack if we lose. So, we never lose."

Kat threw her head up to the sky and drew up that oh so familiar electric current from the depth of her core. Pulling the lightning from above, even though there wasn't a storm, she had the power to conjure the bolt. She let the magnificent blue streak come racing towards her body. The beautiful bolt coursed through her system, then out the tips of her fingers. She knew she looked like a lightning bug, all lit up and glowing, but she didn't care. This feeling was what she was born for, bred for. And the harpy loved it.

With one last screeching roar, Kat lit the lake up like a Christmas tree, the flashing blue sheet hurtling over the lake like a cover, instantly engulfing her victims in her electrical current. She didn't have to push her powers much since the water acted as an outlet to her charge.

They tried to run out of the lake, but her bolt was faster; freezing them in place, as the lightning barreled through their bodies. They tried to pull the blue light off their skin, rapidly throwing clothes to the side, but it was far too late. A few agonizing screams of pain later, it was over. They were burned to utter ash.

Using her gift at this capacity usually only left dust bunnies behind. But at least they were in the river. It made cleanup a breeze.

Smiling her sister doused her flame. "So, that was fun."

Propping her hands on her hips, she returned the smile as she glanced around. It was. She hadn't felt this alive since, well, since Luke. *Don't go there Kat, don't go there.*

"Yeah" she replied, "it was." She walked out the lake, shaking out her boots, and resumed her place at her sister's side.

"Think the Dark Prince will get the hint and leave us alone after his minions don't show up to report?" Sia asked as she walked over to Kat so she could inspect her flesh wound.

She hissed, "Nope." He was just getting started.

They walked back to the abandoned building in comfortable silence. Sia controlled the buildings flame to a faint hum, so it wouldn't cause any more notice that they were sure it had already created. No way the humans hadn't heard something. Their curiosity would drive them out here, even if they were mainly in the middle of nowhere.

"Let's get out of here, shall we?"

"Let's."

They took off at a brisk pace down the street. Tucking their wings away and trying to hide their weapons under their jackets and clothes the best they could. The Knights tried their damnest to conceal their war from humans so that they could continue in their blissful lives. Most phantom creatures worked with them in trying to keep humans unaware of the monsters that lurk in their dark shadows. Others, like those assholes, didn't care.

Creating a camouflage mist to hide their war when it crossed over to Earth was an ability most phantom creatures possessed, yet it was taxing on the body and left one vulnerable. So, they tried to push their war to dark corners and abandoned buildings at late night hours. As modern-day technology continued to progress and camera phones continue to exist, they were going to need to call upon that ability sooner than later. That meant teams were coming, whether they contained the war between the wolves and vamps or not.

"Wanna go to Phantom and have a drink?" Sia threw beside her, after a few minutes of walking.

"Huh?" Kat questioned, she checked her watch. "You haven't mentioned the club in a while. Figured you'd been there, done that."

"Nah. We've just been busy, with being hunted and all that. I was just never in the mood."

Hmm, well that's new. Sia never missed the opportunity to drink; maybe she wasn't the only one changing. But their shift was far from over, and she was still bleeding.

"We should just finish patrolling."

Sia barked out a laugh, "Aww, is Kat finally scared of little ole Sky?"

"Never," she came to a halt and sneered. "You know what? Sure, let's go. And it's Thursday night, which is goth night, so we don't have to change."

"Let's go."

They began their stroll in the direction of Phantom, and she got this tingling sensation in her gut. *Hmm, what the hell?* She wasn't hungry. She had just let off a great deal of power in that lake, so it was going to take her a few more seconds to recharge, therefore it wasn't her powers. *Huh,* could it be? Oh Goddess, she was, wasn't she? Kat was nervous. Taking a deep breath, she tried to still her jitters. By all likelihood, her human wasn't even there... but what if he was?

Chapter Nineteen

Nope, Kat's human wasn't here. Just the regular group of misfits milling around, pretending to understand the dark arts. The disappointment was staggering. But what did she expect? It had been weeks since they had their night together, and it's not like she left her number for him to contact her. Did she think he would just come to the club every night in hopes of running into her again? Kat could be self-absorbed at times.

How did she let a human male get under her skin? It didn't make any logical sense. Kat knew nothing about him. Strangely enough, she felt Luke meant something to her, and she had to figure it out, or she wouldn't be able to focus. It could've been highly plausible that it was only her feeling this, no need to ruin a perfectly fine human's life, but she had to know for sure.

Kat was losing focus in fights, and now that she was teamed up with Sia, she had more than just herself to look after. There was no way she would risk her sister's life. Thus, she had to keep herself alive. Kat thought the new challenge the phantom creatures were throwing at her would be enough to quell her thirst for him; however, it hadn't. It just made her more restless and tense. There was so much pent up aggression that Kat needed to release. Luke was the only one she wanted to help her release it.

The harpy drew back her fifth whiskey, knowing her decision had been made. Kat was going to see her human again. She just needed to figure out how? It wasn't like her ass could walk up to his condo, knock on the door and say, "Honey, I'm home." No telling if she'd saunter in on something personal. And she didn't need that type of full-frontal disappointment. She could maybe show up at his office, but that could be perceived as a little stalkerish. No, she had to keep it casual.

Gesturing to the bartender for another drink, she figured the best course of action was to bump into him while he was out accidentally. Perceptions be damned, it was extremely stalkerish, but that's the only solution she had. Following him, however, meant she'd have to go out in daylight, which required a greater chance of exposure. Kat would have to use a light hum of power to conceal her wings, which could draw her enemies to her location. If they attacked, it'd be harder to disguise the battle in daylight than it would be in darkness. But, as Kat remembered those dark curls sliding through her fingers as she palmed his head, as those powerful hips thrust in and out of her, she knew it was oooh so worth the risk.

Sia came off the dance floor to stand beside her, ordering a seltzer. They had been getting along so well lately, falling into familiar patterns; it was almost as if they'd never parted. Their parents had trained them well. Unfortunately, that was the only thing positive they ever did for them. Teach them how to stay alive.

Their father tried, to the best of his ability, to be more active in their lives outside of training, but it just wasn't in his nature. He was a phoenix, not a harpy male, and the fact that his children turned out to be harpies always seemed to upset him.

When two different species had children, whoever had the more dominant DNA between the two would determine the species of the paranormal they conceived. Their father always felt less of a male since he ended up having two twin harpies, which proved their mother wore the pants in that relationship. There was still a chance that the kids would split down the middle, but that was extremely rare. Their father loved them nonetheless, but he always found a way to let them know that if they'd been born a phoenix, they wouldn't have had to go through such grueling training. Like it was their fault for becoming harpies. But, you can't change the past. Regardless of her history, she was proud of who she was. And having at least one member of her family at her back made it that much more worthwhile.

"Ready to go?" She asked her sister.

"Yeah, I'm beat; besides, we should get back out there."

Kat raised her lips in a smirk, "Chicken."

"Nah. But I ain't stupid either."

Kat laughed, linking their arms together as they walked out of the club. Yes, she was happy to have her sister back at her side and hopefully soon her human.

****

Just one more mile. As Luke came to a stop at a bench along the side of the lake on the path he ran every Wednesday, he checked his Fitbit and saw he'd already beat his previous record, yet he wasn't burnt out, which was encouraging. He lifted a leg, putting his foot on the park bench, and stretched out his tight muscles, bending at the knee. The frigid air frequently did that to his muscles quicker than being inside; however, it was better than running on a treadmill in a crowded gym. Seeing how it was just a few days into March, the gym was still loaded with New Year's resolution seekers trying to lose the fifteen pounds they gained over the holidays. It just made more sense for him to run along his favorite track, besides, he loved being outdoors.

He rechecked his wristwatch, his goal target of five miles flashing complete. Luke rotated his shoulders counterclockwise, gearing up for one final mile before he cramped. Resetting his playlist, he reconnected his headphones and Lil Wayne's "I Am Not A Human Being" came blaring through.

Luke had had a stressful week thus far and running always seemed to clear his mind. He tried to make it out to the track at least twice a week. However, his schedule hadn't permitted much personal time, so he was glad he was able to sneak away today. Destressing his muscles should help get him through the rest of the week.

Clasping his hands together he straightened, then stretched his hands to the heavens, long stepping with his knees up, while marching in place. Feeling loose, he set out.

"Must be my lucky day."

Luke spun around instantaneously, taken off guard by a familiar voice. He hadn't heard it in over a month, yet it was one he remembered. It was one Luke had guaranteed himself he'd never hear again after all this time. His fantasy woman in the flesh. He almost thought he was hallucinating. Hell, after five miles his brain could've started to draw up a mirage, but when she spoke again, he knew she was real.

"How have you been, Lucas?" He stepped back and smiled. *She remembered my name.*

"I nearly didn't recognize you without your glasses."

My glasses? Reaching up, Luke went to adjust glasses that weren't there, then shook his head to clear it. He wasn't doing an excellent job on the conversation front.

"Right, yes, hello, I take them off to run. I hate when they fog up, so I wear my contacts instead."

"Makes sense..." she paused, tapping her index finger to her chin. "So, you haven't answered my question."

Luke lifted a finger to scratch his head. "Huh? Oh um, I'm sorry what was your question?"

"How have you been–" *Say my name, please say my name*

again "–Lucas?"

He almost came right there in his track pants. But seriously, would anyone blame him? Even in her all-black tracksuit with matching black sneakers, scarf, vest, and earmuffs, she oozed sex appeal.

"I've been good. How about you?" He replied with what he hoped was a confident smile, tucking his hands into his pants pocket.

"Same," she responded returning his smile, which lit up her gorgeous face.

He'd been envisioning this very encounter for weeks now, and after countless rehearsal conversations, he still had no clue what to say to her. She stepped closer to him, which made him lose his train of thought, even more so when she spoke her next words.

"I've been thinking about you," she stepped even closer into his space. "I've missed you."

That snapped the awkwardness right out of his body. Doing something he'd dreamed of doing for weeks, he grabbed her, pulling her close to his body.

He whispered down to her, "I've missed you too." And he had. He didn't know why, but it was the truth.

"So, what are you and I going to do about that Luke? You missed me; I've missed you."

Luke ran his hand down the woman's cheek, smiling. He knew precisely what he wanted to do about that; he was just hoping they were both on the same page.

****

Kat slammed Luke's door behind her. Grabbing his arm, she threw him back against the wall to her left and took his lips in a punishing embrace. Kat was so glad he didn't ask questions once they'd left the track. She had told him she'd driven to the trail and she would follow him home, solidifying the lie by telling him not to worry about losing her since she remembered where he lived.

The truth was, she'd followed him to the lake on foot, and he didn't need to know that. It would probably just freak him out since the track was basically in the middle of nowhere. She said she'd park some distance away and ran here so she would meet him back at his place. She had hoped that he wouldn't question it or offer to drive her to her car, and she was right. He had taken her at her word and rolled with it. She was so blissfully glad he decided to run with it. She was so excited to see him she hadn't prepared for any other scenario.

His tongue darted in her mouth past her teeth, fighting for dominance, effectively drawing her attention back to the kiss. As they frantically pulled each other's clothes off without disengaging their lips, she could distantly hear items being knocked over in their haste. She felt that familiar spark of electricity between them again, but she managed to keep it within her. An effort that required a great deal of concentration. Which was exceedingly tricky considering he was devouring her lips and his flavor was intoxicating. She nearly came right there in his hands at its intensity. So worth the wait.

Kat hadn't known what to expect when she walked up on him on the track. He could've been completely thrown off by her approach or acted as if they've never met. Males tended to have a short attention span. In the end, she was semi-hoping for the latter. Maybe if he acted as if they've never met, she'd be able to move on and get him off her mind. However, this situation turned out better. Much better.

As Luke yanked Kat's top over her head, freeing her breasts with a speed that impressed even her, she was pleased to see he wanted her just as much as she wanted him. The wet dreams didn't do this moment justice. And they were both impatient for it. Clothes were thrown everywhere, she was quite sure she broke a few zippers, and she may have unintentionally scratched a couple of tender places trying to relieve him of his pants until they were finally both delightfully naked.

Coming up for air, Kat took a moment to appreciate him as they pulled apart. She loved the fact that he was confident in his nakedness. Allowing her gaze to roam free unashamed. He stood before her proud, and he had every right to feel that way. He was gorgeous. And she could've stared at him all day, but a moment was all he gave her to admire his physique. He pulled a condom out of the walkway dresser, putting it on his massive girth.

She was spun around until her back hit the wall, then was lifted into the air. Kat immediately wrapped her legs around his waist, curling her arms around his neck, as he captured her lips again, plunging inside her with one powerful thrust. He pounded into her forcibly, banging her head back into the wall so hard, that she had to brace a palm above her head to keep her from slamming through it.

They were both panting heavily, requiring them to break their passionate, all-consuming kiss in favor of air. When she peeled her lips away from his, she ran her tongue up the side of his neck and up to his ear. He tasted salty from his run, but she was still able to taste his flavor, which was mind-altering.

Kat felt her climax rise in a rush of glory and he smothered her lips again with a kiss to drawn out the sounds of her exotic cry. Elated, she dug her nails into his back effectively leaving a mark. As she screamed into his mouth, her vagina muscles tightening around his member, he buried his face in her neck as he exploded right behind her. True bliss.

Chapter Twenty

Luke couldn't move; he just stayed there holding his seductress up against the wall with his forehead resting against hers as they tried to catch their breath. He felt like his chest was going to burst wide open if he didn't get his breathing under control soon. Hell, if he didn't have enough oxygen somehow, Luke was likely to pass the hell out. He lifted his head slightly to peer into her eyes. *Please look as utterly defeated as I feel. Thank God.*

Slightly pulling back he looked up, and yes, she appeared just as beaten down as Luke felt. And didn't that just make him swell with pride? Their gazes locked, and he smiled as she opened her mouth to speak.

"Damn."

Luke threw back his head and laughed just as she unhooked her legs from his waist to slide down his body. They stood there for a few more seconds in each other's arms, as they collected their thoughts. Man, he could hold her all day if she let him.

They fell into a comfortable silence, neither of them speaking, just continuing to get their bearings after what just transpired between them. He'd spent most of the afternoon and evening out on the track, and he was sweaty and probably smelled worse. Not that he cared at the moment, but he didn't want her uncomfortable. He needed a shower.

"As much as I'd like to keep holding you, I could use a shower. Not that I don't like smelling of you, but I've been on the track for a while, and I worked all day." Luke pulled back slightly so he could look at her.

"Hmmm, yeah, a shower sounds amazing right about now."

Right, she'd need one too. He grabbed her hand to show her to the guest bath on the other side of his living room.

"Come with me, the guest bath is just down this way." She stilled his hand when he went to pull her away from the wall.

"Now why would I want to shower alone? How about we conserve water and shower together instead."

Yeah, he *so* could get on board with that.

Luke grabbed her hand and drew her toward the master bath. He loved his bathroom. It was about five-hundred square feet with marble his and her style sinks, a jet whirlpool tub to the side, and a shower in the corner that could probably fit five people inside. The power jets overhead and from the front were some of its best features, excluding the bench inside. As he pulled his woman inside, shutting the foggy glass panels after starting the jets, he thought of so many positions that he could put his temptress in on that very bench. Yes, the seat most certainly will be the best feature in his shower.

Closing things up entirely, he turned his back towards the jets from overhead and pulled his lady into his body. In the hallway entrance, they had taken things incredibly fast, no doubt both craving each other's touch, but this time he wanted to take things slowly. He needed to memorize her body. He wanted to watch her face as he pleasured her.

Luke started kissing her cheek then he ran his tongue down the side of her neck as he caressed her breast, pinching each erect nipple in turn. He enjoyed watching them pucker under his sensual caress, proceeding to do it again, loving the exhale of breath his lady took in response. Dipping down a little, Luke captured one red nipple into his mouth and sucked, allowing her more comfortable access to run her fingers through his damp hair. He could feel the energy between them was starting to escalate, but he wasn't ready to take things any further just yet.

He pulled away, grabbing the soap on the stall and lathered his hands with the suds. Luke washed her body from elbow to toes then handed over the soap so she was able to do the same. She took her time working over his body, admiring all his lines and sensitive parts, and planting featherlike kisses to his pecs and abs, making him shiver.

Once they were both clean and free of soap, he resumed his sensual kisses to her flesh. Turning her so she faced the wall towards the bench, he ran a hand down her spine as he kissed her shoulder. Luke propped her leg up on the chair then grabbed his length and positioned it at her entrance from behind. This time he entered her slowly, grabbing her hips to steady his thrust into her. They both moaned in unison as he invaded her tight inner circle. She felt so good, so right.

Keeping a slow, steady pace, he moved in and out of her as he ran his tongue down her neck and over her shoulder. She slanted her head back so it laid slightly over his shoulder, meeting him thrust for thrust. Reaching around, Luke cupped her chin and brought her lips around to capture his as he dragged a hand down her abdomen. He touched the cliff of her clitoris with his fingertips, circling her bud, burrowing his staff in pace with his hips, drawing a hushed gasp from her lips, as their mouths continued to dance. A few seconds later, she climaxed gently in his arms, and he followed a few strokes after, kissing her slowly as he exited her entrance.

The water in the shower had cooled a long time ago, but neither of them seemed to mind as they allowed the cool jets to cleanse their skin. He turned off the faucet; both of them exiting the shower in silence as water dripped from their bodies. Luke grabbed a towel from his stand in the corner and walked back over to dry his girl off. He took exceptional care making sure she was completely dry before he grabbed the other towel and quickly dried himself off. Luke wrapped the towel around his waist, then bent down to kiss her again. When she looked up at him and smiled he knew right then, he was hooked.

****

Luke's confidence started to sprout as the evening progressed. The things he did to her in the bathroom involving his fingers were mind-blowing. She didn't know if it was a combination of the jets teasing her body or just him. It wasn't too often that a girl could have multiple orgasms in one sitting, but the way he used his body with such confidence had brought her over the edge numerous times.

They had finally stepped out of the bath once the water started to run cold. Luke towel dried her off then grabbed his robe to wrap around her. He had been so gentle with her in the shower, treating her as if she was a precious jewel that needed to be polished. Kat had never felt so cared for in her entire life. She loved aggressive sex, the one filled with passion and heat, but what she just experienced in the bathroom was unexpectedly wonderful. She liked it. Kat liked him.

Finishing up in the bathroom, they walked out with him leading the way to the main room. By now the sun outside had dropped in the horizon with darkness taking its place.

"So," he turned to look at her, "can I get you a drink?"

Kat looked over at her clothes knowing she should go. She needed to hunt and staying here any longer wouldn't be a bright idea. Luke must have read her mind, as she looked over, he came around the bar and stood before her blocking her view of her clothing at the entrance.

He ran his hands down her arms, looking at her with those amazing blue eyes. "Please, don't go, not yet."

Kat bit her lip and glanced towards the windows, calculating the time before her sister would arise. She still had a few more hours in the day left, which meant she could stay for a while. But Kat knew she needed just to go. Her itch was officially scratched, yet she heard herself answer.

"Whisky....neat."

Luke smiled that deviously attractive smile and hurried off to the bar.

"So," he cut a glance at her and looked back to focus on pouring her drink into a crystal glass.

Ah yes, here it comes, the questions. *Shit!*

"I never got your name."

"I never gave it." She stuck her hands in her robe pocket, walking closer to the bar.

"That you did not."

Luke came around the bar and handed Kat her drink. She took a swing of the liquid and loved the smooth burn, as it slid down her throat. Yeah, that was the good stuff. Top shelf. She gave it a little swirl.

"So....?"

He looked down at her again, and this time his baby blues held, looking at her in question. He wasn't backing down. Good boy.

"It's Kat." She might as well give him the truth. All Phantom Knights had an alias in the human world; they didn't need anyone digging too hard into who they pretended to be. "Katrine Thorne."

"Beautiful name."

"Thanks."

Luke came and joined her in sitting on the opposite bar-stool across from her, sliding her legs in between his. Noticing he was still extremely naked under that towel. *Focus Kat.*

"So, Kat, what do you do?"

"I'm an electrician." The lie rolled off effortlessly.

Luke paused, his eyes got a little full, and he blinked. "Seriously?"

"Yeah, why? You want me to pull out my tool belt?"

He laughed, "No, I didn't think... yeah I wouldn't peg you for someone who works with their hands. I mean you don't look like someone that could do manual labor. You're just so, so delicate."

"Oh, Luke you can't even begin to believe what I could do with my hands." She ran her hand over his knee. "And as for manual labor, I'm not as delicate as you think." She took another drink from her glass.

"Correct, never judge a book by its cover. Noted." He took a moment to collect himself. "So, I know it's probably too late to ask, but I'm going to ask anyway. Do you have a boyfriend?"

"No, Luke, I don't have a boyfriend." Kat smiled. He was just too cute.

"Husband?"

"No."

"Thank God." She laughed, then took another sip of her drink which was now empty.

"Do you have any family around here?"

"Just a sister," who was probably going to kill her if she

found out where she was.

"What about your parents?"

Okay, this was getting a little too personal. She jumped up from the barstool. She didn't want to talk about her parents to anyone, and she didn't like the direction the questions were taking. Kat couldn't afford to slip up, and she was getting so relaxed she just might.

"I should get going; it's getting late."

Luke slid off his bar stool as well and stood in her way glancing at his watch.

"It's only 8:30, can't you stay a little longer, talk some more? Please, I want to get to know you."

"Why?" Kat stumbled out. She did lose her cool when he was near her, looking down at her with such hunger in his eyes.

"I don't know, because I... I guess I like you. Isn't that what you do with people you like? Get to know them?"

She went to step past him, "You don't want to get to know me. Trust me."

"Give me a chance to make my own decision–" He grabbed her arm to stop her retreat, "–please."

He needed to stop with the "please," she could feel herself caving every time he used it and especially looking as adorably naked as he did now.

"Fine," Kat said walking back towards the bar once more, hopping up on the barstool. "What do you want to know?"

Chapter Twenty-One

Kat and Luke ended up back in the bed after downing a few more drinks and another round of steamy hot sex. Both were lying on the mattress staring at the ceiling talking about nothing and everything at the same time. Kat couldn't remember the last time conversation like this flowed so smoothly for her. And she didn't even have to lie, much. The two of them had a lot in common, which was pleasantly surprising. The two both loved to run, swim, and rock climb. They liked the same kinds of music, which mostly consisted of hip hop and R&B with some rock and roll thrown in for kicks and giggles. They also enjoyed electricity. Sure, his was more the electrical engineering type and hers was more flashing lights, but kind of, not the same thing.

What connected them even more was the loss of their parents. Well, okay, Luke lost his in a plane crash, along with his only sibling, his sister. After hearing his heartfelt story of their death, she understood why he had a catch in his voice whenever he talked about his younger sister helping him pick out this place. They had taken a family trip that he was supposed to attend himself, yet he had got held up at work. Luke was going to meet them in Paris a few days later, yet their plane never made it to Europe. The engine malfunctioned and went down in the Atlantic Ocean, with no known survivors. He had been devastated by the loss and hearing his story made her ice-cold heart melt.

To have family and then lose them all in one tragic accident would be overwhelming for anyone. And, well, her parents might still be breathing, but according to her, they were as good as dead in her eyes.

"Yep, they are straight up assholes," Kat began, "sperm and egg donors; nothing more, nothing less."

"I can't believe parents would treat their children that way. My parents were so loving and caring; I couldn't imagine them not loving me the way they did," he paused for a few heartbeats, "I miss them every day."

"Yeah well, I didn't have that..." Kat said with envy in her heart, "me and my sister Sia were all each other had... All each other still have." She sounded small, *where the hell were my balls?*

"Must have been tough growing up?" He leaned over, propping himself up on his elbow and resting his head on his palm.

"Yeah, but we made it out alive and now she and I are the best war... Ahhhhh wor-kers the firm has ever seen."

"So, I guess the training helped in a way, huh?"

"Yeah.... I guess it did." She replied distantly, throwing an arm over her eyes.

A vibration sounded again in the distance. Kat had heard it a few times before, but she'd ignored it. Luke was talking about his parents and she loved the way she felt laying up next to him as he ran a hand up and down her stomach. But she couldn't ignore it any longer because she was quite sure she knew where the vibration was coming from...yep, by the door where her clothes were...again.

"Shit!" She sat up and shot a quick look out through the windows.

It was pitch black outside. *FUCK!*

Kat reached down and grabbed her robe off the floor and slipped out of bed to grab her phone. She looked down at the screen and saw the time. *Midnight? Are you fucking kidding me?* Where had the time gone? The phone had stopped and started back up again, bracing herself for her sister's wrath she answered on the second ring.

"Hel–"

"WHERE THE FUCK ARE YOU!!!!" Sia shouted through the phone. Yep, she was capital P.I.S.S.E.D, pissed.

"Calm down sister please, I'm okay" she looked over at Luke who had sat up and was looking over at her. He gave her that secret smile she was beginning to love when their eyes locked... wait, love? Did she think that word?

"What do you mean, calm down?! I've been trying to reach you all night. I was so close to calling Sky, Kat, this fucking close."

Kat winced, thankfully Sia had a little faith in her because if she'd made that call, all hell would've broken loose.

"Look, I'm sorry, I lost track of time. Can we meet now?"

"Where are you, Kat?" Sia seethed through her teeth.

She looked over again and thought *why lie?* It was her sister, and they seemed to be getting back on the right foot.

"I'm with Luke... You know, the guy from the club." The silence was so high over the other line of the phone; Kat thought her sister hung up or died from shock.

"Meet me at your loft in ten minutes, Kat. Ten fucking minutes," Sia spat, hanging up.

"Shit," she whispered under her breath. Kat went to grab her pants and jacket from off the floor and started to get dressed as fast as she could without seeming supernatural.

"Hey, look, I gotta go." She directed the sentence across the room towards the bed, not bothering to look in his direction as she got dressed, but Luke was already standing next to her close enough to touch. He was also still gloriously in the buff, which was hauntingly distracting. Luke knew he had a fantastic body and he wasn't afraid to show it.

"Please, wait. I want to see you again. Tell me I get to see you again."

"I don't know, Luke," Kat answered honestly as she finished dressing. "I'm a busy girl. I usually don't let time slip away from me like this."

"That only means this time was special. It means this thing, whatever *this* is between us," he drew his finger back and forth between them, "is special."

Kat paused. Luke was right. Somewhere deep inside her small Grinch-like heart, she felt he was right. This, whatever it was, felt... right. But damnit, she could get him killed. If not by the dark lords in the shadows, then by Sky. She'd freak if she found out Kat was sleeping with a human, even though she was never one to play by the rules this would take the cake in her leader's eyes. She didn't want to push Sky to her breaking point, but it seemed the logical part of her brain was dormant. Besides, it wasn't like she'd let anything get serious.

"How about we go out tomorrow night for dinner? I know a nice restaurant nearby. It has an excellent selection of just about anything."

"I can't do dinner, Luke, I work late nights," she was fully dressed now and easing towards the door. *Just leave, Kat.*

"Okay, what about breakfast?"

"Don't you work in the morning?"

"I'll call out." Kat had to laugh at that.

"No, Luke, go to work," she chuckled.

Luke gave a dramatic sigh. "Then at least meet me for lunch. I know I'm being pushy, and I know that's probably a turn-off, but you got to throw a guy a bone here... please."

There goes that word again. And what do you know, Kat found herself caving towards that gorgeous boyish smile. "Give me a pen."

Kat smiled as he darted over to the dresser in the walkway and grabbed the note pad and pen, skating back towards her once he had what he desired. She scribbled her phone number down onto the pad and handed it back to him, starting to head out. He walked towards the door and unlocked it for her, cracking it a little.

"Call or text me with when and where you want me to meet you."

Luke sighed against the door with relief, "Absolutely."

Luke grabbed her abruptly, smashing his mouth against hers in a scorching kiss that was all tongue and passion. As he released her, Luke gave her his secret smile. She stepped outside in the hallway and heard Lucas lock the door behind her as she walked towards the elevator. Kat ran her hand across her lips. That last lingering kiss was almost worth the verbal ass whooping she was about to take against Sia in a few minutes...well almost.

Chapter Twenty-Two

The next day, Luke probably got about an hour's worth of work done before his lunch break. Glancing at his watch, for the hundredth time, he was elated the thing finally said 11:00. Luke had just one more hour until lunchtime, and he'd finally get to see Kat. On his fifteen-minute break, he'd called her with a bit of nerve in his stomach, hoping she had given him the right number. But when she picked up, with that musical seductive siren's voice, he knew it was his Kat. They talked his whole break about nothing, and it was the most natural conversation with anyone he'd had in a long, long time. He asked her to meet him across the street at Tony's Bar, and she agreed. He couldn't wait to see her.

Looking down at his watch he realized his musing had lasted all of three minutes. *Urrrghh, just fifty-seven more to go* he mused, looking at his watch once more. Turning back towards his computer, Luke moved the mouse. He really should try to focus and work.

Reorganizing his thoughts, Luke pulled up his notes for the day. He was running through his numbers until a balled-up piece of paper hit his desk. With confusion, Luke looked up to find the paper culprit was Justin. Holding up the paper, he looked at him with a question until he mouthed, *incoming.* Frowning his face, Luke looked in the direction Justin moved his eyes to see Casey coming towards his desk. He groaned.

"Hi, Luke, wanna do lunch?" she said after stopping in front of him.

"Hey, Casey, sorry I already have lunch plans today."

"Oh, really, where are you and Justin going, Tony's? I can tag along with you two if that's okay."

"It's not with Justin," and he didn't mention it was in fact at Tony's, but that was none of her business.

"Oh, with who then?"

"No one you know, Casey, so maybe some other time. I really should get back to work. I don't want the boss man to come out here and flip."

"Oh right, so maybe we can get together tonight? Hit Phantom? It's been a while since we hung."

"Sorry, but no. I'll probably stay in tonight." *Hopefully with Kat.*

"What's going on, Luke?" Casey frowned down at him and pushed out her lips in a pout. "I hardly see you anymore. You don't answer your phone when I call. I... I miss you."

No, no she didn't, she missed her lap dog. She missed the fact that he didn't follow her around like every other male tool in this office, with a hope that she'll look his way.

"Nothing's wrong, Casey, I've just been swamped lately. Nothing against you personally, I don't have time to hang out, sorry."

"Well, whenever you finally have time for me, just shoot me a text, okay, Mr. I'm Too Busy For My Friends?"

She turned around and stomped off purposefully back to her desk. He glanced at Justin, and his friend smiled brightly. All boy-next-door smile, giving him a thumbs up. He just shook his head and counted down the minutes until he saw the woman he was beginning to fall hard for.

****

This was a bad idea, Kat thought, as she waited outside of Tony's Bar. She rechecked her phone. Yep, the text message from Luke saying he was in the bar at a booth in the back was still on her message feed. She shouldn't go in; this was a horrible, bad idea. An idea that could lead to very wicked, evil, naughty things. She shivered. Decision made, she was going in.

Kat knew once she crossed that entrance and sat down at that bar, she'd be officially dating a human. And she was okay with that; he was special. She liked her mundane. He was the first thing in a while that made her feel good. There wasn't much happiness in her line of work, so she owed it to herself to see where this was going. Just for a while, anyway. She knew nothing would come of it. Taking a deep breath, she decided to rip off the bandage and walk in.

Tony's Bar was a simplistic, old-school dive bar. It had a few pool tables off to the side, a jukebox that had smooth jazz playing in the background, and a few tables and booths littered around. The bar was modernized despite its rustic vibe and was twice the size it appeared to be from outside. But when you were across the street from a building like Fall Heights one guessed they'd need a pretty big bar. A stressful job equals a lot of booze.

Sweeping her gaze around to the back, she saw Luke in the corner by himself. Kat's mouth began to water, as their eyes linked across the distance. He signaled her over, and she followed his beckon.

Luke looked terrific in his form-fitting grey suit. He wore a crisp white shirt under his blazer, with a dark grey tie with blue stripes that matched his eyes. Eyes that were without glasses. Looking at his gorgeous face now, she kinda missed his other set of eyes. *Okay, time to stop drooling.*

Hi," she said in greeting as he stood. She leaned in and kissed his cheek.

"Hi, Kat, you look great."

"Thanks," she uttered with a slight blush, considering all she wore was a light green blouse with wide black leg pleated palazzo pants. "You look quite edible yourself." His blush was adorable, as she took a seat opposite him.

"Hi Luke, what can I get you and your guest—oh, Kat, hi," the waitress spoke, noticing her for the first time.

Bitty, her name was Bitty, she was a panther shifter just like her boss behind the bar.

Many paranormal hid in the human world to work and find a conceptional life. It was just easier to come up and make money here. Back home, if one wasn't a witch, the market was slim pickings.

Casting a look over to Tony, she gave him a tilt of her head and a smile. She'd been here plenty of times, and Tony was a great ally to have.

"Hi, Bit, how have you been?"

"Good. I haven't seen you around in a while, and with a hu.... ummm with Luke. How do you two know each other?"

"We just recently met, a few weeks ago at Phantom," Luke cut in with a smile.

"Oh well, that's nice. So, what can I get you two?" Bit said with a nervous hiccup in her voice.

She knew better than to question Kat. She also knew she never saw them here together. That's why she loved the panther pack at Tony's. They were loyal to a tee and didn't ask too many questions.

"Kat? What would you like?"

Kat cut her eyes over at Bitty and gave her a reassuring smile letting her know she wasn't here to cause trouble today, which was usually what she did when she came into the bar. The waitress probably thought she was here to kill the poor guy. But, it wasn't her fault most of her perps liked to hide from her in the bar, thinking they were on neutral territory since Tony had a no-violence spell around the place.

Some of the tension left Bit's body as she caught her, peace and promise of no broken furniture, smile. Besides, the bite back when one broke the rules was a bitch.

"Can I get a loaded cheeseburger, fries, and chocolate milkshake on the side, with a glass of water?"

"Sure thing. Luke?"

"That sounds great; I'll have the same."

They handed Bit the menus.

"Wonderful, I'll be right back." Bitty turned to walk back behind the bar towards the kitchen.

"So, it seems you come here as often as I do, huh? Can't believe we haven't run into each other." Luke chucked across the table at her.

"Yeah well, I'm normally a late-night customer."

"Right, you work nights?"

"Mostly, yes."

"Huh?"

"What?"

"I would think you'd need the daylight to do what you do?"

"We don't," Kat answered flawlessly. "Our firm is paid more because we work nights, gets the job done faster if you work through the day and night hours."

"I bet."

"So, how's work so far Lucas...What?" Kat asked, cutting off her line of questioning. "Why are you staring at me like that? Do I have something on my face?" Kat brought her hands toward her cheeks for inspection. He just shook his head, smiled her favorite secret smile, leaning forward with his hands clasped in front of him. "Seriously, what?"

"I just can't believe you came," he replied.

"I told you I would, and I make it a point to follow through on the things I say I would do."

"Good to know," he sat back slightly, still not taking his eyes off her, which left her somewhat breathless.

"You're staring again, Luke," she breathed a little deeper this time. She knew that look. She knew that look well. He wanted her. And didn't that send a gush of wetness through her panties.

"I know," he ran his tongue over his bottom lip.

Luckily, Bit took that moment to return with their food and set it in front of them. Kat was a hair away from jumping across the table to devour him.

"Thanks."

"No problem you two, enjoy."

She focused on her food since that would keep her in her chair. They ate in comfortable silence for a while.

"I'm so glad you didn't order a salad. I hate women who don't like to eat on the first date–umm, not that this is a date or anything," he backtracked. Aww, her strong, silent nerd was back. He was just so damn cute.

"Luke."

"Yes?" He paused, using a napkin to wipe his face.

"This is a date."

"Good," he looked up at her again when his phone vibrated. "Oh, I apologize, this is my coworker Justin," he noticed when he checked the screen.

"By all means," she signaled for him to answer it and he did.

"Hey, Justin, What's up?"

"I followed you."

Kat heard his friend report on the other side of the phone. Enhanced harpy hearing was a nice perk to have, especially since she could turn it on and off on a whim.

"What?"

"To the bar."

"What are you talking about Justin?"

"I'm on the other side of Tony's Bar." Luke went to look around.

Kat noted his friend a long time ago. The harpy noticed everyone in the bar once she entered. Her job required her to remain three steps ahead, always.

"Don't look around, crazy."

"Justin, what are you doing here?" Luke whispered, which was truly unnecessary.

"I wanted to see who you were blowing Casey off for. I had an idea, but you've been so mute lately. I knew you wouldn't answer me if I asked, soooo I followed you."

Kat went to wipe her mouth with a napkin to hide her smile.

"Oh my God, Justin, you are such a child. I'll see you in a few, okay?" Luke replied, covering his mouth with his hand.

Kat could tell he was amused by his friend.

"Okay, but after work I want details. Do you hear me? I'm coming over, and you are fucking spilling, like a teenage girl to her friends after prom night. Got it?"

"Okay, Justin, goodbye," he hung up and looked back at her.

"I'm sorry about that." Shaking his head, Luke tucked his phone back into his coat.

"It's cool, you probably gotta head out, huh?"

He looked at the time "Shit, yeah, an hour went by that fast?"

Wow, he was even cute when he cussed. Damn, she was utterly smitten.

"It would appear so."

Bit came over to take their plates and drop off the check. She went to reach for it, but he beat her to it. He slipped his credit card in the bill folder and handed over to Bit for payment; then he looked back over to her once Bitty walked away.

"So?"

"Yes, Luke."

"Yes, what?" Luke cocked his brow at her in question.

"Yes, we'll get to see each other again."

"When?" He looked eager, and she didn't want to look too

deeply into the feeling, but so was she.

"Can I come to you tonight after I, umm, get off work?"

"Yes, sure, that would be great," his breath was just as husky as hers, which meant he was catching her meaning of the late night/early morning call.

"It'll be pretty late, almost close to dawn."

"I'll be up."

"Then I'll be there. I'll call you when I'm close by."

They went to get up together and walk towards the exit door. She gave Tony a wave and a smile that read "you heard nothing, you saw nothing, I wasn't here" and walked out with Luke. They just stared at each other on the sidewalk for a few seconds, until he leaned in and kissed her. It wasn't a quick peck on the lips either. The kiss was a promise of what was to come later that night. A kiss that made her weak in the knees.

They parted a few moments later, and she turned to walk away from him. It wasn't supposed to be like this. She wasn't supposed to feel like this. Kat thought some steady sex would get her back in the game and keep her on her toes during her battles, but it was turning out to be something entirely different. She was falling hard for her human, and she didn't know what to do to halt her descent.

Chapter Twenty-Three

Luke opened his door and let his friend walk in behind him. Just like he promised, Justin had followed him home so that they could talk about his afternoon. Justin was rather quiet on the way up in the elevator, which made him nervous.

He took off his light winter coat, went to unbutton his grey suit jacket next, then he headed towards his bar for a drink. His friend's silence was about to end, and he needed a drink before he started up in five... four... three...two...

"What the fuck, Luke!"

Yep, at least he waited until he shut the door behind him to yell.

"What do you want to know, J?" Luke took a sip of his drink and sat down on his stool in an exhausted heap.

"Everything, Luke. I want to know everything. You were so vague about her after the night you two left the club hand in hand; I figured it was just a one-time thing."

"Yeah, so did I." He smiled into his glass.

"What changed?"

"We ran into each other at the track, the one up by the lake yesterday."

"Annnd?"

"Annnd, we talked. Then she came back to my place annnd

talked some more." He gave his friend a knowing smile.

Justin came to stand next to him and pushed his shoulder with his elbow, "You dog."

He barked out a laugh, "Hardly."

Justin sat on the opposite barstool. "So, could this be the real thing or is it just sex?"

"I don't know; I want it to be... she's different."

"C'mon." Justin crossed his arms over his chest with a look of disbelief on his face.

"No, seriously." Luke turned to face him fully, "She's not timid at all. She's forceful and direct. I don't have to guess what she's thinking, she says it. She's smart, athletic, and get this: she works as an electrician."

"Get out," Justin gawked at him.

"Not something you'd expect out of a one-night stand, right?"

"You sure you're not just another one-nighter for her? I mean, I know you, you're not the hook up just one night kinda guy. You sure you're not just reading too much into this?" Justin replied with care.

Luke knew Justin was asking out of love for him, but no, he didn't believe that was true anymore.

"Yeah, I thought that too, but after talking to her that afternoon on the track, I found out that she hadn't slept with anyone since her ex. And that was years ago. Said she had started to get cranky and she figured she needed someone to help her work it out. So, she went out with her sister Sia and found..."

"You."

"Me," he and his friend said together at the same time.

"Well, you are one lucky son of a bitch, my friend. She is breathtaking."

"Yeah, she is. And she's coming over later tonight, so you need to leave so I can rest before she shows up," he went to get up and push his friend out the door.

"Need your rest, do you? Why? Is she wild in bed?"

"Goodbye, Justin." Luke was practically pulling him towards the door now.

"Does she make you scream like a little bitch?"

"Get out!" He was laughing so hard he knew the command didn't hold weight.

"Wait, wait, wait. Serious question?"

Luke opened the door, pushing his friend out in the hallway, then paused.

"What?"

"Did you cry after you cuddled? ..."

Luke slammed the door in his face. Justin was such an asshole sometimes.

****

Kat should not be here. She should have gone straight home as Sia told her to. Sia had laid into her ass once Kat got back to her apartment building. Sia made perfect sense, of course, letting her know that seeing Luke would be dangerous. Sia always wanted the best for her; just wanting to make sure she knew what she was doing. Kat told Sia that it was just sex and it wouldn't go further than that, so she did not need to worry. Her dear sister took her word and let the subject drop. If her sex life didn't interfere with their work, then she was on board. And besides, she knew getting involved with a human wouldn't go anywhere. Therefore, Sia dismissed most of her worries instantly. But Kat knew something different. She knew it went beyond sex for her; that's why she didn't understand why she was here.

One of the reasons she had shown up was because Luke hadn't responded to the text message she'd sent, checking to see if he was still awake. He said he'd be up, but when he didn't reply she became worried. A feeling she wasn't too familiar with.

So, here she was on his balcony, looking in his window door watching him as he slept. Luke must have mistakenly fallen asleep since he was sitting on top of his couch in his seating area wearing sweats and a white tee shirt. His feet were bare, with a half-opened book laying on his chest. Those glasses she hated in the beginning, but now seemed to love, were back on his angelic face.

Kat stretched out her fingers, watching her nails extend into claws, then swiped her finger through the panel unlocking the door and letting herself in. Pausing before she went over to him, she went to open his front door, so it appeared that was the way she entered. After that was done, she went over to her man.

Luke was beautiful. Kat knew he'd tried to stay up for her. And that made her tiny heart swell. The TV was still on, and his phone was on the coffee table flashing a blue light that probably signaled her incoming text. Kat kneeled in front of him and started to run her hands up his thigh then back down his legs. He began to grow hard under her sensual caress, lips parting slightly, breathing deeply, as her hand traveled to caress his rather generous length.

"Katrina?"

"Yes?" she replied to his sleepy whisper.

His eyes peeled open slowly until he entirely focused on her kneeling before him. She had to jump back on the balls of her feet, as he sat up forcibly. He righted his glasses up on his nose, then turned on the lamp that set on the table beside the sofa, where he also set the book.

"Kat, God you're here...." He scrubbed his hands down his face. "I'm sorry, I must have fallen asleep."

"It's okay. I texted, but you didn't respond. I figured you might be in the shower or something, so I just came over. Is that okay?" Considering the fact, he smelled delicious, him taking a shower wasn't so farfetched. That ocean smell that was unique to him started invading her senses, which made her ease a little closer.

"Yeah, no, of course. I came over to the couch hoping that if I were as far away from my bed as possible, I'd be okay," he laughed, "guess not. It's been a long day."

"Yeah, sorry, I completely understand. I should have known when I knocked. I turned the knob and saw it was unlocked, so I figured you left it open for me and were just in the shower or something. But then I heard the TV, came over and saw you asleep... maybe I should go so you can rest." She started to stand until he grabbed her arm.

"No." He pulled her forward by her arms, and she landed in a cradle right between his thighs. "Please stay."

"Okay." That's what she wanted to do anyway. He'd get no fight from her. "....You wanna talk then?" She looked at him expectedly. His expression changed from her smart geeky Clark Kent to her strong, powerful, hungry superman in a split second.

"No."

"So..." She ran her hands up his thighs, still kneeling in between his legs. She allowed her fingers to roam up his stomach then across his chest and down his arms. "What do you want to do Luke?"

Silence, just more heavy breathing as she stroked his body.

Good boy.

"Well, since you've had a long day, how about I do all the heavy lifting tonight?"

Luke remained silent. He looked at Kat with fire in his eyes, nodding. She stood up and stripped before him, loving the way he cataloged each movement with his eyes. Dropping back down in front of him, she brought her hands to the top of his sweats, releasing his erection. Once his member was freed of its confinement, she brought his length to her awaiting mouth. She started at the top, circling the head with her tongue. He dropped his head over the back of the couch as one of his hands started running through her wavy red hair. Giving a longing lick to his crown, she widened her mouth, relaxing her jaw and swallowing him whole. She was almost able to take in his full size, yet his girth made it impossible. Kat used her hand at the base of his dick to cover what she couldn't fully take in, bobbing up and down with a steady rhythm. When a moan escaped his lips, she knew he was getting close to his peak. It was a cliff Kat wasn't ready to take him over. She wanted him deep inside her when he came. Popping out his staff, she pulled out a condom, slipping it on with her slick mouth.

She got up, straddling his hips, then slowly guided herself down onto his cock. They both moan in unison when she completely settled down to the hilt of his erection. Kat grabbed the side of his face and brought his lips up to hers for a kiss, slowly grinding up and down his length at a tentative pace.

He reached up to take off his glasses as he kissed her back. "No, leave them on. I find you rather sexy with them on right now," she exhaled into his opened mouth.

He released his hands, only to let them slide down her back to grip her firm ass. Using his strength, he thrust up with his hips and slammed her ass down on his lap, picking up the pace substantially. Kat pulled away from Luke's kiss, throwing her

KD BOND

head back, as she bellowed her climax towards the ceiling. Her tight inner walls milking his stiff thickness in great convulsions brought forth his climax swiftly.

A few minutes passed with them still in each other's embrace trying to steady their breathing. They finally pulled apart after a few deeper breaths and stared into each other's eyes. Another heartbeat later they both breathed out "damn" at the same time. This time they were both out of breath for an entirely different reason. Humor overtook romance.

Once they settled, they decided to stay on the couch and watch some television, since neither of them were tired. Luke had gotten one of his t-shirts for her to wear and they snuggled up on the comfortable sofa together. The sex between them was incredible, but she was starting to look forward to moments like this. He had never seen her favorite TV show "The Walking Dead" so they decided to watch a few episodes on demand from season one. Three episodes in and he was hooked. She was about to start the next episode when he rejoined her on the sofa after getting some popcorn.

"You sure you don't want to stop here? My day is over, but isn't yours starting in a few hours?"

He looked at his watch to examine the time, which she knew was close to seven in the morning according to the sky outside.

"Yeah, I probably have one more episode in me before we call it quits."

"Sounds good to me." She started the next episode.

"You should stay and get some rest. No point in leaving when I do. You can just let yourself out once you wake up."

He didn't look at her as he talked, which made her think he didn't want to meet her eyes in case she turned down his offer. The truth was, she didn't want to leave anyway. Kat enjoyed being with Luke, and besides, his bed was more delicate than hers. Sia wouldn't be looking for her considering it was almost daylight, so she had the hours to spare.

"Thanks, that sounds amazing. I had a long night, it'd be nice to sleep a bit before I leave."

"Then it's settled. You'll stay." Luke pulled her closer and planted a kiss on the top of her hair.

At some point during the show, she'd fallen asleep in Luke's arms. Kat would have remained asleep, but she felt herself being lifted and when she opened her eyes, she noted being carried towards the bed.

This was the second time she had let her guard down, falling asleep in the company of another, but she was too tired to think of the implications. He pulled the sheets down, placing her in his giant king size bed, then pulled the covers back over, tucking her in. She observed his suit absently, figuring it must be time for him to leave for work.

"Get some rest and make yourself at home when you wake up." He leaned down to kiss her lips. "I have my phone on me, so call if you need anything."

She nodded, gradually closing her eyes. Kat heard the door shut a few seconds later. And her last thought before sleep reclaimed her was of home. Kat finally felt she was home.

Chapter Twenty-Four

Stepping out of the wooded cabin in the heart of the forest, Zafrina stood on the porch and breathed in the fresh dawn air. She had been tracking a particular rogue wolf for some time now, and she was finally able to follow him to this cabin. And he was not alone. The war between the vamps and wolves continued to thrive, but the Knights had been victorious in keeping the fight out of the human realm. Mostly. Yet, this wolf was not part of the mostly.

In the process of killing a vampire, he also took out two innocent human children, without a care in the world. He could've attempted to avoid the death of those sweet little girls. However, the wolf chose to favor vengeance over stealth. His anger clouded his judgment, which ended in two human parents burying their children.

Zafrina was the Knight called in to clean up after one of her fellow warriors came across the smell of blood. The parents must have been gone because only a single young teen had been in the house, trying to protect the children from the paranormal intruders.

The young girl had just been released from the hospital a few nights ago. However, the kids later died due to their significant injuries. Zafrina had staged it to look like a home invasion, one a sick sociopath would concoct. Her power to manipulate the mind helped her persuade the police force and news reporters to believe their elaborate ruse. She used mind manipulation to plant the assailants in the memory of the babysitter.

Criminals that committed similar crimes but were still at large. Once that was complete, she told her leader she needed some time to herself. And so, the hunt began.

Zafrina was known to her colleagues as calm and docile, as opposed to Sky's impatience and quick temper. And it was true; however, she was just as deadly as all the other Knights. She possessed a power that could only be rivaled by her leaders, with a temper to match; only she knew how to control her rage.

Z rarely lost control of that temper. The last time she could remember losing her anger, a once beautiful building became permanently tilted. The Torre Pendente di Pisa in Italy, the Leaning Tower of Pisa, was supposed to be a freestanding building. However, she caused a mild earthquake which caused the tilt during construction. Since then, Zafrina had tried to maintain steady control of her emotions. Dreadful things happened when she lost her temper, so she did everything in her power to reel it in until today.

Sky materialize directly beside her as she continued to take in the morning sun, attempting to quell her anger. It was easier for her to calm the emotions of others, yet when it came to her own, it took more control and focus. She could feel her friend's stare leveled in her direction, yet she did not turn to her leader nor did she comment as Sky walked into the cabin silently behind her. Z knew what her comrade would find.

It wasn't just the body of Casper in the cabin, the wolf she was after, but also those of his followers. She had allowed them to flee, but they chose to stay and fight with their master, as opposed to continuing to live. Only two cunning wolves finally realized that continuing to follow Casper would eventually lead them to their graves, so they left their leader without so much as a backward glance. Which meant a total of six bodies remained littered around the cabin.

Four of them stood up to her bravely, and she awarded

them with a swift and painless death. Casper and his beta did not. Once they discovered they would lose this battle, after four of their minions quickly met their demise, they tried to escape through the back door of the cabin. Z figured she'd help them stay in place by rapidly cutting off their legs, then their arms, saving their heads for last, knowing they would be able to feel the pain as long as their heads were attached. It's what the humans deserved. She couldn't bring their children back, but she could give them this.

She felt Sky's presence behind her once again, knowing she observed blood splattered on the walls and various body parts thrown throughout the living area. The scene was grotesque. She hadn't used a weapon for the dismemberments, and the evidence of her lost control was all over her teeth and claws. Zafrina's long jet-black hair was wet with the liquid. And she knew her face was no better. Thank the Goddess they wore black.

She closed her eyes and breathed in the fresh, crisp air once more before she turned to face Sky. She had lost her temper once more, and she knew better. With powers like their own, they required more restraint.

"At least you tracked him here. We don't need more heat on us in this day and age." Sky responded.

"Yes, I would have to agree."

Sky took a moment to study her features, coming over to cup her chin and wipe some of the blood off her face. "Do you feel better?"

Z took a hesitant breath for reassurance before she answered. "Yes. Did I cause any other disturbance?"

"No, well, a few trees fell when you unleashed some of your powers, but other than that nothing. I'm surprised the house didn't fall," she pointed at the structure behind her

"Wolves tend to build sturdy homes."

"I suppose they do." The silence stretched between them before Sky backed up and spoke again. "We must speak to Luther soon, Z."

"Yes. I will go to him personally and tell him I have slain six of his brethren."

"Need me to go with you?"

"No, I am much better now, but thank you."

"Good. I knew seeing those kids like that would mess you up, but I didn't think you'd go nuclear."

"Yes, and for that, I am terribly sorry. I should have used the week it took to locate Casper to suppress my feelings."

"It's alright, Z." Sky came closer, turning her back to the porch rail leaning up against it. She shrugged, "Shit happens, it's not like they didn't deserve this ending."

Zafrina took a moment to study her friend's face. All she saw was mild contempt. "Very well then, I should be going."

Sky nodded, "Before you go, how about you stop at home and shower? I'll take care of the cabin."

"But of course," she looked down at herself, "it would be disheartening and cruel to arrive as I am. I know Casper was rogue, but I'm sure losing any member of your pack would be difficult."

Sky looked at her deadpan and replied, "He understands our place in this war. He knows what happens when the rules were broken."

"Indeed."

"Go."

Z bowed a little, then teleported out of the wooded area. She went home to shower and changed swiftly before she dematerialized again. Once she resurfaced, she strolled along the Alpha's border.

Out of respect, they never teleported into another's domain unless necessary. Knowing a soldier would find her shortly and bring her to his alpha, she took that time to regain the last of her composure. Even though Z was going into the wolves' den alone, she was unafraid. They may have the numbers, however, many of them would fall before they finally got the best of her. Luther would never risk his people unless the Knights betrayed their alliance. She knew she was justified in her killings, but out of courtesy Sky and the others had agreed to notify the Alpha and new vampire king of each slaying they were involved in. So, here she stood.

Stopping her repetitive pacing, Z turned her head west and listened to the young soldier's approach. The wolves were evolving in the talent of masking their approach; soon it would take her undivided attention and concentration to sense their advance, which was quite impressive.

The wolf emerged through the trees and barked a greeting. She returned the reception with a smile of her own. Zafrina fully extended her lips, showing her full set of pearly whites, as the familiar calming sensation coursed through her body. Finally, she was once again the calm, docile Knight. And just in time. Looking up, she lost her bright, welcoming smile. Luther had also come to greet her arrival.

Chapter Twenty-Five

Kat was once again sitting atop the room of what was becoming her new favorite building, swinging her legs back and forth over the edge, against the wind. She had just sent Luke a message, letting him know they were still on for their afternoon brunch across the street at Tony's Bar. A lunch date that was starting to become routine.

Her feelings for the human were starting to enter the danger zone, but she couldn't seem to stay away. They'd been together nearly every day since their pretend run-in at the track, and even that time didn't seem enough. She wanted more of him. And the realization should have scared the hell out of her. But it didn't.

The phantom leaders continued to send their best soldiers to try to take them out, yet that thrill wasn't nearly as exhilarating as being with Luke. She even started to dispatch the fighters their masters would send quickly so she could get back in enough time to see Luke. Kat knew what she was doing was reckless, but she didn't care.

They'd spent their off morning and afternoon together running or using the gym in his complex to either swim or rock climb. He'd told her he'd like to take her in the spring a little further up north close to Canada, so they could embrace the mountain climb. She'd agreed to the trip without qualms. It sounded exciting, and with the way they'd been besting the phantoms lately, Sky would give her the time off, hopefully.

Swinging her feet with glee, she started typing Luke a

naughty text when she heard a voice from behind.

"Thought I'd find you up here." Kat jumped suddenly, nearly falling off the roof. She did, however, watch her phone sail down the side of the building.

"Shit!"

"You see, little sister, had you not been so caught up in your dreamy fantasy you'd have known you weren't alone." Sia declared behind her.

Swiveling around, Kat swung her legs over the ledge, to face her big sis. "Sia, hi. What...What are you doing up here?"

"I came to talk to you," Sia replied pointedly.

"Oh yeah," she tilted her head in inquiry, "Sure, what's up?"

"Sky called."

"She always does." Kat started to massage her temple in exasperation, "What the hell did I do now?"

Sia shrugged, "Nothing, she wanted to thank me for bringing you back around. For turning you back into the focused killer you used to be." Sia narrowed her eyes and crossed her arms over her chest.

"Huh." She plopped back down on the ledge, *get the hell out.*

"Yeah... you're coming back to meetings, not taunting– well, not as much–with the phantoms. It's like you did a total one-eighty and she thinks I'm the cause."

"Well, that's great. Always good to get bonus points with the boss lady–"

"But I'm not," her sister cut in, "am I?"

"Not what?" Kat played dumb, raising both eyebrows in confusion.

"The cause of your change."

"Listen, Sia..."

"It's the human." Not stated in a question, but fact.

"Sia..."

"You're playing a dangerous game, Kat."

"I can take care of myself," she threw her legs up on the ledge and laid down, crossing her arms behind her head, then overlapping her ankles.

"And what of him? What if your enemies find him and break him, to break you?"

"I can take care of him too."

"Can you, Katrina? You're just learning to take care of yourself."

That did it. She was over in her sister's face in the blink of an eye.

"Back the fuck off, Sia."

"You can't do this, Kat. You have to stop seeing him, please."

"No." This wasn't her place to tell her what to do.

"What are you going to do if he finds out about you, about us? It's only a matter of time before your power slips. What then? Or worse," Sia walked up meeting her nose to nose, "what happens if Sky finds out?"

She recoiled, as her sisters' words sank in. *No.* Sky would kill him, and there wouldn't be a damn thing she could do about it. Sky was the one foe she didn't want to face, not because she was afraid, but because Kat knew she couldn't win. Fighting her, though noble, would be futile.

"Sky's not going to find out now, is she Sia?" She gritted out.

"Kat, please listen..."

"No, you listen, I'll be careful, okay? I promise. And if I see it getting out of hand, I'll end it, I swear." She didn't like this feeling of desperation and Sia didn't look convinced, so she grabbed her upper arms and pulled her close. "Sia, c'mon, please, don't take this away from me. I'm going to have to let him go soon anyway. I know he's a mortal. I know it can't go anywhere. Just let me hold on a little while longer, he's... he's just different. He's funny, smart, caring, not something I would expect out of humankind. And he's a great lay."

Kat smiled. Even Sia could understand that last part.

Sia let out a breath and lagged, "Fine. But if you fall for him any more than you already have...." she raised her hand to stop her denial with a lie, definitely a lie, "don't bother, I'm your twin. I know you, and I'm pulling the plug if this gets out of hand. And it's not a matter of if, but *when* it gets out of hand. Understood?"

Yes, she did. Sia always wanted the best for her, their relationship had been strained in the past, but she knew the love between them would never change. They were twins. Kat straightened her body, clicking her black booted heels together, and saluted her sister. Sia shook her head and left.

Walking back over to the edge of the building she hopped up to stand on the corner looking down. Kat had a million and one things to be concerned with. Sky finding out about Luke, the other world salivating on the fact that she had a weakness for the fairer species, the price on their heads. So many obstacles, yet all she could think about was her shattered phone below.

****

When the boss is away, the kids will play. And play they did. Someone had turned the radio on, and everyone was milling around Fall Heights. It was Friday; the boss had left early for DC on business, so needless to say, no work was getting done today. Luke was sure they could probably leave early, which a few of them did, but others wanted to stay and clock in their required hours for the shift. His numbers were up; Heights was doing great, relieving some of the pressure off his shoulders. Luke was taking a leisurely day right along with the others; they deserved it.

Most of them had been working themselves rigid these past few weeks, trying to make sure their boss continued to come out on top. Things were finally starting to turn around for Luke. After losing his family, he never thought he'd feel this kind of happiness again. And the woman he was meeting later for lunch was a big part of that change.

Luke was sitting on the top of his desk with his feet in his chair talking to Justin, who leaned against his office cubicle in front of him. The two were busy talking about their weekend plans when Casey walked over.

"Hi, guys, what are we talking about?"

"Nothing." They both replied in unison, as they peeked towards the unwelcome intrusion.

"Oh, okay." She paused as they continued to stare at her but not speak, "Well, Justin, you mind if I talk to Luke for a minute, alone?"

His ex-best friend got up from his relaxed position against his wall and cast him a look of amusement, throwing his hands out as if to say "sorry" as he walked away. Narrowing his eyes at his enemy's back, Luke looked back towards Casey and mustered a smile. She hadn't said anything to him in a few weeks, ignoring his good morning greetings, so it was surprising that she had anything to say to him, considering they were supposed to be "friends." It was astonishing how quickly he realized how shallow and narcissistic she was. The woman knew she was beautiful, and Casey used her looks to get what she wanted. He was a puppet. Now he had no strings.

Taking a resigned breath, he addressed his former crush, "What's up Casey?"

"Nothing." She smiled her best seductive smile and leaned into him, putting her breasts on display. "I was just wondering if you had any plans this weekend, like maybe Saturday?"

In fact, he did, he was planning to take Kat on that trip to the mountains they'd discussed. She'd told him that she had the weekend off, so he was going to take advantage of that—and, hopefully, her—all weekend. Casey, however, didn't need to know all the details. They probably could've remained friends if he didn't recognize how much she used him and, when he was no longer a commodity, ignored him, as she has done to so many.

"Yeah, sorry, actually I do. I can't club this weekend." He pushed his glasses back up off the bridge of his nose; he needed to get them readjusted.

"Oh, so I see you're starting to wear your glasses again. You looked better without them."

Yeah maybe he did, to her, but it turned out a certain red-head was turned on when he wore them. So clearly, he opted for his glasses rather than his contacts.

"Was there anything else I can do for you, Casey?"

"Oh umm, no, I guess not. I was kinda hoping that you'd be free for dinner Saturday night. Like you know, for a date."

"I don't need you to set me up Case, I'm good, thanks."

"No," she placed her hand on his leg "it's not a setup. I was hoping you'd like to go on a date with me?"

Luke paused and stared. He was about to remove her hand from his knee before she spoke, but now he couldn't remember what he was about to do. After all this time. Why now? She'd never once showed any interest in him on a romantic level, so he didn't understand what she was asking.

"You're asking me out?" He looked at her with confusion.

"Yes, silly." She flipped her long golden locks over her shoulder dramatically. "I started to miss spending time with you, and I thought, you know, we could maybe take our friendship to another level. I knew you had a crush on me, but I didn't want to risk our friendship, but now, I don't care." She ran her hand further up his thigh, "So, what do you say?"

Um-fucking-believable. He wanted to laugh, but he kept his face neutral. He would have killed for this chance a few months ago, now, not so much.

"Sorry, Case, I'm seeing someone right now," he removed her hand from his leg.

"Seriously?" she balked like she either couldn't believe he was seeing someone else or turning her down. He didn't care either way.

"Who?" She propped her hands upon her hips as she stood and cocked an eyebrow in question.

"Me."

Casey turned to face the voice who spoke those words. Luke looked around the blonde beauty, capturing the eyes of the woman that belonged to that voice and smiled.

What a pleasant surprise. His redheaded temptress was here in the flesh. She was dressed in high waisted, faded, skinny blue jeans and a long-sleeved black crop top with his favorite black boots. The office had gone uncharacteristically quiet. Luke caught those forest green eyes attention and his grin deepened.

"Hey, baby," Kat purred returning his smile.

"Hey."

"You... I know you. You were at the club that night." Casey threw out the accusation like Kat had no right being there.

"I was," Kat said turning her eyes back to Casey. "So?"

"So, only senior VPs are allowed up here on this floor, and last time I checked, you don't work here." Casey crossed her arms across her chest, with her head cheerleader *I'm better than you* attitude.

"I'm sure Roman wouldn't mind." She gave Casey an unfriendly smile, "after all; he was the one who gave me the code to get up here after I called him to see where I could find Mr. Mason."

"Roman... Mr. Heights gave you the code?" Casey asked with disbelief.

"Of course, he did. Roman and my firm have done a great deal of business together. He has become one of our best clients. Would you like to call him for verification? He was still on the turnpike headed to Washington DC when I called."

"I don't have his personal cell," Casey uncrossed her arms, losing the fight.

"Really? What a pity. I'd be glad to give it to you...." Kat gave the most wicked smile he'd ever seen, "Got a pen?"

Casey turned bright red with embarrassment, and Luke had to fake a cough to hide his laughter behind his closed fist.

"No, whatever, I don't care." She turned back to Luke waiting to see if he was going to respond. He didn't.

Casey stormed off, heels clicking as she went back to her desk. Luke tried to hide his laugh again and failed miserably.

Kat strolled over and filled the spot Casey was standing in. She ran her knuckles across his face, then leaned in to kiss his cheek.

"Hi again."

He wanted to greet her properly, but he knew the others were still watching him. "As much as I enjoyed the show, and don't get me wrong, I love seeing you, always. But what are you doing up here? I thought we were meeting later."

She leaned in to twirl her finger around his tie. "I dropped my phone, ahh on the side of the road when I was stepping out of my car, and it shattered. I didn't know what time it was or how to contact you, so I decided to come up."

"I'm so glad you did," he continued to smile, raking his eyes over her body.

"Me too."

He grabbed her hips and pulled her closer for a kiss, almost forgetting where he was. Luke looked around his office and yep, everyone was staring at them. They pretended to get back to work when he brought his head up to glance around. Was this high school or a corporate office? He shook his head.

"How much time do you have left?" Kat brought her arms around his neck, seeming oblivious of the presence of the others.

"We aren't doing anything, just killing time until 3."

"So, can you leave early?" She leaned in and whispered into

his ear. "I promise to make it worth your while."

Luke didn't voice his answer, knowing it turned her on when he delivered his reply by silence. He grabbed her hand from around his neck, stood up, and gathered his things to leave. As they headed towards the elevator, Justin stepped in their way.

"So, where are you two lovebirds off to?"

Luke was going to answer his friend with a snide remark, but Kat beat him to it.

"We're going to fuck, Justin," she said in a muffled voice so only they heard "...and the sooner you step out of our way, the sooner I get what I want. So why don't you be a good little boy and move so I can enjoy your friend's company? He'll tell you all the hot and sweaty details Monday, you have my word." That last part was said loud enough so others, such as Casey whose desk sat by the exit, heard. Her jaw dropped as a result.

"Do you have a sister?" Justin swooned, placing a hand over his heart.

Luke stepped around his friend pulling Kat behind him, dragging her towards the elevator doors. They waited patiently as the light pinged and the doors slid open. Amusement littered Kat's stunningly beautiful face, while hunger darkened his.

Stepping in together, he allowed her to hit the first-floor button as he waited for the doors to close. As soon as the doors glided shut, he grabbed her forearm throwing her back up against the elevator wall. Capturing her lips in a punishing embrace, he grabbed her wrist and hoisted them above her head. Luke slid his hand up Kat's shirt, moving her bra out of the way so he could rotate her nipples with his fingers, drawing a slight gasp from her lips. He ran his other hand down her stomach, past her navel, landing right between her thighs. Creating friction, Luke could feel her began to dampen between her jeans, as he continued his carnal stroke. Moving his hand rapidly, he could feel her start to reach her peak, so he bent down to suck her breast through her shirt, effectively bringing her over the edge.

Righting her clothing quickly, he kissed her cheek then stepped to the side to readjust himself. Kat was breathing heavily, with her hands still raised as the elevator reached its descent. She collected herself just in time, as the doors swung open revealing a busy lobby below. Whistling, he walked out ahead of her, holding the elevator doors at bay, as she straightened off the wall, all amusement wholly erased from her face. She walked over, stopping directly beside him as he held the doors open wide.

The look they shared between them said a thousand things and meant a thousand more. She reached up and planted the gentlest kiss on his lips as she walked towards the exit. Luke looked after her with longing. He was falling for this woman, wholeheartedly, and he was prepared to show her just how much every chance he was given.

Chapter Twenty-Six

Matthias sat on his skull throne made of his victims' remains and fumed in his own territory in the demon realm. He was the ultimate demon High Lord, a demon known for his strength and supremacies. The strongest of his kind, with a body made for destruction. He was 6'8 and 300 pounds of full muscle and steel. His body bore a magnificent set of dark green scales, a feature which dictated his species of demon, the Optatis.

Optatis was one of the deadliest breeds of a demon, possessing extraordinary abilities like conjuring up lost souls from the underworld to do their bidding, for a price of course. His small, shallow horns and black claws also verified his race, and he wore them proudly. All revered Optatis. Everyone but the Knights.

Matthias had sent some of his finest combatants to take out the two illicit Knights he'd come to hate. Their conniving leader, Sky, had killed some of his excellent warriors over the years in their rivalry, and it was time to return the favor, especially now. Outer realm leaders were gearing up for the ultimate coup; taking over the human world, and finally destroying the Knights. He wanted to be the one responsible for the Knights' demise.

He'd created an alliance with the old vampire, King Victor, thinking he'd be able to control his bloodlust enough to be a formable ally; however, he was wrong. Like most vampires, he was weak, falling prey to the Knights' blade.

Deciding to take matters into his own hands, he'd sent his underlings to collect the electric and fire Knights' heads. It was only fair since they were responsible for Victor's demise.

Knights frequently worked independently of each other, but those two were always together, and taking out two Knights simultaneously would let the other dark High Lords in the Phantom realm know he was the supreme King. So far, his subordinates had failed.

The energy around him was practically sizzling with anger. Looking down from his throne at his number two kneeling before him, Hawk, a rare demon shifter, he let his aggravation show.

"Why do I not yet have a new set of twin skulls to add to my collection, Hawk?"

His follower, Slate, answered instead, bowing before his throne.

"Because he's been too lenient, my lord. Allow me to take his place and prove to you that it can be done."

Matthias waved his hand, engulfing his slave in flames for speaking out of turn. He didn't need false promises or unruly minions. He needed results, and he wanted them now.

"Hawk!?" He barked.

"I need the blood demons, master. These Knights aren't like the other harpies we've killed throughout the centuries. They're stronger, faster, and deadlier. If you want to kill the best, we must send the best. I need the Bloods, my liege."

"Hmmm," Matthias mused, getting up from his throne to pace. His long cape draped over his shoulder flowed as he walked.

Perhaps his lieutenant was right. However, summoning the

demons was no small feat. Blood demons were rare; they required his powers as an Optatis to bring forth the dead demons from the shallow pits of Hell. It also required great sacrifice. One he was willing to pay to bring Sky to her knees before him.

Matthias would begin the summons notifying the kings of the Underworld.

"Fine," he answered his second after a few minutes of musing. "I will summon three and no more. If they don't bring me their heads... I will take yours."

Hawk left with a deep bow, no doubt to get his battle plans together for his new champions.

Resuming his seat on his throne, Matthias thought of Sky, the Knight warrior's dark, ferocious leader. That leather-clad sadistic bitch was almost as deadly as he was. They'd always clashed over the centuries, neither one getting the upper hand. There was just something about those mystic creatures his demon brethren craved. The thrill of torturing the mystical harpy females was quite pleasurable for them and in return, Sky would slaughter his men in retaliation.

He longed to get that Knight to submit, and he was close. They were diminishing their numbers until there was one harpy to every five demon-breed. That was until Sky took over the Knights. They were faster, stronger, and better trained; thus, solidifying his decision.

They all needed to be destroyed, and whatever the cost, he was willing and able to pay. And he'd start with two that threw a wrench in his plans, Kat, the one that took the Vampire King's head, and Sia, the fire Knight, her twin.

This job required the most skillful of predators, a King among Kings. He lifted his distorted lip, smiling, envisioning the carnage that was soon to follow. The Knights were as good as dead.

****

Kat and Luke lazed about in bed all day, into the night. They were supposed to go up into the mountains this weekend, but they never made it out of Luke's comfortable, silky sheets. They had an all-day sexathon with breaks in between to either eat or shower. And she wouldn't have had it any other way. This was looking to be, undoubtedly, one of the best weekends she'd ever had.

Now she laid, with her head on his pecs, running deep circles around his bare nipples, enjoying the comfortable silence after their latest bout of sex.

"This is nice," Luke spoke into the silence.

"Hmmm."

"I was planning to take you out of here, honest."

"Sure," Kat chuckled.

"Really..."

"I believe you had good intentions."

"Good," he kissed the top of her hair.

"So, what do you want to do now? Wanna watch a movie?" He asked after more silence.

"Hmmm." She ran her hand down his stomach and over his abs, loving the slight shiver that overtook his body in response.

"I feel like if we don't get out of bed soon, we'll never leave." He closed his eyes, savoring her intimate touch.

"Would that be so bad?" Grabbing his erection and stroking lightly, his hiss was answer enough.

"No," he choked out eventually "I guess it wouldn't."

Kat pushed up with her elbow to apply her lips to his, to

initiate another round of mind-blowing sex. She was an inch away from sealing his lips with hers when all hell broke loose.

Chapter Twenty-Seven

The loud smash as glass shattered inside the room drew Kat's lips from Luke's. She jumped up fast into a crouch after sliding her hands under Luke's pillows to grab Hansel and Gretel. She looked over towards the balcony as glass came crashing in.

The harpy was gloriously naked, but she didn't care, she was ready. Luke jumped up with her; however, Kat was quicker, and this time she had her boys palmed and ready. She shifted to the front of the bed slightly, remaining in her crouch, so she was completely in front of Lucas. Baring her teeth in a hiss at their assailant, she aimed her boys, releasing the safety, ready to fire. When Kat came to realize her would-be attacker's identity, she recoiled, then straightened, blinking her eyes rapidly in shock.

Sia stood before her, decked out in Knight hunter gear, a black mask covering her face. Kat's sister was strapped to the nines, with weapons secured all over her body, looking like a dark angel from the apocalypse. *What the hell?* This couldn't be happening right now.

"Sia, what the fuck are you..." she didn't get a chance to finish; her sister threw a camouflage duffle bag at the edge of the bed hurriedly.

"Suit up, and fast. NOW!"

"What, why?" Kat questioned, as she and Luke scrambled off the bed, quickly covering their naked bodies with the clothes littered around the floor.

Luke looked as if he wanted to speak; however, he was still in a state of shock after witnessing a woman come barreling through his penthouse window.

"Matthias sent his Blood demons, and they tracked your sloppy ass here. I sensed a dark aura in the city, so I followed it. It turns out it was their soulless, brought back from the grave, dirt-ridden, asses. They're on their way up now. We probably have five minutes before they breach, so move your ASS!!!"

Fuckity, fuck, fuck, fuck! This was the moment she'd feared. She thought she was careful, yet Kat let her emotions cloud her judgment, and now she'd risked all their lives.

She turned to look at Luke and saw he'd thrown on some sweat pants and a t-shirt. He looked frightened and confused, but he still reached out a hand towards her with trust. A trust she was about to shatter. In a few seconds, she was about to lose everything she was beginning to care for. That is, if they lived through these next few minutes.

"What's going on Kat?! Who is this and how did she just come hurtling through my window like Trinity from the Matrix?"

"We don't have time to explain, lover boy," Sia answered before Kat could respond. "You either come with us, or die. Either way, I don't care. We're out in four."

Trying not to take her eyes off Luke, she unzipped the bag to pull out her cargo pants and muscle top. Her beloved sister had packed some of her best blades, but she noticed she didn't bring her sword which was a pity. Guess she didn't have a right to be picky. At least she had her favorite twins palmed in her hand.

Finishing dressing using her full speed, since there was no point in hiding her abilities now, she took a deep breath and addressed Luke, who was staring, eyes wide.

"Listen, I didn't mean for you to find out like this. Hell, I didn't mean for you to find out at all. None of this was supposed to happen, Luke, we weren't supposed to happen."

"What's going on Katrina?" Luke's hushed whisper pierced her heart, "Find out what? What the hell are you talking about?" He glared at her, but so far, he was still semi-calm.

"Please, can you trust me for now? I'll explain everything when we get to safety. I promise."

Sia ran to the front door and laid her palms on the panels, no doubt to test the vibration in the hallway, hoping to predict when the blood demons would arrive at their doorstep.

"Please, Luke I need you to come with us. If you stay here, they'll kill you, or torture you to get to me, then kill you."

"Who will kill me? Is this some sick joke!?" He threw out his hands and shouted. "I want to know what the fuck is going on, and I want to know right now. And why are you fastening all those weapons to your body?"

"I have to Luke. I need them for protection. They're a part of my job."

"Your job. Your JOB!!!" He started pacing, then walked over to his closet, throwing on sneakers as well as a hoody. She wondered was he even aware of what he was doing.

"What's happening, Kat?" he asked again in a shaking voice.

"Short answer. Some very dangerous creatures have been sent to kill me, and we must get out of here now. If you come with me and stop asking questions, I promise I will give you an hour to ask every question you want. I'll answer everything truthfully, you have my word, but I need you to give me an hour of your complete trust in return. Right now, I have to ask you for that hour, Luke. If these past weeks meant anything to you, you'll trust me for sixty minutes. Come with me, please."

She wanted to cry in frustration, but now wasn't the time. She couldn't afford to break down; she had a job to do. Sia darted away from the door swiftly walking towards her.

"We have to go, Kat." Sia glanced towards the door and back. "They're here."

"Okay, okay." She finished putting the blades in her boot "I'm right behind you. How many?"

Her sister's ears twitched slightly. "Three."

"Fuck! Why couldn't I feel shit?"

"You must've subconsciously tampered down your abilities when you started your…" She cast her eyes in Luke direction, "activities. But that doesn't matter now. We can't fight them here. We have to make a break for it."

"Safe place?"

"Yeah."

They knew without speaking that it was safer for them to split up. They needed to draw their enemies in two different directions, hopefully confusing their scent. Defeating one blood was difficult, eliminating three without a solid plan, impossible.

Kat covered the distance between her and Sia, throwing her arms around her neck in a punishing hug.

"Don't die. Please," her sister whispered in her ear, "if he holds you back…"

"I know, I know. And I'm sorry." Kat whispered back; then she let go. "See you there."

Sia nodded slightly, then took off with paranormal speed

back through the shattered glass door she came.

Kat turned her focus back in the direction of Luke, seeing his jaw nearly on the floor, his gaze directed at the balcony, her sister just sailed off.

Luke's gaze slid back towards her, mouth wide. "What are you?"

She took a step forward and was crushed as he took a step back. Lifting her palms out, Kat spoke.

"Please, just one more hour of your trust. I know I don't deserve it but remember our time we shared. Surely that counts for something. After I get you to safety, you can choose never to see me again, never remember me again. But right now, I need you to come with me. I need for you to be all in for sixty minutes, Luke."

Finally releasing some of her powers, she sensed the menacing Bloods' approach. They seemed to be testing the durability of the front door, soon realizing a swift kick would suffice. Kat started to panic, which would be reckless. She wanted him to come willingly, but she would take him by force if she had to.

Just as she was about to make her moved, a look of determination passed through his eyes. Their gazes locked and Luke gave her his answer by slightly nodding his head. At that moment, Kat knew she had lost her heart to this brave male. There was no reason to deny her feelings any longer; she had fallen in love with a human.

Chapter Twenty-Eight

Luke knew he was crazy, but he'd never seen Kat look so afraid. The fear in her eyes couldn't be faked, which was enough for him to realize that what was happening right now wasn't a game. His mind was desperately trying to piece together what he'd witnessed her sister do a few minutes ago, and the other part of his mind was with Kat. A small part of his brain was whispering to him that this was real, and Kat had the speed to escape on her own. Here she was trying to convince him to go with her, as danger loomed at their doorstep. No, Kat wasn't afraid for herself or of those who come for her, she was fearful for him. Kat cared about him. So, he'd take a leap of faith for her.

"Thank you. My Goddess, thank you." She walked up to him and dragged him towards the balcony exit, "I promise you'll have your hour, now let's go."

They exited through the door and walked up to the railing outside. The sun had fallen in the horizon, replaced by a full moon, and they were greeted by nothing but darkness.

"I need you to jump with me, Luke."

He balked. *Ha! She must be out of her goddamn mind.*

"You said you'd trust me, remember?" She pleaded with her eyes up at him.

He remembered all right. But that was before she asked him to jump off a goddamn building. This was crazy. They'd never survive a fall from this height.

As Luke continued to glare, the front door behind them smashed in. He risked a look behind him, and the three scariest mother fuckers he'd ever seen, burst through the destruction of the door. Three distinctly tall creatures dressed in all black from head to toe. He squinted his eyes, trying to focus in on their bare faces, *did they have skull heads?*

Kat yanked on his arm drawing his gaze back to her. "Luke, please."

He cut his eyes back near the dark figures, their deformed hollow eyes locating them outside on the balcony the same moment he looked in their direction. Flames lit their eyes as they created giant fireballs from the palm of their hands, balancing them in midair. With evil smirks that promised pain, they let out a battle yell so loud the floor beneath them began to shake.

Luke was having an out-of-body experience. He had to be. None of this was real. Any moment he would wake up, and this would all be over. And since this was just a dream, he had no problems stepping up onto the railing. He would step over, and before he hit the ground, he would wake up. No problem, Luke could handle that.

Closing his eyes while taking a deep breath, he jumped.

Cold air rushed through his face as he plummeted towards the ground. Luke opened his eyes and had enough time to realize that this was not a dream. Surely he would've woken by now. He'd jumped out of a building to escape three giant disfigured creatures, with skulls as heads and could shoot fire out of their hands. What about that didn't say dream. As the ground came deviously closer, nothing happened. Just as he closed his eyes to pray, Luke's fall abruptly stopped. Stumbling back on the sidewalk, his eyes frantically caught those of the little redhead before him.

"What the hell just happened?" He tried to compose himself as Kat pushed him aside and grabbed his hand after stopping his fall to certain death.

"Let's go, they're coming."

Turning around and looking up he noted the three walking skeletons setting up to jump down from the railing he just stood on.

Shit! "My car..." He tried to pull Kat in the direction of the garage.

"No, Luke, we gotta run, I'm faster than any car."

"What?"

"I need you to hop on my back."

He gawked. "You can't be serious?"

"I tell you to jump off a balcony, and you do that no problem, but this, *this* you can't get behind?"

"I thought I was dreaming." *Fuck!* Luke ran his hands through his hair in frustration. Kat was right, but it was so, so emasculating.

"Luke, they are going to hit the ground in five seconds. I'm fast, but I'm not that fast."

To hell with it. "Okay, okay."

He threw his arms around her neck, and as soon as he settled securely on her back, she took off.

His body was notably larger than hers, so his positioning felt awkward, but only for a moment. After a few seconds, he didn't have time to think about anything else. *Sweet baby Jesus, mother of God, it feels like we're flying.* This was exhilarating. She couldn't be moving this fast, could she?

If it weren't for the realistic night chill cutting through his eyes, he'd revisit the possibility of this fantasy dream. However, this was not an illusion of his imagination, and neither were the creatures closing in behind them. Frankly speaking, his mind just wasn't that descriptive.

Sneaking a peek to the immediate threat trailing behind him, he noted they were gaining on them, fast. A few elongated strides and they could reach their long boney fingers out and grab them.

"They're right behind us, Kat!" he yelled over the whirling wind.

"Luke, I need you to hold on as tight as you can. You're crushing my wings, but I'm going to speed up and try and lose them!"

"Your what!"

Did she say she had wings?

Luke's grip became punishing around her neck, and that seemed to be all the response she needed. Kat shot off like a rocket in the night. *Damn, she was fast.* He didn't think a fire jet could beat Kat in a foot race. He didn't understand how he was still conscious, let alone how he was able to turn around and glance over his shoulder trying to see their assailants. Who were barely noticeable.

They ran forever, it seemed, before they came to a stop at some dusty broken-down building in an area where he'd never been.

Sliding off her back, he took a moment to catch his breath. He bent over, laying his hands on his thighs and began to dry heave. He distantly felt small circles rubbing his back in comfort. Running at that velocity must have affected him after all.

He looked up at the same time the woman that came

crashing through his window walked out of the building behind them. She was still wearing all of her gear, yet this time her mask was pulled down to reveal some of her face.

"Get him inside."

Luke didn't have the strength to argue, so he allowed himself to be led into the building by Kat.

Once he finally got his breathing under control, he was able to take in his surroundings. The ancient structure was modernized, with an inside that was surprisingly clean and furnished. It had a computer desk, a table with chairs, and a few couches facing a huge flat screen TV. Despite its outer appearance, the inside looked like a regular home, which was surprising.

"So, the human didn't faint when you turned on the jets... impressive." The brunette remarked absently, talking to Kat.

The mystery woman's face was revealed under the florescent light. Features that was nearly identical to his woman, except her coloring was slightly different. He eyed Kat in question.

"Luke, I'd like you to meet my twin sister, Sia."

That explained the similarities, but right now he wasn't feeling the family reunion. He took a menacing step towards Kat, pointing an accusing finger in her direction.

"Start talking, and right fuckin' now!"

****

Yeah, Kat could tell the shit was about to hit the fan. Luke was pissed, and she couldn't blame him. His world was turned upside down. Nightmares he couldn't fathom coming true were banging down his door, literally. She'd put him directly in the line of danger, and for that, she'd be eternally remorseful.

"Are we safe?" Luke questioned, folding his arms across his

chest.

"For now." Sia answered, crossing her arms in turn, "the Bloods track by scent, their master must have something that belongs to Kat since they chose her to follow. But our scents are muted here. The area is surrounded by garbage, so they shouldn't be able to find us before dawn draws them home."

"Great," Luke replied never taking his eyes off Kat. "Now talk. What the hell is going on?"

"Kat," Sia groaned in warming.

"No, Katrina, I want answers. You promised me, I deserve to know what's going on, and I want the truth."

"And you'll have it as I promised." She took a tentative step towards him, and her heart shattered just a little bit more as he, once again, stepped back. Her face fell, body sagging, as she looked towards her sister.

"Fine. It's your funeral." Sia threw her hands in the air, "because when Sky hears about this, all hell is going to break loose."

Sia stomped off towards her bedroom, slamming the door shut. Both jumped at the sound.

Finally alone, Kat redirected her gaze to Luke. "What do you want to know?" She walked over towards the dining table. "I'll answer everything to the best of my ability. You'll have an hour, as promised, but that's all I can give. There are some things I have to plan out with Sia."

Kat set her watch, hopped up on the table, bracing her hands in front of her. Waiting. Luke started pacing in front of her, seeming to collect himself before he began.

"So, you aren't an electrician?"

Kat laughed. She didn't mean to, but she didn't expect that as the first question he'd ask.

"No, Luke, I am not."

"What are you?"

"A harpy." With this, he stopped and finally met her eyes.

"A what?"

"A harpy."

"What's that?"

Kat cocked her head to the side and studied him. "Luke, you're a brilliant man, you know what a harpy is, or at least you've heard of us in old human folk tales."

"But that can't be true; harpies aren't real." That wasn't a question, so she kept quiet. He seemed to be talking to himself, anyway.

"What were those...those things after us?"

"Blood demons. Soulless beings from the Underworld, ruled by a demon prince with too much time on his hands."

"Demons are real too?" He placed his hands on his hips.

"Yes."

"What's next, Katrina?" He threw his hands up in the air, "Are you going to tell me the Tooth Fairy is real? What about the Easter Bunny, Santa Claus?"

"No, I'm not, Lucas, but I will tell you most paranormal creatures such as harpies, demons, vampires, and werewolves are real. There are more to that list, but I think you get the picture. They aren't just urban legends, Luke. They exist... we exist."

"But how can this be?" She felt this was another moment where he wasn't directing the question at her, but she answered anyway.

"Every story or folk tale starts with a little bit of truth. Think about it. The theory had to come from somewhere. You just don't magically come up with the idea of a vampire without something to compare it to. Over the years, the tales just started to get water down and become myths, fairytales. Humans were able to create such elaborate tales because there once was a time when we didn't have to hide who and what we were from humans. But as your species started to evolve, wars commenced amongst our kind and yours. The Phantom creatures, which is what we call ourselves, decided to pull our subjects away from the human realm back to our own for a time. It was just easier to leave, so we wouldn't be killed or be forced to kill. Centuries went by before any of us returned to the Earth realm, and by then humans didn't have any recollection of what we were. They turned our image into creatures your kind feared in the darkness. We became the boogeyman, and we collectively decided to keep it that way."

Luke looked like he wanted to throw up, as everything she shared began to sink in. "This can't be happening," Luke said to himself. Again, it wasn't a question, so she kept to herself, watching him. Waiting for the moment he snapped and tried to kill her. Humans were known for that. Their kind usually wanted to destroy things they couldn't explain.

Surprising her once more, Luke took another deep breath before he began another round of questions. "What are the other realms you mentioned?"

"We can leave your world and enter ours through underground passageways. There are portals beneath the Earth's surface that only paranormal creatures can see or create to exit this world."

"Are there any humans where you're from?"

"Yes, but not many."

"So, humans can cross into your world."

"Yes."

"How?"

"It has to be with another paranormal or the portal may not open. But it's not a good idea to take humans over to our world for a long period. Simply better for everyone if humans never knew our world existed."

"Why?" He looked at her with renewed interest.

"Because..." She looked down at her watch, *shit, ten more minutes.*

"You promised Kat."

She sighed, Sky was going to kill her. "Because humans stop aging in our world after repeated exposure."

"Seriously?"

"Yeah."

"How...why?"

"We aren't one hundred percent sure. Could be many things. The magic in the air, or maybe because time runs on a different wavelength in our world than yours. We don't know, seeing as how none of us make a habit of bringing humans into our realm. But I do know you can feel the power as you walk through the breach. For humans, it'll keep them youthful while they're there. If they returned to Earth after a year, they wouldn't have aged a day. Prolonged exposure, of unspecified time, will halt their aging, making them immortal, permanently. So, we don't want humans finding out that the cure for immortality is right in their backyard."

"My God, the chaos." Luke sunk into an empty chair at her feet.

Kat hadn't even noticed how close he'd gotten. She didn't want to get her hopes up but having him close made her heart swell.

"Precisely."

Luke sat there for an awfully long time in silence. She knew he would bolt soon, and it'd be the first time in history where she wouldn't want to see someone run from her. When he spoke again, she jumped at his unexpected voice.

"So, what now?"

Kat didn't answer that question, because she didn't know how. This had never happened to her before, or anyone she knew.

"Are you..." he looked up and swallowed, "are you going to kill me now?"

Kat just stared at him, Goddess above, she fell in love with a human, didn't she? How could she have let this happen? She shouldn't have allowed this to happen, because now the man she loved was looking at her expecting to die. By her hands, nonetheless. Kat wanted to assure him that he was safe with her. However, if there was one thing she learned in all her years as a Knight was never to fight a losing battle. And if she had to go up against Sky to protect Luke, she would lose. So, she decided not to answer his question, and when her alarm sounded on her watch, signaling his hour was up, Kat was grateful she didn't have to.

Chapter Twenty-Nine

Kat didn't answer his question, which meant there was a high possibility that she was going to kill him. Hell, why wouldn't she? She'd just spilled all her secrets about her hidden world to a human. And that's what he was, to this extraordinary woman, just a plain and simple human being.

Luke saw what she could do, seen her speed, her strength; he knew she possessed the power to annihilate his very existence. But right now, at this moment, once he finally was brave enough to look into her eyes, she looked broken. On the table she sat silently crying, with her head down. Against his better judgment, he stood before her. Easing his way between her thighs and lifting her chin so she was forced to look at him. Those forest green eyes were mesmerizing and looking into her eyes reminded him of the reason he jumped. At that moment he didn't care what she was.

He lifted his hand and wiped at her tears.

"Hey, hey, please don't cry." His words only seemed to make the tears fall faster.

"This is just so messed up; this wasn't supposed to happen Luke. You weren't supposed to find out. I was supposed to leave you. Why didn't I leave?" She choked out.

"Shh, shh yeah, I know, it's okay. I understand." He embraced her in his arms.

"I don't want to kill you." Kat looked at him with sadness.

"I believe you." He laughed without humor.

"I wasn't supposed to fall in love," she mumbled to herself, "I despise humans. I wasn't supposed to love one," she whispered, still loud enough for him to hear.

"You what?" He pulled away and blinked down at her.

"Ummm, what?" Kat looked at him and wiped her eyes in confusion.

"You said you loved me."

She recoiled. "No. I didn't. "

"Yeah, you did." He smiled, "you said it twice actually."

"Luke."

Kat tried to push him off, but he took her chin in his hands, capturing her lips with his. Despite all the paranormal activity happening around them, Luke still knew for sure that he loved her as well. How could he not? He didn't care that she was a mystical creature from another realm, he only knew how he felt, and that feeling was pure, unfiltered love.

He didn't know where that confession would lead them, but he was willing to take a chance. He broke apart from her to tell her as much when the door to the entrance burst open, and a beautiful angel of death walked through.

For some reason, he felt this new foe was even deadlier than the blood demons that were tracking them. Kat jumped in front of him, and he noticed a flash of light in the corner of his eye. Refocusing towards the front entrance, Luke saw Kat's sister had rejoined them in the front room. Somehow, as they faced off against their newest adversary, Luke knew it wasn't going to be enough. He was praying Kat had more sisters in that back room.

****

"Sky, please, listen, I can explain," Kat begged her boss.

She would've dropped to her knees, but she needed to remain alert. She couldn't let Sky kill Luke. No matter how she felt before, faced with the possibility of his death was unfathomable. She knew she'd die if she lost him.

Sky just cocked her head to the side and dropped a death stare. Closing the door behind her with the powers radiating around her body, she took another step forward. Kat had never been more afraid than at that very moment.

"Sky, I don't know how this happened. I thought I was careful. I know I usually fuck up, but not like this. Never, like this."

She cut her eyes at Sia, briefly. "How could you call her? I trusted you. How could you betray me again? You could've at least given me some damn time to think," she fumed, baring her teeth at her sister.

"Oh, Sia didn't call me, little one," Sky spoke while taking another menacing step forward.

Both her and Sia resumed a fighter's stance.

"Oh." For a split second, Kat glanced over at her sister. "Sorry." Today just wasn't her day.

"Yeah, we'll deal with that outburst later, sister." Sia squared her stance, never taking her eyes off Sky.

"Then how did you find us?" Only Kat and Sia knew about this hideout. They'd picked it once they were ordered to work together.

Sky tilted her head more, as her midnight eyes began to swirl with suppressed rage. "I received a tip that Matthias was sending his blood demons to the human realm. And I knew exactly who he was sending them after. I've been keeping an eye on you both ever since, of course."

And if anyone could follow them undetected, it was Sky.

Her gaze swept to Luke. Kat shifted her stance, so she was blocking Sky's vision of him once again. She knew Sky would strike quickly, so she had to concentrate as best she could. Maybe they could hold her off long enough for Luke to escape.

Her leader modified her stance again, seemingly unaware of Kat's heighten awareness of her boss's movements. Fear was a powerful tool to have in your arsenal.

"Please, Sky, don't do this."

"You dare to protect him from me...a mere human."

"Yes."

"Why?"

Might as well put all the cards on the table, the only thing she had to lose was everything. "I love him."

A gasp sounded all around the room. Even Sky's step faltered a little at that announcement. She understood their surprise; Kat never loved anyone as much as she loved herself. Well, maybe Sia.

"That is an extremely dangerous emotion in our world Katrina; there are those that would use that love against you. Those that would torture him to get to you. Creatures like Matthias would capture him and force you to choose between him or us. That is a risk I am not willing to take. A risk I will not take. There are rules for a reason child. And they will not be broken. Not even by you."

Sky shifted again, and this time Kat understood the movements. She was placing herself in a direct path to Lucas, where she could run straight through them and cut off his head before either of them even knew what was happening.

Kat shifted closer to Sia hoping her sister understood what was about to happen. Sia seemed just as aware as she was.

Deciding it was probably smarter to strike first, she locked in her crouch, preparing to spring forward when another figure suddenly appeared by Sky's side. *Fuck!* Zafrina.

If Sky was the captain, then Z was the lieutenant. Separately, they were deadly, but together, they were unstoppable.

Their hopes of ever getting out of this alive had just vanished. Kat knew when she was bested; there was no way they could hold off both while Luke ran.

Kat stood out of her crouch, backing into Luke. She grabbed his hand without looking and squeezed. She was reassured when he squeezed back. Sia also resumed standing, knowing a losing battle when she saw one.

Kat was so thankful Sia had picked this moment to stand beside her, after everything they'd went through. She would always remember this moment. Turning to her sister briefly, she waited until their eyes met, then smiled weakly. Sia just shrugged and mouthed *sorry* with sadness in her eyes. Kat returned her gaze to her two leaders and spoke.

"If you try to kill Lucas you must know I will not stand idly by and allow you to take his life. You will have to kill me as well. But please if I can ask just one thing, I'll ask that you don't kill Sia." She focused on Z, the sane one. "Sia had nothing to do with this; she tried to warn me weeks ago."

Zafrina's calming aura seemed to melt through the air, instantly helping with the tension.

"No one is going to die, child." Zafrina smiled in her direction. "Sky knows I could alter his memories, making him forget everything he knows about us. Don't you?" Z turned those stunning hazel eyes onto their leader. Sky still seethed with pent up rage.

"What good would that do if he lived and was captured? You can not alter Kat's memories; she'd still have her weakness."

"We talked about this, Sky. Love is not a weakness; it's a strength. We knew what was happening between them. You didn't come here to kill that poor male, did you?"

Sky turned that dark focus on her second in command, notably not answering the question. "How did you find me here?"

"Come now, do I need to answer that?"

Sky exhaled, seeming to let out some of her anger, closing her eyes and taking a deep breath, she answered. "No. But Kat could've gotten them all killed. The Bloods were at her doorstep, and she didn't even know! Innocent people could've died tonight, and the blood would be on their hands."

"Yes, a dire mistake Katrina will never let happen again. Isn't that right Kat?" Z looked at her.

"Yes, never again."

"See?"

That didn't seem to appease Sky at all. "Love is a foolish emotion," Sky stomped out, "it will only lead to their demise."

"Yeah, how's that working out for you?" Kat spat at her boss.

Sia grabbed her arm and whispered, "Careful sister."

No, Kat was done being careful. Luke's life was on the line here. "You heard some underworld gossip about Bloods coming after us, and you took time away from the other Knights to focus on two harpies. Why?"

"Because you're mine." Her boss replied.

"You have hundreds of Knights, boss, threatened every day, right at this moment. But as soon as you thought that little, Dark Prince prick sent his best warriors to take our heads you came running...why, Sky?" Her boss remained silent, gaining a smile from Z. Her silence was answer enough.

"You love us... you don't know when it happened or why, but you do. You fell in love with all your Knights, that's why you take special care with us. That's why you stop by the bar to check in on us after we don't report back. That's why you almost sent a hundred Knights to come to find one. That's why you shut down mothers when they lash out, because of LOVE!"

Kat was so pumped by the end of her speech that her gift started to push through her fingertips. Luke laid a hand on her shoulder, centering her, allowing her to calm further.

Still, Sky said nothing. She just stood there unblinking. After a few moments, she spoke.

"So." Sky replied.

"So...? Is that all you have to say after that, is so?"

"You want me to admit what you already know?"

She glanced at Sia, "Umm, yeah, that would be nice to hear."

"Well, I won't. Not after the shit you just pulled. Jesus Kat, you could've gotten everyone killed."

"But we didn't," Kat tried to reason, "we got the fuck out of there as you taught us. We weighed our odds of survival, and we knew it was better to run, so we ran. Pride be damned."

"That is true," Zafrina spoke, "nothing needs to change here Sky, you know what you must do."

Sky narrowed her eyes, unmoved, "They were gearing to attack me, Z."

"To protect the ones we were created to defend. They were just."

Sky turned that lethal gaze on Zafrina. "Fine." Sky stepped back, taking off her long wool jacket to hang it by the door.

It was almost spring, but nights here were still frigid. She started walking forward, and Kat tensed as Sky stopped in front of them.

"May I talk to your mate? Just talk."

"Umm yeah, sure, Luke?" Kat asked nervously.

Kat didn't know how Luke was taking all this as he went to step around her, to address one of the deadliest immortals in her world.

"Um yes, hello."

"Hello, Lucas Mario Mason."

"How do you know that name," he questioned – a little shocked. "No one knows my middle name?"

"I have to. It's my job to know everything about those who threaten our existence, Lucas... Are you a threat to us, son?"

Kat could practically feel the tremors in his body. He was nervous, but he answered with confidence and truth.

"I'd never bring any harm to Kat if I could help it."

"And why is that, young one?"

"Because.... I love her too."

Sky moved so fast Kat would've missed the movement if she'd blinked. But she was too anxious to blink or breathe.

Capturing Luke by his throat, Sky pulled him forward, looking directly in his eyes. Kat went to crouch, once again gearing up for a fight, and she noticed Sia had done the same. *My girl.*

"That would be unwise my twins..." Z spoke to their defensive positions, while she twirled her hair between her fingers, "Sky could kill him and still have time to fend off your advances."

Kat still didn't relax her stance she did; however, give her boss time to do whatever she intended to do.

"Fearless little warriors... indeed." Z, forever calm, turned her focus back to Sky.

"Luke, you have a decision to make," Sky spoke ignoring them all.

"Okay," Luke choked out.

"There is no way I could allow you to live in your world with the memories of our kind engraved inside your head. So, listen and listen carefully. You could either enter our world fully, allowing you to stay by Kat's side or... I get Zafrina to wipe your memory of everything that happened after you met Kat at that night club, returning your mind to a state of ignorant bliss. Do you understand what I am telling you?"

He nodded his head up and down.

"Good." Sky pushed him away, and Kat was right there, helping him up as he coughed, rubbing his throat.

"So, what will it be, Lucas?"

Luke looked up in confusion, as he collected himself. "Wait, I have to answer, now?"

"Yes."

"Sky, you're being unreasonable. You want him to decide to give up his whole life, his job, his friends and enter our world right now? That's a lot to ask, and he's been through a lot tonight."

"I don't think I'm unreasonable at all. I could very well kill him now. I should kill him now. But Z's right, we could use someone with his computer skills on our side. Your male is smart, which could work in our favor. You get to keep your human, and we get a computer engineer." Sky shrugged, "win-win either way."

"Wait. You almost choked the life out of me, and now you're offering me a job?"

"Yes." Sky's expression never changed. Kat couldn't tell if she was bored or still angry.

"Unbelievable."

"Yeah, now you see what I've been putting up with for two centuries," Kat added, rolling her eyes

Luke recoiled away from her, "You're two hundred years old?"

"Give or take a decade. I didn't mention that?" She looked at him innocently.

"Umm no!" He shouted.

"My patience is running thin," Sky cut in

"Your patience is always thin," Kat mumbled.

Turning to Luke, she grabbed his face and considered his eyes. Those lovely Bahama blues.

"Listen, I'm sorry I dragged you into this. I know it was selfish, I should have let you go, but I couldn't. Even if you decided to have Z swipe your memory, I'd understand, and I won't love you any less. I will remember our time together enough for the both of us. Know that I regret nothing."

Luke just stared at her. Saying nothing, even though she begged, pleaded, with her eyes for him to do so. He ran his knuckles over her cheek, and she turned her head, leaning into his caress, kissing his palm. With one last longing look, he pulled away from her.

It took everything in her power not to crumble to her knees, as he walked away from her towards Sky. Luke stood in front of their leader silently. She knew this was it. He was telling her goodbye. How could he not? No one ever chose her. Why would today be any different?

"What's it gonna be, Mr. Mason?"

Luke's decision was made at that moment. She saw her shy, timid, nerd stand before the Dark Knight, one of the strongest beings in Phantom, as a reliable business professional.

"Since you know so much about me, you know how much I made at Fall Heights."

"Yes."

"I need you to double it. I've seen the weapons you carry; you can afford it."

"Still planning to work on that charitable organization in honor of your sister?"

"How did you... no one.... forget it. Yes, but I can do it anonymously if that's okay. I prefer it that way."

"As you wish."

"And I need to know the ins and outs of your world if you expect me to help you. I can't work efficiently blind."

"Of course, just know if you're working for me, I require absolute loyalty."

"You'll have it."

"Any betrayal will be met with a slow, agonizing death," Sky retorted, casually.

"Understood."

"Good."

Kat's mouth dropped as they concluded their negotiations. She looked to the side to see her twin was just as shocked as she was. The only one who seemed unfazed by the discussion was Zafrina. It was like she knew this would happen.

"I'm guessing you'll make my old life disappear. But there are people around me that know some of my data configurations. If I were to hack into national databases, which I'm sure my new job will entail, I need to know no one will be able to trace me to you."

"You mean your best friend, Justin? You let me handle that, and no, I won't kill him."

"I see why you're the boss... fine. Then I guess you have yourself a new employee." Luke reached out his hand and Sky clasped his hand in her slender palm.

"Just fuckin' swell... now," Sky turned to them after pulling back her hand, "Zafrina, Sia why don't we circle the area and see if our new friends have abandoned the hunt? Let's give these two some time alone to discuss our new arrangement. It'll also give me time to think of your punishment. Don't think I'm just going to let you two off the hook."

Shortly after that command, they all vanished. Still confused, she waited for the love of her life to turn and face her. When he finally did, she realized her world had changed, yet again. But this time she welcomed the new direction, with arms wide the fuck open.

Chapter Thirty

Kat couldn't believe what just transpired. Certain death was imminent, and she had excepted her fate. And had Zafrina not showed, Kat was quite sure Sky would've taken their heads. She owed that harpy everything.

There were so many emotions going through Kat at the moment, but the most prominent was confusion. How could Luke give up his whole life, for her?

"Luke, do you understand what just happened?" He turned around to face her then but didn't speak, just stared at her with those ocean blues eyes she loved. "Luke, you can't go back after this. You're in my world for good. This is it, do you understand that? No Justin, no more Fall Heights. You can't tell anyone goodbye, everyone you've known over the years is gone. We can't risk you being seen. The world as you knew it is over, you're... you're a phantom, Luke."

He closed his eyes briefly, taking a deep breath. "I know Kat. Your boss, our boss, was pretty clear about that when she was about to kill me."

"Why?" Kat couldn't understand his choice. She backed up and sagged against the table, closing her eyes until she felt warm palms on her shoulders. Looking up Kat saw Luke had closed the slight distance between them to stand before her.

"Because like I told them, I love you, Kat. I haven't felt like this for a woman in all my life, and if that means I have to jump worlds to keep you, I'll jump. Don't get me wrong, we have much to discuss and relearn about each other, but I'm willing to try. Besides, I'm not leaving much. I'll miss Justin, though." He frowned.

Kat tried to wrap her brain around his words, but she was still having trouble. "I just don't understand."

Luke laughed. "You can't understand how anyone could love you or jump worlds?"

"Both." She leaned her head against his chest.

"Okay, what about this. If I asked you if you were given the opportunity to leave your world and come live with me, what would you say?"

"I'd say you'd need to stock your bar with more whiskey." They both laughed. "It's different for me though; I never wanted this life. I'd leave it in a heartbeat if I could."

Luke lifted her chin and looked into Kat's eyes. "It was either leaving my world or forgetting I ever met you. Losing my memory just wasn't an option for me. I am wondering one thing, what are they going to do about my job, my life?"

"Sky will probably report your accidental death. Stage a body with your DNA, car accident or something. Zafrina has power over the mind, so she can use her influence to persuade people to believe you're dead."

He exhaled. "Ahhhhh, okay."

"Okay?" Kat looked at him with hope.

"Okay."

"Thank the Goddess," Kat whispered leaning forward, grabbing his jacket to pull him close, inhaling his scent.

"So... How much time do you think until the others return...think we have time to..."

Kat knew the answer to that, but she didn't reply, only because she was dying to feel his touch. Looking into his eyes, she unzipped his jacket, then slid it off his shoulders. Luke leaned down to capture her lips, while he released the zipper from her coat.

They didn't rush, taking their time undressing each other while savoring their taste. He released her lips, trailing his tongue down her neck. Luke used one of his hands to caress her breast through her top pinching her nipple, making her moan. Kat ran her hands through his hair, massaging his scalp with her fingernails, as he worked his way with his tongue down her stomach, circling her navel.

Luke dropped to his knees to unlace her shoes, helping her step out of her boots. Kat started to pile the majority of her weapons on the table but abandoned the task when Luke unzipped her cargo pants and pulled them down. She hadn't had time to don any underwear, so she was completely bare to him. Luke ran his hands up her calves then around her thighs till he settled his hands on her hips pulling her forward. He kissed her knees while running his hands behind the back of her legs. Placing his palm on her stomach, he pushed back, so Kat was lying flat on the table. Settling between her legs, then swinging her thighs up over his shoulders, he continued to run his tongue up the side of her thigh. It was erotic torture.

Kat didn't know how much more she could take. Luke's gentle caresses were killing her. She needed him at her core, like now. Kat tugged on his hair a little, guiding him towards her center, hoping he got the hint.

"Impatient, are we?"

Kat dug her heel into his back pulling him closer. He chuckled but finally brought his lips to her heated sex.

By the time he finally reached her center, she was liquid.

Her arousal had already started to seep between her thighs, and when he brought his warm mouth to her throbbing pussy, the floodgates burst open wide. Kat dropped her head back against the table, as he thrust his tongue into her canal.

Kat was trembling so badly, it was embarrassing. How this mere human could bring her so close to climax in such a short amount of time was staggering.

Biting her bottom lip to suppress her moans, Kat burrowed her nails into her palm, trying to prolong the sensual ecstasy. All hopes of lasting died when he inserted two fingers deep inside her, pumping fast as he sucked on her clit. She screamed as a release that could only be described as legendary came roaring through her. He continued to work her, helping her ride one of the best climaxes of her life until she sagged on the table in defeat.

Luke kissed both of her thighs before he stood up between her legs. Leaning down, he kissed her stomach, then pulled her by the hips to the edge of the table, so her ass was almost hanging off the side. When she looked up at him, the heat in his eyes and the way he licked the juices off his lips with his tongue almost made her come again. He was gloriously erect, stroking his staff slowly up and down his palm. Luke placed one hand on her hip as he positioned his cock at her entrance. He started to ease himself in, pausing mid-way. His control was astounding.

"It's okay; we don't contract human diseases. And I'm only fertile once every three hundred years, so stop making me wait. I want you inside of me NOW."

"Yes, you have much to explain."

Not wasting any more time, he grabbed her hips and thrust inside of her swiftly to the hilt. They both moaned at the invasion.

Beginning a steady pace, seeming to savor the feeling of

their union, he rotated into her, gently pulling out, then pounding back in. The friction was incredible, but the pace was driving her insane. They were both on the same page. Luke began to pump harder into her, causing her to lock her legs around his waist, bracing her arms around his neck as he bent lower. He captured the back of her neck, pulling her up so he could catch her lips as he continued to impel himself into her. She ran her hands up his back, scoring him with her nails as yet another climax soared through her. Her inner walls tightened, clenching around his staff, pushing him over the edge.

After a few minutes of holding each other, as they gradually came down from their sexual high, he brought both of his hands to the side of her face and kissed her, gently. Pulling away a touch, he gazed into her eyes. "I love you, Katrina."

Allowing herself at this moment to be vulnerable, she let a single tear escape from her eye. All her life she was told to be strong, never to allow anyone to decipher a weakness and here this man was, effortlessly professing an emotion that could quickly get them both killed. And he looked at her unafraid. She had much to learn from this male, and she planned to treasure every moment. "I love you, too."

****

They both leisurely dressed, talking lightly. It was nice not to have to hide anything from him, now that he was officially one of them.

Kat talked to him about her kind and what made Knights so special. He got a kick out of the whole electric thing, making her show a light demonstration. They discussed more about the Knights and their specific roles played in the war. He wasn't fond of how dangerous it was but understood it was a necessity.

She answered more questions about her world, trying to help him understand as much as he could in the short amount of time they had. The male was smart, so he caught on quickly. Kat knew he had more questions, but he stopped speaking for a few minutes, probably allowing time for everything to set in. Luke had just stuck his hands back into his hoody when he seemed to notice they were still alone.

"Hey, are the others okay? It's been a while; do you need to check-in?"

Kat yanked on her boots, lacing them up as she stuffed weapons back inside. "Nope. They're outside, waiting for us to finish... talking."

"What?! Seriously, for how long?"

"Long enough," Sia stated as she and Sky walked in. "And thank the Goddess you're finished; it's cold as hell out there." Sia stomped in, throwing herself on the couch.

Kat looked at Sky.

"Nothing. They must have left when they lost your scents, no doubt not wanting to draw attention to themselves, but they'll be back. Especially when Matthias finds out you two ran. He'll think he has the upper hand. He will send them again."

"Yeah, I know. Fuck." Kat hopped up from the table and paced, as she ran her hands through her hair. "This is bad."

"So, why did this prince send demons to kill Kat and Sia?"

Kat went to answer Luke's question until she realized he wasn't looking at her, but Sky.

"Blood demons are the strongest guard dogs the Demon Prince, or King, whatever he calls himself these days, can summon. They are conjured up from Hell by his blood. Because of this, they're nearly impossible to defeat, since you can't draw blood from them or they'll strengthen, but not nearly as much as if they've drawn blood from their opponent. Matthias has a standing kill order against all my Knights, but Kat killed one of his allies, so I'm assuming he'd want to take out her partner, Sia, as well." Sky folded her arms and continued. "It takes a great amount of plasma to summon a Blood. I'm not completely familiar with the dark arts, but I've heard from reliable witches you'd need at least ten sacrifices to create one. The prince wants them dead because he knows it will hurt me."

"Wow." Luke looked at Kat with worry.

"Yes, defeating them is problematic, but not impossible. We have to make sure they're killed quickly, with minimal blood drawn."

"Easier said than done." Sia spoke up from the couch "What do we do, Sky?" All three turned to their leader. Huh, guess she was Luke's leader now, too. *Wow, what a difference a few hours makes.*

"I'm sending in more Knights. You'll need help."

"We can handle three Bloods, Sky," Kat grunted out. She loved Sia, but she hated working in teams. She may have found love, but old habits die hard.

"Yes, you can, but four? Five? What then? I am not willing to take that risk. Are you willing to risk even one Blood getting past you?"

She didn't need to answer that; she'd already done the risk assessment in her head. Three, yes. Four, no, not without casualties at least.

"Didn't think so."

"Who?" Sia and Kat asked at the same time.

"Who do you want?" This question not from Sky, but Luke.

Kat pulled him closer to her. "Ummm, honey, I don't think that's how it works." She looked at Sky, who was eyeing Luke with interest.

"Why not?" He threw his arms across his chest.

"Because, umm," she threw a look at Sky all *help me here,* but the leader remained quiet. Luke continued when no one else spoke.

"You're saying these demons are stronger and extremely dangerous, right? It would just make more sense if you got to pick the Knights you work well with. The last thing you need is to be in a battle, fighting to the death, with people that won't compliment your fighting style. I saw how you interacted with your sister in that short amount of time; you counted on each other; it was instinct. So, it makes sense to pick your team."

Sia and Kat just stared at him with their mouths hanging open. *Damn, he was hot when he got all analytical.* Maybe he was meant for this world after all.

After a few heartbeats, they all peeped over to see what Her Majesty had to say. What she saw was utterly astounding. Amusement was plastered on that angelic face.

"Well?" Sky said.

Kat looked at Sia and back again. "Well, what?"

"Who do you choose? I'm sending two extra Knights. Who do you want?"

She couldn't believe her ears. Sky was letting them choose their team. *Get the fuck out.*

"Asia," Sia said not missing a beat, probably assuming, like her, that this was a setup. Asia was an appropriate choice though. That Knight was an impressive fighter, and her gift was wicked. With Kat and Sia having two offensive gifts, it would be nice to have a little defense as well.

"Zelda," she decided.

Zelda was a borderline sociopath. Some say it was her gift that turned her humanity cold, but Kat didn't believe that. They got along great, and she showed emotion when Kat was around. And Zelda was as loyal as they come. If she had to work with anyone, other than Sia, she'd pick Zel any day of the week.

"Very well, I'll make the call. In the meantime," she looked at Luke, "I need you to get us better communication devices. The Knights can't keep relying on their phones in the heat of battle to keep in touch with each other. They need to be able to go a vast distance, since as you know, harpies can run exceedingly fast. Kat, Sia find a new place, somewhere in upstate New York away from civilization. I don't want you two staying in that building anymore. I want all of you to stay together, so your lofts must go. Cover your scents well. Luke will work on surveillance and security. I'll need your oath of loyalty to the Knights in blood writing, but we'll do that when you have everything settled."

Finish with her commands, her boss flashed out.

"OH MY GOD! She can teleport," Luke gasped.

Kat didn't respond; she was sure there would be several things that shocked him in the future; her attention was on one particular thing Sky had said. She turned to her sister with suspicion.

"You've been staying in my building, this whole time?!"

"Yes."

"Why?"

"How else was I to keep an eye on you?" Sia said matter-of-factly.

"I can take care of myself, sister." Kat rolled her eyes.

"Well, not back then you couldn't, sister." Sia sneered back,

"You were one feather away from tipping your scale into crazy."

"Fine, whatever. Guess it's moot now, we'll be living together. It'll make spying that more efficient."

"Yeah, whatever bitch." Sia seemed to think about something. "Where should we go?"

"Hell if I know. If it were up to me, I'd go back to my loft."

"Mind if I look for us?"

They both looked at Luke. Kat almost forgot he was here; he'd been so quiet. Kat lifted her eyebrow.

"You two have enough on your plate. This is my department anyway. I need to find an area that's isolated and secure, but close enough to cell towers where I can still broadcast signals to the satellites orbiting Earth. It'll be easier for surveillance purposes if I'm able to see everything around us. And I know you four are going to need space, so I can probably find a place big enough for all of us and have all the things I require faster than you can."

Kat swooned over her man. She loved it when he went nerd. He was soooo getting laid.

"Good idea, Luke, we'll leave it up to you. But the place has to be big; we aren't well versed in sharing. " Sia replied.

"What's the budget for this kinda stuff?"

"We normally wouldn't have one; we make a ton in investments in your world. Something I'm sure you'll learn soon enough when Asia arrives. Plus, I boosted boss ladies Master Card ages ago. We're set." Kat rubbed her hands together in evil glee.

Luke shook his head. "Give me two days, and I should have something. Until then, you two should stay in until Sky gets your back up. I'm sure those things will be back, and there's no telling how many there will be."

Kat was about to tell him where he could stick that idea, but Sia spoke up before she could snap her response.

"You're right." Kat's jaw dropped. Luke lifted it shut. "We'll stay in. We need to formulate a plan anyway. And Sky would find a way to kill us if we died before she sent us help."

Two against one. Damn reasonable bastards. She wanted to get out there and track down those fuckers and show them just how bloodthirsty she could get.

Running never sat well for her, and Kat had a reputation to protect. But they were right, of course. Staying in was going to suck ass. But she refused to die being foolish. Those days were over.

Kat glanced over at Luke, and he smiled in return. She had so much to live for.

****

Kat had been laying low the last few days, waiting for Asia and Zelda to get their affairs handled before their relocation to New York. Both welcomed the change and challenge they were soon to face.

As Knights, battles over the centuries could become repetitive. Even though the possibility of death was higher, the adrenaline from being the ones hunted would be enough to appease them for the time being. The latest report was that Matthias indeed heard of them fleeing and assumed fear, causing him to increase his minions by two. Which now totaled five blood demons.

Sky ordered them to stay rooted in the safe house until they were able to set up camp in the new location Luke provided. However, Kat hated being on defense, she wanted action, but she'd never risk Luke's safety. Worse, if they were to engage in battle at an unsecured location, the consequences could be catastrophic.

Kat was on the couch, laying back, tossing one of her daggers up in the air repeatedly, catching it by the hilt. She knew one thing that would keep her mind off retaliation, but her better half was busy. She looked over from her laid-back position on the sofa to see if her favorite nerd was still on his computer.

Halting her next toss, she peeked over the back of the couch. Yep, still nose to screen, setting up surveillance that would allow Luke to use the camera and media systems all around the city on his laptop. He'd been at it all morning. He said it would give them a leg up on any activity that seemed out of the ordinary. Meaning if any human snapped a picture of something they shouldn't have and uploaded it, they'd know about it. Which would be extremely valuable, the sooner they could get ahead of any possible supernatural reveal, the less clean up there would be. Kat understood why Sky needed someone like him the more he explained his work. They needed someone that understood their species, and it couldn't get any better than a human.

Luke had also found three possible locations to transfer to. Sky had taken him out to each site, and he had narrowed it down to one. They were waiting until sunup to go and check it out and see if they approved. She didn't care as long as she got out of this hell hole. They didn't have much as far as entertainment, seeing how they didn't want to draw unnecessary attention to their location. Which only left her with two possibilities, fuck or fight, and right now fighting didn't seem like an option.

Kat placed her dagger back in the strap at her thigh and got up from the couch. Luke was sitting at the table near the kitchen, so she went over to him. He was so engrossed in his work that he didn't even sense her approach. Placing her hands on his shoulders, she began a slow massage. He moaned a little but didn't stop his frantic typing. After a few minutes, she became frustrated, so she leaned down to place light kisses on his neck. That got his attention.

"Katrina?" Luke whispered.

"Hmmm?"

"I need to get this done, and you're distracting me."

"Can't you take a break?"

Kat ran her tongue up to his earlobe. "Fifteen minutes is all I need." She ran her hands down his stomach towards his growing erection. Once she reached home, she started slow circles through his sweats which caused him to drop his head back against her shoulder, abandoning his task completely.

"Where's Sia?" he murmured.

"With Asia, they'll be here at dawn," Kat responded, continuing to stroke him through his pants.

Luke pushed his chair back, captured her arm, and pulled her down on his lap to straddle him. Kat had worn her black leather skirt with no panties praying for this exact situation to happen. She wanted to be ready in case he could be easily seduced. She was so glad he could.

Luke grabbed her neck and started to kiss her with urgency. Kat was so desperate for him that she kissed him back with the same intensity, causing their teeth to clash. He pulled her top over her head, freeing her breasts. After he finished, she ripped his shirt off as soon as her hand was free.

Their hands were all over each other as they both tried to dominate each other's kiss. He slipped his hand up under her skirt moaning when he realized she wasn't wearing anything underneath. Kat gasped when he slid two fingers into her throbbing pussy, coating his fingers in her honey as he rubbed her clit. She broke away from his lips, throwing her head back as she rode his talented fingers, yet it just wasn't enough. Kat needed more. She needed a deeper connection. She needed to feel him inside her, and she needed it sooner than later.

Kat knocked his hand away and went for Luke's sweats, pulling the drawstring, freeing his length as quickly as possible. She palmed his dick, eased up on her toes, lifting her bottom off his lap, then plunged on his girth.

Grabbing his face in both hands, she brought their lips back together as she used her legs and thigh muscles to bounce up and down on his erection. He ran both hands down her back, cupping her ass so that he could meet her thrust for thrust. Kat was so close to shattering; she could barely hold herself steady. Knowing she was close to the edge, Luke brought one of his hands around and placed it between them, rubbing her clitoris as he continued to thrust up into her. Her orgasm came rushing forward, her walls milking his cock in spasm. Whispering his love for her in her ear, he followed her into paradise a few seconds later. His warm jets shooting up into her deep channel.

As their passion started to dwindle, their kiss turned less frenzied and more serene. She loved the feel of his lips on hers. She could kiss him forever and never get tired.

Luke gave her one last peck on the lips and pulled back to look up at her. "No panties? You don't play fair," he chuckled.

"And I never will when it comes to you," she replied returning his peck on the lips.

Kat got up from his lap and rearranged her skirt, grabbing her shirt from the floor, she pulled it back over her head. He fixed what was left of his clothing, as well as discarding his torn shirt.

"When did Sia leave?"

"Sky came and got her a few hours ago. You were still deep

in your hacking, so they decided not to bother you." She hopped up on the table beside him as he brought his computer up from sleep mode.

Kat felt a whole lot better now that some of her tension was released. She crossed her legs and lounged back on her elbows.

"Sorry about that. When I work, I tend to focus on nothing else...." He smiled up at her, "think Sia will make it back okay?"

"Yeah, she's tough, always has been. Even when we didn't see eye to eye, I never had to worry about her. They'll both make it to the safe house by dawn, unharmed."

"You never told me why you two fell out in the first place. I mean, you told me about your parents, but from my recollection, you and Sia have always been close. What happened?"

"That's a long story, baby."

He leaned back in his chair, his top half still bare and very distracting, and folded his arms, causing his pecs to pop forward. "We've got time; it's going to take a minute for my data to download on my hard drive."

Kat barely heard anything he said; she was too busy drinking him in with her eyes. The last thing she wanted to do was talk when he sat in front of her half-naked and looking edible.

She uncrossed her legs and went to push a foot up the inside of his thigh, but he captured her calf and reclosed her legs.

"No. Kat, I want to know. You know so much about me already, I feel like I have to get to know you all over again. Well, the real you, anyway."

That cooled her jets. Kat hated it when he reminded her about her deception. Luke never threw it in her face, but he wasn't afraid to let her know that she kept a valuable part of herself from him. "You know why I had to lie," she responded guiltily.

"Yes. And now you don't. So, what happened?"

Kat dropped her head back and stared at the ceiling. Her eyes sparkled, then she felt her electric pulse scale out down her arm and threw her tips. She brought her hand up and looked at the electricity sparking out her fingertips. Kat always called upon her gift when she felt uncomfortable. It calmed her and allowed her to clear her head. She hated thinking about the past because it brought her nothing but pain, but she owed it to Luke. He'd told her about his path, and she loved him too much not to return the favor. He didn't rush her either. Luke just sat there quietly watching her play with her electricity on her fingers.

Finally gathering her courage, Kat brought up the old memories she tried so hard to keep buried.

Buenos Aires, Argentina Twenty-Seven Years Earlier...

Kat and her team had finally followed these low-life demons to a location in South America. At first, they weren't sure of the murderer's species, but the fact that they left no trace behind as to who the killer could be, they figured it had to be phantoms. And they were right.

Sky had put five Knights on the task of finding the culprits responsible for snatching up women and children to feast on, then later discarding their bodies for the human police to find. They'd all been tasked with tracking missing person reports for nearly four months now and every lead they ended up finding turned into a dead end. They were all beyond frustrated. It wasn't in their nature to fail, and every time a mother and her child went missing, each and everyone one of them took it personally. They were breaking cardinal rule number one in their world. No children. They were utterly helpless and too trusting, so they needed to be protected among all others. Which meant the killings needed to end and they were becoming ex-

tremely disheartened with the fact that they were nearly untraceable. That was until this day.

They'd finally caught a break. A demon had been caught bragging about killing a set of twins in front of their mother in the Pug, the Phantom Realm's very own prestigious bar. Paranormal creatures from all walks of life visited that bar to get shit-face wasted in peace, which the witches no-violence spell allowed them to do. Gypsy, a.k.a Ghost was sitting in the back of the bar drinking fairy wine when the demon began boasting about his conquest. He was so drunk he couldn't understand the implication of his actions. Ghost sobered up quick and focused on the idiot spilling his beans to a shifter.

Once the demon finally collected himself enough to leave the bar, Ghost was right on his heels. Her teleportation gift, hence the nickname, allowed her to follow him without notice. Once she got the location of their hideout, she immediately called Sky. They moved on the hideaway instantly.

Kat and Zelda scouted out the area for two days verifying their intel. They hadn't been able to completely guarantee the authenticity of the location, because the only movement that had been made was between the demons. Using their heighten hearing, they weren't able to hear the voices of their victims either. They were about to leave and circle the bunker again when they heard a Jeep speeding up from the dense forest around them. They waited in the trees for the new arrivals and Kat's heart dropped in her chest.

Two demons got out of the Jeep, reaching into the back and pulling two small kids along with them. One girl and one younger boy, both clutching a dead human female to their bodies. The female, who must have been their mother, had a single bullet hole between her eyes. A shot, she was sure, had instantly killed the poor woman. The kids were crying and kicking, but their screams were died out by the two demons' laughter.

Kat felt her powers boil over and it took every ounce of strength she had to keep her planted in that tree. Zelda sounded the alert, sig-

naling for her to follow her out. They both dropped from the tree soundlessly and ran for the rendezvous point.

Once they were out of earshot, they spoke.

"They must have an underground bunker. That's why we can't hear them on the surface; they're down below." Zelda spoke as she paced.

Kat remained quiet. What she had just witnessed froze her ability to speak. Sia arrived a few minutes later, having gone a few miles away to scout out around the perimeter.

"Report," Sia asked.

Zel gave her the rundown as Ghost came through the trees a few seconds through the story. Zel started over from the beginning, so Ghost understood the situation as well.

"Fuck!" Ghost shouted. "Sky and Asia got pulled away to Canada for an emergency. Since this place was quiet for a few days, they figured they'd dip out quickly and help before they returned. Sky said we couldn't move without her. Damnit, they're going to kill those kids!" Ghost ran her hands through her silky black hair, her Egyptian features prominent in her frustration.

"What do we do?" Ghost asked no one in particular.

Sia pulled her phone from her ear, another call to Sky going to voicemail. "We do nothing. We wait for Sky; those were our orders." Sia forever the responsible one.

But Kat didn't hear that. She stood static, the eyes of that lifeless woman hunting her as her kids clutched ahold of both arms in desperation. No one deserved that kind of pain. Her power was humming through her in waves, and she was tired of waiting.

"I'm going," she told no one.

"Hell yeah!" Ghost backed her up.

"No! Sky said—"

Kat wheeled around to face Sia in a fury. "Sky isn't here, and I'm going. Come or don't. I don't give a fuck!"

Kat took off like a bullet towards the bunker, she distantly heard footsteps behind her, but she didn't particularly care which one of her comrades had balls. She pulled her lightning from the sky, letting it course through her body. Coming in closer on the abandoned building, she sent the strike right through the front door as she came up towards the building. The blast took the door off its hinges. After the explosion, all hell broke loose. Thinking back on it, Kat should've used more stealth and thought through her approach, but fear for those kids controlled her actions.

Gunshots erupted, grenades were thrown, and fighting commenced. However, throughout all the chaos, she was focused on trying to find the underground basement.

Kat zoomed in on a demon pulling a latch on the floor then jumped down into the darkness. She didn't think twice; Kat followed suit. She was utterly reckless, but she knew she had to find the kids before the demons decided it was best to kill them first before they fled.

Dodging bullets, Kat ran to where she saw the demon disappear. Using incredible strength, she grabbed the hooped barbell and pulled. Looking below she saw nothing but a dark tunnel. Not wasting another moment, Kat dropped to what could've been the gates to Hell for all she knew.

Landing effortlessly in a crouch a few feet below, Kat took a moment to examine her new surroundings. The underground bunker was a dingy, dirty, prison. The cells were rustic and filled with women and children. Some were aware and others, well, she didn't want to think about that right now. Kat was focused on the demon in front of her holding the young boy she saw in the car in his arms with a knife to his neck. The harpy was so angry she was shaking.

"Come closer, and I'll kill the kid." The gray, scaly demon replied.

Kat focused on the young boy, who despite the dire situation they were in, the kid seemed calm. She guessed she understood his acceptance of death; he'd just seen his mother killed in front of him. And to be taken to a place where so many others had already met their demise, why fight? The life had already gone out of his eyes, and the sight of his soulless gaze broke her.

Kat wasn't going to let this kid think he was going to die. Using her senses, she put out a beacon to make sure there weren't any other demons below. Satisfied with just the one, Kat relaxed her rage, honing in on her gift, trying to focus her power on one direct strike. Taking a deep breath, and praying to the Goddess above, she released her electric pulse directly at the demon's forehead, causing a burned hole to form between his eyes.

The demon dropped the knife and fell backward, releasing the boy. The young kid, who was dressed in nothing but a torn t-shirt, looked down at the demon below his feet. As silent tears ran down his face, he walked up to Katrina, pointing to the cage that held the little girl that was in the car with him. She looked up and saw the young girl had come up to the bars, peering through as tears ran down her dirt ridden face.

Dropping to her knees before the little boy, Kat turned his face to hers. He had stopped crying and was looking at her expectedly. She went to wipe his face, but he pulled back, shaking so badly she thought he was having a seizure. She went to embrace him, but he spoke first.

"Please.... please... don't hurt her; you can do whatever you want to me. I can take it."

Someone so small and innocent shouldn't have had to voice such an honorable request. She grabbed the little boy as tight as she could, holding him in her embrace. Distantly, she could hear the battle up above start to dim as two figures dropped to her side. She knew *instantly they were allies, so she never let go of the boy.*

"My Goddess," one of them whispered as they took a look around.

Asia zipped passed her, unlocking the prisons with speed and accuracy.

If Asia was here, that meant Sky had arrived as well. Fan-fuckin-tasic.

"Where's Sky?" She asked Sia, who'd come to help her with the women and children.

"She had to take Ghost to a medic," Sia replied not looking at her. Kat's stomach dropped.

Freeing the little boy, she ordered him to start helping with the care of the others, as she began to aid those released. "What happened? Is she okay?" She turned to Sia, as she patched up a little girl's bleeding arm.

"She was double teamed when she ran in after you," Sia sneered, "you left her to fend for herself. She was trying to back you up, and those fuckers ripped off her wings." Sia spat with controlled anger.

Kat could hardly move, let alone speak. She hadn't thought, she just acted. She had heard another come with her; she just assumed the others would follow as well. And to leave Gypsy up there with all those demons alone without even assessing the area. Rookie mistake. And she paid for it through her friend.

A harpy's wings were a part of what made them who they are. Their powers, their speed, it all centered around their wings. It took months for wings to regenerate once removed and years to become fully functional again. Not to mention the process hurt like a son of a bitch, which is why they always took great care of them during battle. And because of her blinding fury, she'd caused one of her closest friends to lose hers.

Kat wanted to leave and check on Ghost, but they still had to clean up the bunker. It had taken hours to get everyone out and treated by the medics, but they were able to save quite a few. Yet, there were so many others beyond their reach.

Zafrina had to come and implanted a different narrative of the scene that happened, so the humans didn't know it was phantom creatures that abducted them. She made it seem as those there was a group of older men that were taking people and torturing them before finally putting them out of their misery. They had saved seven women and children, four were in critical condition, and four were dead. They planted in the local police's heads that they were the saviors, successfully following a tip they received to this abandoned warehouse in the middle of nowhere.

She was good with the story. They knew to save some of the victims was a victory, however now that she had time to think, she didn't feel like it was. So, when Sky brought down the hammer, she took her punishment in stride. She was suspended from the Knights until Ghost's wings were healed, and she deserved every day. The damage was done, and she couldn't take back the mistake she made.

Present Day...

Kat had ended up being off the Knights for five whole Earth years. Enough time for her to develop grudges. There were so many things she wished had gone differently that day, but she never regretted her actions. She just prayed she hadn't gotten her friend hurt in the process. Ghost was the only one that had her back. She would forever be in debt to that crazy, down for anything, reckless bitch. Gypsy had received the same punishment as well since she went against orders. Even worse, they had never paired again. Damn, Kat missed her friend.

"So yeah, I know I fucked up, but I thought Sia of all people would have my back. Looking back on it now I didn't deserve her support. I went against direct orders and got a Knight's wings ripped off. But maybe if Sia been there that wouldn't have happened. Maybe if she believed in me, trusted me, Ghost wouldn't have had to experience that." She put her head in her hands, not wanting to look at Luke, "That's almost a fate worse than death for us."

Luke pulled her hands away from her face, and she noticed they were wet. She had begun to cry.

"Everyone makes mistakes, Kat."

"Not ones that could risk another's life."

"Yes, but what would've happened if you hadn't acted right at that moment? Who knows how many more would've died had you waited. Every great sacrifice comes with the possibilities of risk. You saved those women and children. People that didn't sign up for the risk you and the Knights take every day just by breathing. I don't know this Ghost, but I bet she doesn't blame you one bit." Luke wiped at her tears.

"No, she's forgiven me, and her wings have since healed, but I still feel guilty whenever I see her. Our friendship kinda ended because of it. She stays in South Africa, so that makes it easy to avoid her."

"Well, maybe it's time to make amends and move on, Kat."

Kat knew he was right, she should be brave enough to face her fuck ups, and besides, not having Ghost around was dull. Those two could always find something destructive to get into. Sky hated when they linked up, which made her wonder if she wasn't waiting for the best possible moment to ban them from being together.

"Yeah, you're right," she sighed, "I'll call her tomorrow and check up."

"Good. If there is anything else ever troubling you, remember you're no longer alone." Luke cupped her chin bringing her face forward, "you have me now." He kissed her slowly.

Pulling back slightly, she whispered, "I love you." His returning smile was infectious.

"As I love you."

Kat recaptured his lips, tugging on his hair to deepen the kiss. He stood to pick her up off the table, and she immediately wrapped her legs around his waist. They continued to kiss as they made their way towards the bedroom, where they made love well into dawn. For the first time in over two centuries, Kat finally felt at peace.

Chapter Thirty-One

Luke couldn't believe how much his life had changed in the past few weeks. He'd been working with the Knights the entire time and everything he'd been missing throughout his existence finally started to link together. Luke felt he had a purpose; this was what he was meant to do. His intellect was given to him to help others, not sit behind an office chair. Luke owed everything to Kat, and he was going to show her as much as he could how thankful he was. He just never knew all those sleepless nights learning to crack cryptic codes would be used to help immortals protect the human race.

It had only been a few weeks, yet he could already tell this was where he was meant to be. Luke didn't miss much from his old life, besides his best friend, Justin. He wished there was a way for him to keep that friendship still, but he understood why that wouldn't be possible. Sky had explained to him that too much memory tampering could leave the person braindead, and he didn't want to risk that kind of damage to Justin's mind. So, he had to let him go without so much as a goodbye. Luckily, he was starting to make new friendships. Asia, another harpy Knight who was standing right behind him, was beginning to become one of those friends.

They were in his brand-new tech room, which they'd officially called the command center, setting up his fancy and highly expensive toys. The computer system they were finishing setting up rivaled some of the best across the world and he was sitting in front of one of his six monitors. When Sky had told him to get everything he needed, without a budget cap, he went for the latest and most exquisite. Luke was even able to use some of his old connections on the dark web to get some military-grade equipment. It would help keep them hidden, broadening security. The girls had already persuaded some witches to do a spell that masked their scent around the perimeter, so that left him with the surveillance. Which, he'd have to say, turned out amazing considering the amount of space they had in their new place.

The large wooden cabin that they'd chosen in upstate New York had nine bedrooms, six baths, a library, and three studies. There was also a guest house in the back with two additional bedrooms. He'd picked the place because it was miles away from anything and it had a long, flat, grass field, so he didn't have to worry about enemies hiding in the surrounding trees. Also, the mansion was built out of five foot thick cement, even though the outside made it appear like a wooden cabin. It had taken him a week to set up the latest state of the art security system, but he didn't mind as long as it kept everyone safe. The Knights didn't seem to care how long setup took since they loved their new home. They were all happy to be out of that garbage hideout, that they let him turn one of the studies into his personal man cave. Where he currently sat in one of the leather armchairs around his ten feet long, u-shaped desk.

Luke was so in love with his office and its new toys that he almost forgot he had company. It was just natural for him to get lost in his work, now more than ever.

Asia had walked up closer behind his chair, leaning over in fascination. "Wow, what's that?"

"That, my dear, is the latest IBM cloud and cognitive computing tool. This baby can help me deliver personalized Knight experience to all the warriors that missed the live action. Who need folders when I can broadcast all the information we gather together over Skype? Knights that miss the meetings can download all the information from an email server."

"Handy."

"Damn right. You'll know as soon as everyone else does if there's a threat in the area that might cross over to the next Knights stationed. I can send the alerts all from this bad boy. I should be able to connect it wirelessly as well, soon as I get everything downloaded. That way I won't even have to be here to control it. I'll show you everything as soon as it's set up. It'd be nice to have someone to bounce ideas off of that gets this stuff."

"Where have you been all my life, Luke?" Asia said to him placing a hand on his shoulder.

"Back off Asia, he's mine." Kat scoffed, rushing through his office door, dressed in all black with her red hair pulled back off her face, looking stunning and deadly, very deadly.

"I can share," Asia shrugged, "your man's smart, I like smart."

"I don't share Asia, you know that. He's mine." Kat stalked closer, drawing out her claws.

"How about gift against gift? Winner takes the human," Asia replied, checking her claws for lint.

Luke swiveled around in his chair. "Ladies, ladies, please, I'm flattered truly, but if you're going to fight, take it outside. Not in here. Please, anywhere but here," he said hugging one of his new babies.

"Let's go," Asia said, stomping out the room.

Luke shook his head. He swore those two got into a fight every other day. They were both utterly exhausting. He knew Asia wasn't interested in him romantically; she just loved getting under Kat's skin. And she knew the quickest way to get to her was to go through him. But in all their fights they never used their gifts against each other. And they both had some pretty intriguing gifts.

"LUKE!!" Kat stomped her foot at him in frustration.

"Outside, Kat." He pointed out his office.

Kat looked like she wanted to argue, but eventually turned around and walked out of his office. He waited a few minutes and listened to see if they'd gone outside, but a quick look at the monitor showed they were in the living area. Walking out into the living room he noticed Sia and Zelda on the couch watching the action with popcorn.

"I can't believe you two. You aren't going to help me stop this?" He directed towards the Knights on the couch.

"Nope." They both said in unison.

"Let's do this," Asia moved her neck from side to side, rotating her shoulders counterclockwise.

"I'm not fighting you with my gift, Asia." Kat put her hands on her hips.

"Why not, scared?"

"Of course not, but I'm not dumb. You can get in my head faster than I can draw up my current. I'd nuke the whole house before I touched you."

"And we don't want that. There isn't another place like this, and you all wanted to stay close to town, so the house remains standing." Popcorn was thrown at him once he finished talking.

"Booooooooooo."
"You're no fun."
"Let them fight." His hecklers yelled out. Mostly Sia, since Zelda rarely spoke.

He was living with two-hundred-year-old children.

"Fine, no gifts, hand to hand, no weapons either Kat. Give Hansel and Gretel to Luke."

"Fine." Kat unstrapped her twins from her thighs, walking over to Luke to hand them over reluctantly.

"Babe, why are you baiting Asia? You know she doesn't want me. She does this to get you all riled up."

"Exactly. Don't wave an arm in front of a lioness and expect her not to bite. Besides, I need the exercise, haven't seen those Bloods since we doubled our team and I'm getting restless." She walked away cranking her neck.

"Rules?"

"No rules."

"There soooo will be rules," Luke stated. More popcorn was thrown—more booing.

"Shoot, Lukie," Asia winked at him, and Kat bared her fangs.

"No speed, no extra strength, no powers. This is simple hand to hand. Do not take this house down; got it?"

"Got it," they both said readying their bodies.

It was still hard to wrap his mind around how much fights like this would be a part of his life. Harpies had so much pent up aggression that if they didn't release it somehow, things could go wrong. For them, it was either battle or sex.

He brought his hand up to massage his eyes under his glasses, "Fine. Fight."

The battle began a few seconds later. He hadn't noticed that they'd moved a few of the furniture aside to make room for their fight, but their judo skills allowed them to stay practically in the center of the room.

Leaning back against the couch, he got so caught up in watching his beautiful, seductive, red-headed temptress move as fluidly as the ocean waves, he didn't notice that Sky had joined them. Not that she didn't specialize in stealth.

"Asia hit on you again?" Sky asked tilting her head towards the fight but looking at him.

"Yes," Luke breathed in exasperation.

"Doesn't Kat know she's being baited?" Asia liked humans even less than Kat did.

"She knows, Sky, yet here we are," Luke answered. "You going to stop this?"

"No. Why would I? They seemed civilized enough. Your doing?" Sky cut her eyes at him.

"Yes. We've already had to replace two walls and a countless number of furniture pieces. So, if they fight, they fight clean, end of discussion. Any more damage to the place is coming out of their accounts."

"Seems I'm starting to like you more and more, human." Sky folded her arms across her chest, her lips curving in what could've been her version of a smile.

And he understood why she didn't change her facial expressions often, because when she did, it was somewhat distracting. He loved Kat, but even an idiot could see Sky was breathtaking.

"Yeah, and you're just a ray of sunshine yourself, angel." They looked at each other smirking, just as Kat slammed Asia on the ground, straddling her legs.

"Stop coming onto Luke, or I'll kill you, got it?" Kat spat as she grabbed ahold of Asia's throat and squeezed.

"Yeah, okay fine; I'll stop," Asia choked out, spitting blood on the hardwood floors.

Kat nodded, seeming satisfied by the proclamation. Letting go of her death grip on Asia's neck, she jumped up off her opponent and backed away, giving her space.

"Children," Sky and Luke said at the same time.

"Oh, hey Sky, what's up?" Asia said, pulling herself off the floor as if nothing happened.

"I just came to see how you all were settling in. And to see if you all had any other reports on the Bloods."

"No," Zelda replied walking around the couch to face Sky, forever professional, her snow-white hair braided in a knot almost landing on her hip. "We were only able to kill one before the other four split. I got injured in the fight causing blood to spill, so Asia and Kat got me to safety while Sia distracted them in the opposite direction. Thankfully, she was able to retreat, so we could regroup. I held them back once; it won't happen again." Zel finished impassively, lowering her head.

Sky nodded, expecting her declaration.

"One blood down is still good. Losing one of them will hurt Matthias tremendously. He won't be able to conjure up more without seriously diminishing his powers. Keep taking them out one by one if you have to. Luke, the new com earpieces are amazing by the way."

"Thanks," Luke beamed at the praise, "I'm still working on the distance though. A hundred miles is the max before static."

"Still good work."

"Appreciate it, but I'll keep working on it."

"I know human, glad you're on our team. Very efficient."

"That he is," Asia cut in, looking at Luke, licking her lips. "You should see the things he could do with a stapler; I'd like to piece together that ass......"

Kat tackled Asia to the ground, and just like that, the fight was back on.

****

Fate had a wicked sense of humor. Kat was back, once again on the roof of Fall Heights, swinging her feet as she sat on the ledge. She was sucking on a Tootsie Roll pop, using one hand as she tossed a dagger in the sky and caught it with the other. It was just after midnight, as she waited for her man to do his thing with Sia at her side.

It'd only been a few months, but so many things had changed in their lives. Spring was now in full bloom and the night air was light and crisp. She was in a phenomenal mood since she was about to do one of her all times favorite things, which was rain havoc. Second only to lying in bed with Luke.

Things had been going great for her lately, and she owed everything to him. Kat still had a long way to go as far as her mental health, but not trying to kill herself in battle anymore was a tremendous start. She understood that everyone in life was dealt with some shitty ass cards now and then, but it was up to the individual to decide how to play them. And Kat decided it was time for her to accept her role and play her hand to the best of her ability. It helped she had someone who was starting over in life as well. Luke indeed was a gem.

Her new outlook on life came with the acceptance of fully being a Knight, which meant attending meetings, reporting in, and following orders, which she was doing exceptionally well in. Okay, that was a lie. Kat could follow some directions now. But if it didn't make sense, she wasn't doing it. Old habits died hard.

One thing that was surprisingly easy for Kat to adapt to was her willingness to work with others. Her newly assembled team was getting along famously, making their battle mission success rate more efficient. Harpies weren't used to working in groups, yet they made it seem as if they'd been doing it for years, which was great for them, yet sucked for rogue phantoms. Especially those they hunted tonight.

"Okay everyone, the security feeds will be disabled in about five minutes. The freeze frame will only last for about four minutes, five tops, before someone notices the video feed hasn't changed," her man said in the com in her ear.

They were waiting for Luke to kill the cameras in the area. They needed to go in undetected and rescue a group of humans from vampires that stole them from their homes. They had to remain vigilant, keeping a low profile in the age of technology was of high importance. They also didn't want to run the risk of drawing out the blood demons while they were out on one of their missions. They needed to remain focused on one task to keep all the victims alive. So, killing the cameras in the surrounding areas was a brilliant idea. They'd be able to use their supernatural speed to get in and get out without being detected.

And of course, it was Luke who came up with the suggestion. He was turning out to be a valuable new member to their team. He may not fight, but without him, their job would be ten times harder. He was the smartest, sexiest, most conscientious person she knew. Kat just loved everything about him. Luke was her true match in every way. A mate she never expected, yet was everything she needed. So, Kat decided she'd let him know, again.

"Baby?"

"Yes, darling?"

"I love you," Kat blew him a kiss.

"I love you too, babe." Groans from the other Knights came through the line, along with a couple of "get a room" chants.

"Okay ladies, you all have four minutes left. I've been keeping an eye on the heat signals in the area, and I'm just reading bloodsuckers, no Bloods, so set your watch for the countdown."

Kat and Sia set their watches as directed. Sia stood on the ledge waiting, but she remained sitting for the time being. Switching to a private line as Luke taught her, she signaled to him, so he'd catch the switch.

"Luke?"

"Kat, after this, you come right back here, you got it? Don't strip; I want to do that for you." She shivered at his seductive words. "I want you in those thigh-high fuck me pumps you were in when we first met. Do you remember those? Just those boots and nothing else, as soon as you're done. Are you listening?"

"Yes." Kat breathed, starting to pant.

"I want them on you right after I strip you with my teeth, then I want to make love to you until dawn. I want those pumps wrapped around my neck all night. Which means you must come back to me safely for that to happen. Can you do that for me?"

"You know I can." Kat was ready to get this job over with more than ever.

"Good. Now switch the line back over so you can go rip those fuckers throats out and come back to me, got it?"

"Yes, sir." She saluted into the air, then switched over.

Smiling, Kat stood up next to Sia who was looking at her with amusement.

"You know I'm still right here." Sia said looking over at her, "I can still hear you two perverts."

Asia came over the line "Wait, what? What we miss?"

"Nothing. Focus ladies. One minute."

Sia pulled her twin swords from her back; at the same time, Kat palmed her two best friends. It was time to get her siblings some candy.

"Okay girls, ready for some fun?" Kat heard Asia say on the microphone a few blocks down where she and Zelda were stationed.

"Oh yeah, let's bring the rain." Zelda, cocking her gun, came through loud and clear.

"Time to play." Sia.

"Game time." Kat.

"Okay ladies ten seconds...." Luke cut in.

Time stilled. All manners of play evaporating from their bodies. They didn't move; they didn't speak; they didn't dare breathe. This was what they lived for. This is what they were bred to do. This moment right here, as Phantom Knights.

Their watches sounded.

"All clear ladies, go fuck shit up."

Sia looked at Kat and smiled, "Shall we?" Kat motioned with her hand, "After you."

Without further thought, Sia jumped off the roof.

Looking down, as she watched her sister step off the ledge, Kat thought of the time she was sitting up here, in this very spot, reading fairy tale stories. The harpy thought of everything she'd been through these past couple of months and how she'd overcome so much adversity–having to deal with backstabbing sisters and a bitch of a mother. Coping with the introduction of new sisters-at-arms, and one couldn't forget Sky. If she had to have a stepmother, she couldn't choose one better. And her prince...yum. She was in no way trying to compare her wild life to Cinderella's fable, but maybe she was living in her own fairy tale story. Katrina Thorne placed a foot off the ledge and smiled.

Nah, this isn't my ever after. Happily ever afters were for people whose stories had already ended. And theirs, well, theirs were just getting started.

Kat called up the electrical current that lived deep within the depth of her soul. She watched the pulse dance all over the outside of her body, as she looked down at the world below and jumped.

PKS: Book Two

Keep Reading for an exclusive sneak peek into the next novel in the series, "Phantom Knightmares."

Chapter One

Hawk stood pacing in his diabolically miserable tomb in the temple of his master. He was deep in the gloomy depth of the Phantom Realm, encircled by useless objects that weren't his own. The surroundings in his jail cell were utterly distasteful, but Hawk was forced to call this wicked abyss home. The metal bed frame with a stone surface and a literal pot to piss in were paradises as opposed to being anywhere near his captor.

Hawk loathed his controlling leader, the Demon Prince, with all the fire within the pit of his misguided soul. Matthias, Prince of Demons, was a high lord of the six demon realms on Phantom. A ruthless ruler, Matthias was known as one that favored dismemberment rather than redemption. And Hawk was his slave.

The temple Hawk was obligated to call home was enormous, an impressive feat, considering the palace was leveled underground. The Prince had countless enemies and barreling his home underground was a necessity, not a luxury. Despite the massive cement structure, guarded by thousands of lethal demons, it was easy to feel small and alone; as any prisoner in hell would.

Hawk continued his long strides up and down his chambers. He contemplated his current predicament of being an unwilling participant in a war he was immersed in because of his affiliation with the Prince — a contest he had every intention of winning. Looking down at the gold bands wrapped snuggly around his wrist, Hawk knew losing was not an option.

Hawk was one mission away from freedom. One battle away from the bracelets snapping free and releasing him from the blood oath binding him to the sinister Prince. Lifting his arm out in front of him, Hawk glanced menacingly at the golden rings encircling the bottom of his arm. Staring, he felt a desperate urge to try and rip them off his flesh. Hell, Hawk didn't have much to live for lately, so trying to remove the bands while experiencing excruciating pain would be a walk in the park for him. But the promise of vengeance from the Prince lowered his arm.

Hawk walked toward the back of his tomb, sinking on his iron bench. Placing his head in his hands, Hawk tried to control the tremors of anger as they coursed through his body. The bangles weighed heavily on his arms. The gold bands were a constant reminder of the reason for his entrapment. It was seemingly impossible to concentrate on anything other than the female who'd led him here.

Bottling up his rage, the demon warrior allowed himself a moment to dwell on the bitch who subsequently led to the reason he had to sell his soul to the devil. Hawk owed his ex-mate a slow and agonizing death, which required him to stay alive and get through this last mission to fulfill his real purpose. After centuries of enslavement, Hawk would be given a chance to break free of his bindings.

Matthias had officially given Hawk his one-hundredth mission, which would terminate his contract with the Prince. The assignment? Bring the Dark Lord the heads of two phantom Knights. A job Hawk wasn't sure the Prince thought he would be able to complete.

The gifted Earth protectors were nearly impossible to get near, let alone kill. Those vicious harpy warriors were deadly, skillful opponents. One had to be virtually invincible to defend the planet from creatures that had the power to conquer the universe — supernaturals like vampires, werewolves, shifters, and demons.

Most of his brethren lived on Phantom, another world in the infinite universe. However, a variety of creatures decided to call Earth their home. Those of their kind that were able to keep their existence a secret were typically left in peace. Those who couldn't, like most of his demon species, fell victim to the Knights' blades, which was why his variety of demon usually kept to themselves.

Hawk was part of the nomadic shifter tribe. Regardless of their rarity, they were still within the demon ethnicity, even though his appearance could pass for human if it weren't for some minor demon discrepancies. With small scaly horns that were nearly hidden by his lengthy chocolate-colored hair, Hawk would stand out amongst the earthlings. If it weren't for the tusks, his warm sun-kissed caramel skin would've helped him blend in.

Hawk's people came from a small colony. Their tribe just wanted to be left alone in their territory outside of the Prince's domain. Hawk still somehow ended up within their walls, due to the unconditional love for the one that bore him.

Out of all his years, Hawk still couldn't believe he allowed another to betray the trust of his family. The numerous chances he'd given, all wasted on such an insignificant soul.

Hawk got up and began to pace, his long muscular legs making quick work across the distance of his large tomb. He would make sure that a similar lapse in judgment would never happen again, once he got out of here. To let another have possession of his decisions was a foolish error. However, mistakes always allowed one to learn, and he'd discovered sympathy was an emotion best left for the weak. And Hawk was anything but soft.

Keeping up his pace, a knock on his chamber doors pulled him from his self-destructive thinking. Knowing it wasn't

Prince Matthias, since he would've just barged in, Hawk told
whoever it was to enter. Stopping his pacing and settling his
stance, he looked towards the door as Daze opened things up.

Hawk relaxed his posture, nodding to Daze, his only ac-
complice in this fucked up realm. The demon entered the room,
grim. Like him, Daze wore matching gold slave bands wrapped
around his wrist. Looking at Daze, he never would've thought to
make a comrade in this abyss, but then again Daze was basically
in the same predicament he was. But it wasn't a packmate who
betrayed his trust; something far worse landed the male here.

Daze was slightly shorter than Hawk's 6'3 frame but built
just as tough and as sturdy as he was. One needed strength to
survive in a dwelling such as this. It was easy for one to go mad
in their situation, some even deciding to take their chances
in the Bliss, Phantom's spiritual world. However, the two were
united in their quest for vengeance and as such, whoever made
it out first swore a blood oath, to aid the other to freedom. And
as he looked towards his only ally over the centuries, with the
first real chance at escape, he knew he'd be glad to keep his word.
They both just had to survive a little while longer.

Glancing towards his confidant, Hawk sneered. "What
does he want now?"

"Same ole, same ole; death and destruction, as well as the
heads of those Knights." Daze responded, running a hand over
his nape, "it's as if he'd almost like you to succeed. Which would
be a first." Daze finished coming in and sitting on the edge of his
bench in his rather large jail cell.

"The Prince could care less about my freedom. I don't
think he even knows this is my hundredth mission. With everything that's been going on, how could he pay attention?" Hawk
questioned. "The hate Matthias bears for the leader of the
Knights has clouded his judgment. If he hadn't gifted me with
the mission to destroy a few, I'd be on their side. " Hawk pro-

nounced, leaning his solid frame on the stone wall.

Daze crossed his arms over his massive chest, "I feel as you do, brother. So, what's the plan?"

Hawk walked over to his colleague and sat on the bench and glanced at his friend briefly. As humble as he could be, Hawk knew he was attractive for a demon; with rugged features, there was no shortage of females throwing themselves at his feet. However, Daze was in a league of his own. The male was a living god, and Hawk was secure enough in his masculinity to admit it. The demon had a face that had every species of female falling to Daze's feet in worship, hell, even males paid attention. His friend was classically handsome, with skin the color of smooth chocolate, his eyes a piercing violet. The male was beauty personified; however, years of captivity turned his features harder, darker.

"I don't know, D. That bitch, Sky, brought in more fucking Knights and they succeeded in killing one of the Bloods"–some of the most powerful assassins in existence– "so naturally Matthias is pissed."

"I would imagine," Daze looked over at him. "Blood demons are rare commodities; losing one will hurt him." His friend rubbed a hand across his five o'clock shadow.

"You're looking tired, my brother," Hawk muttered. He'd been so wrapped up in his shit, Hawk hadn't noticed his friend appeared drained, defeated.

Hawk placed a hand on his shoulder. "When this is over, I will find a way to free you. You must still have faith, trust me D, I will find a way."

Daze released an exhausted sigh, "Don't. I renounce our vow. I want you to leave this place and never look back. We both know coming back would be suicide, and you don't deserve that. Who knows, once you're freed I may move back up in rank. Finally start having my missions roll in again."

Hawk folded his hands in front of him, resting his elbows on his knees. They both knew that wouldn't be true. Daze had been Matthias's slave for over five hundred years and has only had thirteen missions, which meant eighty-seven remained. How the demon managed to retain a hold on his sanity throughout the years was a testament to his character. Daze was a good male.

As anger surged through his system, Hawk grabbed his friend's jaw, making him look directly in his eyes. "I will come for you. Say you trust me." Hawk grunted through his teeth.

Daze stared long and hard, letting slip a fleeting glimpse of vulnerability. Hawk never lowered his gaze, making his truth and determination shine through. After what seemed like an eternity, Daze finally nodded his acknowledgment of Hawk's oath. His word was law; Hawk would find a way to get them both out of this mess.

"Good," Hawk stated, then released his friend, forcefully. "Now about the Knights? I may have to go after them myself if Matthias doesn't give me more Bloods."

"What!!" Daze squawked, recoiling as if he had been struck. "You can't. It's too dangerous. Scouting alone in their playground is not wise."

"So little faith, my friend?"

"Au contraire, my brother, I have faith. But you don't know how many Knights that dark fairy brought in. Not to mention the gifts each Knight wields. Their powers are deadly. Going in blind is just not smart."

"And what other option do I have? If I can get in and get out without being detected, I'll be able to formulate a solid plan."

"They'll know. You can't underestimate those winged harpies. If you're detected, the Knights will know you belong to Matthias. And if they see the bands, they'll kill you on sight. "

"And if he doesn't give me any more Bloods. What then? We're stuck here for eternity. Do you want that? Going in and assessing the situation is the best play I have. Taking them out one by one seems to be the only feasible solution. And I must do it. The Bloods are destroyers, not trackers."

Daze seemed to contemplate his words, but in the end, he knew Hawk was correct. "Fuck, fine, but at least send the remaining demon Bloods you have at your disposal one last time. See if they can do some damage and then have them report what they find out, maybe you won't even need to go."

Hawk thought about it intently for a moment, but ultimately he knew it wouldn't work. In all his years of service, Hawk had never known blood demons to be very vocal about their missions beyond a success-failure analysis. If he asked about the Knights or the gifts they recognized, they would probably look at him in confusion. The demons only knew to destroy; anything else the dumb logs wouldn't comprehend. And Daze was well aware of the Blood's flawed design. Hawk also knew where the reluctance lied. The demon was getting soft in his old age.

"Okay, I'll send them out again; maybe we'll get lucky and kill one."

Hawk's conviction failed to have the impact he desired. Glancing at his friend whose grin never quite reached a full smile; Hawk knew Daze didn't believe in luck any more than he did.

Made in the USA
Columbia, SC
02 August 2022

64140786R10157